OTHER BOOKS PUBLISHED BY FRANK LARUE

by
Frank LaRue

TOTEM
POLE

BOOKS

Vancouver • Toronto

Library and Archives Canada Cataloguing in Publication

LaRue, Frank, 1948-
    Finding Carrie George / Frank Larue.

ISBN 978-0-9735840-3-5

    I. Title.

PS8623.A7738F56 2008   C813'.6   C2009-900157-8

First Edition
Printed in Canada

Editors: Kelly O'Connor, Morgan O'Neal
Research Consultants: Donald O'Connor, Kim Kirton
Layout: Low Profile

ACKNOWLEDGMENTS

The author would like to thank those who have made possible the completion of this manuscript. Much appreciation to Kelly O'Connor, and Morgan O'Neal for providing editorial input. Special thanks to Donald O'Connor and Kim Kirton for their insight and research assistance. Thank you, Bernard Low for the cover designs, and thanks to Low Profile for arranging the story between them. And thank you, my reader, for reading this book.

CHAPTER 1

The office building was built in 1927, and little had changed since then. The elevator was tiny. Four people in there at one time and you knew what kind of aftershave everyone was wearing. Mike sat behind his oak desk in a leather chair inherited from the last tenant; his dog Benny stood by the window observing the couple who just came into the office. Phil and Mary George now sat across from his master.

"Carrie wasn't bad. An honor student in high school. She had lots of friends. We never had any problems with her. I mean, there was the usual," Mary George said as a hint of a smile softened her weathered face, a small woman who looked younger than her 46 years. The smile vanished quickly as the memory of her daughter's childhood flashed through her mind.

"Do you have any children Mr. Morningstar?" she asked.

"No, been married to a badge most of my life."

Mary laughed, then looked at her husband sitting next to her in stone silence. "Well I'm sure you know what I'm talking about. Never any drugs, and if she did drink, it was on special occasions. Carrie was getting ready to go to the University of Victoria." Mary swallowed hard and pursed her lips. "Then everything changed."

Mike leaned back in his chair. "Something happened to Carrie?"

"She and her friend Susan Wabigon went to Vancouver for a weekend. It was a few weeks after she had graduated. We didn't think anything of it, and she never told us that Susan remained in Vancouver."

"What happened in Vancouver?"

"Susan's friend was a crackhead." Mary turned away. Her husband put his hand on her shoulder. Phil was ten years older than his wife. He was tall, with a body sculpted by years of working in the construction trade.

"The woman's name was Candace Webber," Phil said. "She turned Susan and my daughter on to crack. Susan was the first to get hooked."

Mike pretended he didn't know what was coming next, but in the fifteen years he spent with the RCMP he had heard the story repeated again and again. Even if the names and faces of the kids were different, their fates were always the same.

"Your daughter," Mike said in a forced monotone, "she got addicted?"

"The story was Susan had found a job in Vancouver." Phil rolled his eyes, hinting the whole story was a lie. "Carrie went there trying to find a summer job."

"You kept in touch with her?"

"For the first month or so she called us two, three times a week." Phil threw a glance out the window. The lines on his face hardened; he had told the story once too often. "Then it was one call every second week or maybe once a month until we figured out what was happening."

"She wasn't working?" Mike would regret asking this question. Mary broke down and had to be comforted by her husband, who remained stoic but was slow in responding.

"That Candace woman was a prostitute!" Phil's voice filled with anger, then went silent for a moment as he finished his thought. "She used the money to buy her crack."

"When did you find out?" Mike asked.

Phil tilted his head and gave Mike a cold stare. "I drove to Vancouver. I thought I'd surprise her." He took a deep breath as if unable to continue, but finally in a strained voice managed to finish. "Carrie was down to 96 pounds. I couldn't believe what had happened to my little girl. I got her into a rehab in Victoria, and she cleaned up and moved back home."

"She was clean and healthy," said Mary.

"She was." Phil smiled for the first time, a flicker of optimism in his eyes. "We figured she was going to stay that way."

Mike asked, "How long was she home?"

"Two months and she was back to her old self." Phil looked at his wife who simply nodded. The vacant expression on her face was reminiscent of someone forced to recall an unpleasant memory. "Then one Saturday afternoon, we came home from bingo and Carrie was gone."

"When was the last time you spoke to Carrie?"

"She called us from Calgary. She was in rehab again; she had cleaned up and wanted to come home. I paid for a plane ticket, but she got off in Vancouver."

"Has she called since then?"

"No, that was the last time I spoke to her," Phil said painfully. "Then we heard that Susan died in a hospital in Edmonton; heart failure because of drug overdose. Her funeral was in Victoria. We were sure Carrie would come home. Susan was her best friend since grade school."

"She didn't show up for the funeral?" Mike asked, feigning surprise.

"No. I figured Carrie never knew what happened to Susan."

"You've spoken to the police?"

Phil turned to his wife who slowly lowered her head in sadness. The depth of her sorrow made the grief a cross she would carry for the rest of her life unless her daughter showed up alive. The loss of a child could only be truly understood by another parent, someone who has experienced the same misfortune. The effort required to make it through the day feeling that loss and wondering what could have been done to prevent the tragedy was painful. She blamed herself as a mother; she felt responsible for her daughter's mistakes.

"Carrie's been listed as missing for the last year," Phil said, "and the police have come up with nothing."

Mike could sense the couple was not happy with the police's handling of the affair. He also knew that the police never broke a sweat when the missing person had anything to do with drugs or prostitution. "I understand your frustration," he said, "but I know from experience that unless there has been an arrest it's hard to track down anyone caught up in that vicious circle."

"They don't care," said Mary, her voice rippling with anger.

"What my wife is saying, Mike, is that we're not the only ones. There is a whole group of families who have a daughter or relative gone missing, and none of them feel the police are doing their job either."

"I doubt if it's high on their priority list, but that doesn't mean the investigation isn't active," Mike responded.

"If you're willing to look for our Carrie, I'm sure you will be surprised how badly the police have been handling it so far." Mary lowered her head in her now habitual manner as she rose from the chair and took her husband's hand.

Mike listened as their footsteps faded down the hall; he made no promises. He would make some inquiries, and if the police had no answers, then he would take the case. Carrie George had been missing for an entire year—not surprising for someone trapped in the world of addiction. She might still be crawling the streets looking for that next fix, or she could have moved on and started a whole new life. Carrie could also be dead, and that was the one reason Mike had never taken missing person cases. He had delivered the death message to parents too many times while he was in uniform. It was never easy. It was like telling someone they had cancer. He tried to avoid the situation since he retired from the force. Doctors were trained for this kind of thing; cops weren't.

He called his buddy Jimmy Secola at the RCMP office in Mission. Mike waited on the line for several minutes before his friend picked up the phone. They went through the usual small talk before Mike explained his reason for calling.

"I can do a search for Carrie George Canada-wide, but don't get your hopes up," Jimmy said in a formal voice.

"Why's that?"

"If she's an addict working the streets and has only been arrested once, unless we pick her up for something again, we don't keep tabs on people like her. Jesus, Mike. Things haven't changed that much since you left."

Mike could hear the office noise on the other end of the line, a reminder that Jimmy could not really speak freely from where he was sitting. "I appreciate you looking into it. I have another name, Candace Webber. She was one of the few leads the father left with me."

"I can't place it right now," said Jimmy, "but Candace, yes that name rings a few bells. I will be at home on Sunday, and if I find anything before then, I'll call you."

Bill Roberts drove down Broadway on his way to the Downtown East Side with one thing on his mind: find a woman and bring her home. He wanted someone he knew; he was not in the mood for a stranger who might try and rip him off. Any hooker who had the nerve to steal from him would have to be punished, better to find someone who had been to his house and knew the rules. He liked a woman who appreciated the stash of drugs he kept in his home, Grade A heroin and crack cocaine; she could help herself on the condition that she satisfied him. The game was simple, but somehow he occasionally stumbled on a rotten apple, a hooker who made the fatal mistake of treating him like he was some kind of sugar daddy to be used and abused. That kind never lived to brag about it. It was his duty to punish manipulating, dishonest women who took advantage of his generosity and underestimated him.

He turned right on Commercial Avenue and drove towards Hastings Street. It was five o'clock on a Friday night, and he knew from experience there would be several women on the street selling their asses for a fix as soon as the sun went down. The thought of having a selection excited him. He considered picking up two women. He hadn't tried a threesome for a long time; perhaps tonight was the night. He turned up the radio when Lou Reed's "Walk on the Wild Side" started playing and sang along with the chorus as his black Ford 4x4 stopped at an old garage on Hastings. He needed to pick up a new carburetor for one of the motorcycles he was working on, and Harris Motorcycle Parts was his best supplier.

The owner met him at the door, took him around the back of the garage, and showed him a brand new Indian. It was a beautiful bike, but too Hollywood for Bill. He liked old Harleys; they had tradition behind them, and bikers who drove fancy bikes like the Indian models were pussies. Bill went into the garage. It was greasy and grungy, his kind of workplace. He made some small talk, paid for the carburetor, and left. The traffic rush had just begun, so he decided to stop at the Waldorf Hotel to have a few beers and wait until darkness before going on the great beaver hunt.

CHAPTER 2

Outside, the traffic was building into a crescendo of white noise, the first rumblings of the nine to five crew returning home. Mike slowly put the phone back in its cradle; he could read through Jimmy's reluctance. Passing on privileged information was not acceptable to the RCMP, yet a blind eye was cast on the practice if the request came from a retired officer. In Mike's case, since he had resigned, there wouldn't be any leniency. Jimmy was taking a risk helping out his old partner. Mike had not handed in his badge because he had lost faith in the RCMP, but because he felt betrayed by the justice system—the system he was paid to uphold.

Mike was working in Regina when an incident that happened in Tisdale changed his career. A sixteen-year-old Native girl had been raped by three white men after being lured into a hotel by the ringleader. The investigation was short. The three men were arrested, and a trial was held several months later. The police and the crown shared the same sentiment: a belief that justice would make these men pay for the heinous assault on the young girl.

The high paid defence lawyer had different ideas, and as the days in court went by, he convinced the jury no crime had been committed since the girl had come to the hotel room of her own free will. The fact she had been raped by all three men and was taken to emergency for internal bleeding didn't seem to make the point clear enough. The verdict of "not guilty" rang in Mike's ears for weeks until for his own sanity he decided to leave the life he had put his heart and soul into for fifteen years. He handed in the badge, the uniform, the police-issued handgun and holster before walking out the door for the last time. He later became a private investigator on the insistence of his old friend Jesse Crowchild.

The Calgary rehab was his second call. He wanted to know if anyone could remember Carrie, hopefully a counselor. This was the logical place to start, although it could be a dead end. The receptionist wasn't much help. His only other lead was Candace Webber, and finding her would solve a lot of problems. He decided to Charlie Feathers, his friend from *The Native Times*. Charlie was his best source of information about people who

6

dwelled in the lost world known as Vancouver's East Side. He found the phone number in the masthead of *The Times* and punched the numbers. The desk manager informed him that Charlie was in a meeting but to hold just in case he might take the call. A few seconds later, Charlie was on the blower.

"Charlie! I'm calling to make sure my subscription hasn't run out." Mike listened to his friend rant on about people who never called him unless they need something. "I know what you're saying Charlie. I hate those kind of people. What do I want? Why the pleasure of your company, of course. Are you still the rising star of the karaoke scene?"

Mike smiled down at Benny, signaling the change in their mutual friend's attitude. The dog was aware of Charlie's love of singing. Charlie knew Benny for years, and whenever they came in contact, Charlie would break into song and the dog barked along while slipping and sliding on the hardwood floors like a young Husky on a sheet of ice.

"I knew it," Mike said. "Charlie the crooner. So when can I catch the next performance? Wednesday night at The Sit & Bull? Perfect. I'll be there."

Mike noticed Benny walking towards the door, a sure sign someone he knew had just left the elevator and was headed towards the office. The dog sat down facing the entrance, his ears alert and pointing in all directions. "Who is it Benny?"

The dog jumped up on the visitor the moment she walked inside the door. Theresa knelt down and patted Benny. She was wearing a brown shawl over a red wool sweater, and her long black hair fell loosely on her shoulders. She had brown eyes that missed nothing and cheekbones that became more prominent when she smiled.

"What's the verdict?" Theresa asked. She worked for Sisters in Spirit, an organization set up to deal with the growing number of missing Native women. The George family had approached her to arrange an appointment with Mike.

"I told the family I would check out what the police have done, and if there is a chance of finding her, I'll give it my best shot." He was still not convinced, however, that he could make much of a difference.

"Thank you Michael." Theresa stood up, wiped the dog hairs from her dress, sat down on her husband's lap, and gave him a warm kiss.

"I said I would help. No guarantees I'll get anywhere."

"You've given them hope, Michael. That's something they had lost, and now they can pray something good will happen with you on the trail of their daughter." Theresa smiled as she stroked his hair.

"What happens if I find out their daughter is no longer on the planet?"

"It will be tragic." Theresa looked away, and the smile vanished from her face. "Mary will be devastated. She's close to a nervous breakdown right now."

"It's a no-win situation. The odds are one in a hundred that Carrie is alive," Mike said coldly, remembering a past experience.

Theresa, eye to eye with her husband, was searching for that flicker of belief she was accustomed to seeing when he took on a case. "I think Mary knows the odds," she said, "but at least there is a chance."

"I wouldn't have accepted if I didn't believe there was a slim chance Carrie has somehow survived."

Theresa smiled and gave him another kiss. "We have to stop at the Friendship Centre before we go home."

"What's happening at the Centre?"

"Margaret Bluetail has released her book of Native recipes. I promised we would be there. She's made a special lunch for everyone who shows up."

Mike agreed the change of scenery would give him a chance to let things settle in his mind. He left a list of "must calls" on his desk before locking the office. "Oh yeah, I nearly forgot. The garage called. Your car won't be ready until tomorrow."

"What! You mean we're driving in your car?" Theresa rolled her eyes back into her head as they squeezed into the elevator. When they arrived at the parking lot, she stared at the nemesis of their relationship: a '62 Cadillac Eldorado, Mike's pride and joy. It was cherry red with black trim, white leather interior, long fins on the back, chrome hubcaps, and triple red taillights that resembled miniature rockets. Everything was impeccable. The original radio, built in a time when there were fewer alternatives, had only two gold knobs: one for changing the volume and one for finding the station. This Caddy was the statement of automotive elegance when it came out of the factory in 1962 and still was, as far as

Mike was concerned. Benny took up his usual position in the back seat as Mike's co-pilot. Theresa sat uncomfortably in the front seat, shaking her head in dismay. She was convinced that certain things about men weren't meant to be understood by the opposite sex.

"Please don't drive on Hastings," Theresa pleaded, sliding down in the seat, hoping no one she knew would see her.

"Don't put me through this again." Mike felt compelled to defend his Eldorado, the automotive classic Theresa referred to as the Pimpmobile. She not only hated everything about the car, she was also embarrassed by the stares she got from other people when she was in the front seat.

"I can't help it," she said. "The only people who drive old Cadillacs are pimps and people with an Elvis fetish."

"You're forgetting the rap crew."

"No, Mike," Theresa said flatly. "Puff Daddy, P. Diddy... whatever-his-name-is wouldn't lower himself to driving an old Cadillac."

"That's his problem," Mike said, with a touch of contempt in his voice. "Probably drives some old Chevy Impala."

The Caddy rolled down Cordova until they hit Second Avenue, a stone's throw from the Pacific Ocean. As they approached the Friendship Centre, the landscape became desolate as the terrain between the road and the water gave way to the ruins of an abandoned coal warehouse that stretched for almost two blocks. The exterior had decayed into the grey ghost of a forgotten past. The windows, shattered beyond recognition, gave the impression of a concrete corpse with hollow eyes. Mike took the Commercial Street exit and was within a few blocks of the centre when Theresa broke her silence.

"Please do not park this monstrosity in front of the Friendship Centre."

"Margaret will be disappointed if I park anywhere else," Mike said facetiously as he pulled close to the curb, not far from the entrance of the large one-storey building. They were greeted by a carving of a whale on the wall. The Friendship Centre spread out for almost a block, and the interior was filled with Native art. The centre room from which everything else emanated was finished in polished redwood; two totem poles stood guard at the entrance. Inside, there was a stage built to accommodate dancers from the different tribes who held their powwows here. Traditional masks looked down from a slanted ceiling that was meant to resemble a longhouse. Another wing of the building was filled with offices reserved for the administration and organizations working with the centre. There were also a few shops stocked with traditional Native paintings and clothes designed for Native ceremonies.

The book launch was held in the centre room where several picnic tables were set up with a variety of gourmet dishes. A line was already forming at the foot of the stage where two more dining tables were laid out with examples of Margaret's culinary creations. Theresa greeted Margaret with a hug, and Mike congratulated her as she gave him a copy of her book. He pulled out a pen, opened the front page, and demanded an autograph.

Theresa gave a short speech about how Margaret had brought a new awareness to traditional native cooking with her restaurant and introduced Aboriginal cuisine to the mainstream population. Margaret thanked Theresa and the audience for showing up and encouraged everyone to help themselves to the food. Mike and Theresa were seated at the front table; they took their plates and joined the others in the food line-up. Mike marveled at the dishes Margaret had prepared for the occasion: steaming bowls of seafood chowder, plates of wild salmon, braised partridge with wild mushrooms, bannock, mashed potatoes, and Jerusalem artichokes. There were salad bowls filled with wild greens and watercress, dandelion leaves, and wild onions. For the crowning touch, there were loaves of cornmeal cobbler made with wild berries and topped with homemade strawberry ice cream. An hour later Mike and Theresa, with books in hand, left the Friendship Centre. As they drove away, Benny munched on the treats Mike saved for him, and Theresa seemed content with going home after a full day.

They drove down Hastings, where working girls appeared out of the shadows. There were pockets of women on certain street corners waiting for johns to pick them up so they could score the drugs that had driven them to the oldest profession in the first place.

"What I will never understand," Theresa said, "is why those women risk their lives selling themselves in the most dangerous part of the city."

"You mean, why they don't work for an escort agency that sends drivers out with their escorts?" Mike said with a touch of sarcasm.

"Michael listen…" Theresa tried to choose her words carefully. "I'm not putting the stamp of approval on prostitution. It's just that all of the missing women were working the streets in the East End before they disappeared. If they had been with one of the agencies, they might still be alive."

"No escort agency would have them. Agencies may be sleazy, but they're not stupid. Junkies and crackheads can't be trusted; they have a habit of ripping off customers and employers. There's a high stroll and a low stroll. These women are off the map; they're on the crawl." Mike noticed a trio of young girls hiding in a doorway with a crack pipe.

"Are you saying there is difference between them?"

"Most street hookers were abused when they were young, and that's why they ended up wired. The only way they can support their habit is to work the street."

"You think Carrie could be one of those women?"

"No, but she's been there." Mike slowed down to take a right on Isabelle where several more young women were crossing the street. A brunette in her early twenties stopped and smiled at Theresa, who hesitantly gave her a wave.

"You know her?" Mike asked incredulously.

"I interviewed her for the documentary I did for APTN. Her name is Kim. I can't recall her last name, but she had quite a story. Hells Angels murdered her father when she was just a kid. She was abused in a foster home. One day while a friend was fixing in her washroom, a social worker dropped in to see her. They came and took her baby away two hours later."

Theresa watched as Kim walked into the Patricia Hotel. She was in her early twenties, short and slim, with shoulder length brown hair. The smooth brown skin of her round face needed very little makeup because her brown eyes sparkled and twinkled and her mouth was locked in a perpetual smile.

CHAPTER 3

Kim Lawrence stopped for a second at the curb before entering the hotel; she remembered the woman in the Cadillac from the television show. Kim thought she recognized the car as belonging to a local dealer, and she began to wonder what the reporter was doing with him. Her thoughts were fleeting as she made her way through the familiar lounge lizards in the bar and sat down with two women at a table in the corner. A three-piece blues band was onstage playing a tired version of "Sweet Home Chicago." The music sounded good to Kim, mixed in with the individual conversations that floated over the audience. It all sounded sweet and brought a welcome relief from the hostility at home. Sometimes a crowd was more intimate than being alone, and since her boyfriend Frankie was spending less time at home, she felt a sense of relief being surrounded by people. On most nights she could handle the loneliness, but lately it was bothering her, and tonight she had a more urgent reason to be downtown. Kim needed to fix. The pain was increasing, and she knew it would escalate until it became unbearable.

Mona was already sitting at the table. Jet black hair gave away her Native bloodline, and her dark brown eyes flared up in anger with little or no provocation. She was not beautiful in any ordinary or even exotic way, and the mascara overkill gave her a tough look, which made her attractive to a certain kind of man. Next to Mona sat her wasted friend Lucy, a veteran of the streets and its bad habits, trying hard to maintain some kind of normal posture.

"I did one of your regulars today," Mona said to Kim, finishing her Vodka Seven.

"Oh yeah, which one?"

"Chubby little fuck. I think his name is Dave."

"Enema Dave," Kim said, smiling. "Did he pay you extra?"

"No fucking way was I gonna shove something up his fat asshole," Mona said, unable to resist laughing. "No fucking way!"

"He's actually a nice guy."

"Yeah, fucking sure; they're all nice guys." Mona laughed, waving her empty glass at the waitress. Her fake nails covered in gold lamé caught the light and, for a moment, Kim's attention. "Your so-called regulars are a collection of sick fucking freaks."

"No worse than some of yours." Kim was already pissed that Mona was stealing her clientele, but at the moment had no desire to give Mona a reason to unload on her.

"Fuck off!" Mona said nastily. "What about the doctor who takes you to that XXX theatre? You know, the one who likes getting a blow job while he's watching some porn movie and the other twisted fucks in the theatre stand around jacking off, watching him."

"He was a big tipper," Kim said with a touch of sarcasm.

"I fucking hope so! Sick bastard. I wonder what his patients would say if they knew his little secret?"

"Who cares? I haven't seen him in months," Kim said, wishing she could reach him right now because he would give her the cash without wanting anything. "I've been calling everyone tonight. No one's around except for Rick, and he doesn't want to see me until midnight."

"Don't worry," Mona said, realizing what the problem was and having the immediate solution. "Get Jackie to front you a point; she's got some killer shit."

"I need more than a point," said Kim. A point was just a quarter gram, not enough to get her through the night.

"You know what you gotta do," Mona replied.

"Yeah, Kim," Lucy piped in. "Do what you gotta do." Lucy was 35 going on 50, with blond hair that came out of a bottle and skin as tough as leather; twenty years on the street and still standing. Old hookers don't smile, but tonight Lucy was sporting a junkie grin as her eyelids fought to stay open. "By the way," she slurred, "have you seen Howard?"

Mona shook her head in disgust as she took in the condition of her friend. "You sent him out for some rock."

"When's he comin' back?"

"How the fuck should I know? He's your boyfriend."

"Maybe I should go look for him." Lucy's fractured voice sounded like it was coming from a torn speaker out of an old car radio.

"Maybe you don't move your shaved pussy from that chair and just wait for him to come back," Mona said as Lucy was getting ready to leave. Lucy quickly settled back to her drink.

"I'm gonna walk down to the Carnegie Centre." Kim stood up and took another look around in case a dealer she knew was in the bar. "If I see Howard, I'll let him know you're waiting for him."

"You tell him," Lucy said to no one in particular.

The traffic on Hastings Street on any given night slowed the vehicles down to long lines in both directions, and everything on wheels—from long white limousines to old beaters—was pressed grille to tailpipe. The people on the street were a swaggering, staggering parade of junkies, crackheads, pill poppers, and over-the-hill hookers mingled with a mob from the low end of the gene pool. Welcome to the jungle, where life was worth less than a $20 rock of crack cocaine.

Kim walked around the corner of the hotel, then turned right on Gore Street where several girls had already staked their turf (the usual ten feet of curb that became their office until someone picked them up). Kim kept walking until she was on Isabelle Street where the real stroll extended for the next three blocks. Working girls waited on every corner, lingering in doorways and under streetlights, waiting for sex-starved johns. Kim stopped and turned towards traffic as a black Ford pick-up truck with a Harley Davidson logo painted on the side pulled over to the curb.

She recognized the driver immediately. He wasn't exactly a regular, but she remembered his house and the name on his mailbox; it was William Roberts, but he'd said to call him Bill. He lived somewhere beyond New Westminster. He was in his late forties, tall and heavy set, a big man with a close-shaved head and a beard that made him look intimidating with little effort. Kim had also noticed that he spoke with the hint of a French accent. He wasn't real friendly, but he didn't try and lowball her when it came to payment, plus he was known on the strip for having huge stashes of heroin and crack.

"Get in," he said coldly as he opened the door on the passenger side.

"Are we going to your house?"

"That's right." He gave Kim a glance that seemed to say "where else would we go" then he asked, "You got a friend? And I don't want anybody too fucked up."

"No problem. She's at the Patricia right now."

"What's she like?" Bill queried in a voice that suggested he wouldn't tolerate any attitude.

"We've worked doubles before."

"You better be telling the truth."

Kim rolled down the passenger window and waved at Mona, who was outside smoking a cigarette. "There she is. Pull over here." Kim got out and walked up to Mona, and after a brief conversation they both returned to the truck and got in. Bill undressed Mona with his eyes and cracked a sleazy smile before driving away. The two women exchanged small talk until the city lights disappeared into the rear view mirror and they were on Highway One headed for New Westminster.

"My name is Mona, by the way. I think I met you before," Mona said to Bill, though she really wanted to say that the ride was boring the shit out of her.

"I don't remember you," he replied flatly before turning to Kim. "I did come across some of *your* family friends."

"Yeah?" Kim asked, "Who were they?"

"You wouldn't know any of them. Friends of your father," Bill said with a hint of malice, not taking his eyes off the road.

Kim didn't reply. With the exception of her neighbors, she was too young to have known anyone in her father's many circles of friends. After his death, the period of time she and her family spent in Ontario under police protection had eliminated any connection she had with everyone who knew her father.

As Kim seemed unwilling to talk, Mona decided to intervene. "Are you sure you don't remember me?" Her ego was hurt by the lack of recognition. "It was at a party. There was a band and a lotta people; they called the place The Last Chance."

"That's right, it's my private club, but I still don't remember seeing you there."

"I was with Blackie."

"Is that right?" Bill took a second look at Mona. "I know Blackie. Hells Angel. I haven't seen Blackie for over a year."

"He's not the kind that stays in touch," Mona said, as the truck left the highway, turning on to a dirt road.

"Blackie's solid and he's loyal," Bill said, "not like some people." He shot a contemptuous stare at Kim, but she missed it because she was concentrating on the countryside. The farmhouses passing in and out of view reminded her of her childhood home.

Bill turned into a driveway that was secured by a wire gate. "You remember how to open it?" he asked.

"Of course," Kim said, getting out of the truck and walking over to the corner of gate. She lifted the latch and pushed the gate open; she could hear a dog barking from the barn. After the truck came through, she closed the gate but didn't return the latch. They would be leaving within the hour, so why bother. She got back in the truck, and they drove slowly down a long dirt road bordered by a fence on each side and ending in front of a large house with a garage and barn behind it. The house was old but well kept, too clean for a bachelor living alone, Kim thought to herself. She and Mona sat in the living room while Bill disappeared into the basement and came back with a pipe and a rock of crack cocaine.

Mike arrived at Jesse Crowchild's law office at five-thirty and explained his meeting with the George family. Over the years, Jesse had employed Mike to do investigative work, and they worked together so often they felt like a team. The duo operated like a well-oiled machine. Jesse was well aware of the missing women issue. He lobbied on behalf of the Sisters in Spirit, and he understood only too well how parents felt when a child's life was in danger. Jesse lost a son in a tragic car accident that also nearly cost him his career and his marriage. If Mike could help the George family find out what happened to their daughter, it would force the police into taking more immediate productive action in trying to solve the disappearance of so many Native women.

"I've met Phil George," said Jesse. "He's not looking for miracles, Mike. He just wants to know what happened to his daughter."

"He didn't give me much to work with. Carrie was last seen in a

Calgary rehab, and about the only other thing we know for sure is that her friend Susan died in Edmonton. That's it," Mike said, perusing the office to see if anything had changed.

"Start with Calgary," Jesse said intently. "There's always the slim chance that someone who was in therapy at the same time might have known Carrie."

"I've called the rehab, but the receptionist was reluctant to give up anything." Mike was not in the habit of expressing false hope or forced optimism. "The person I talked to wasn't working there when Carrie was in rehab." Mike forced a smile, but he was no Houdini, and the chances of him finding anyone who knew Carrie George was a long shot at best.

"People in rehab get most of their counseling from the old timers at compulsory AA meetings." A note of personal emotion crept into Jesse's voice. "What goes on in those rooms stays in those rooms." Jesse was speaking from experience; he had not had a drink in over ten years and had spent many hours in similar rooms listening to life stories that echoed his own struggle with alcohol.

"Tell me something I don't know."

"What about Candace Webber?" Jesse queried.

"Nothing so far. I was going to talk to Charlie Feathers about her. If anyone knows anything, it will be Charlie."

"Tell him I liked his editorial on Native veterans."

"He will love hearing that, especially when I tell him it came from you," Mike said on his way out. Jesse followed him and gently put his hand on his friend's shoulder to let Mike know he believed in him.

CHAPTER 4

The Sit & Bull was on Hastings just a block east of Pigeon Park. It had been built back when the best scotch in the house set you back a dollar and a night with a honky-tonk angel cost another nine. The price of a party had changed since then, and so had the clientele. The new patrons were the upper echelon of the welfare crowd. These were serious skid row drunks who had no time for crackheads or junkies. They were especially alienated from the new bohemians who felt drinking with the downtrodden proletariat was way cool. In reality, the skids were about as cool as a turd in a punch bowl, but for the middle class poseurs with their blue jeans ripped and torn in factories before they bought them could only see as far as the next trend.

Charlie Feathers was sitting at the bar. Wednesday was karaoke night, and Charlie was knocking back a cold Kokanee in preparation for his first song. A few beers always bolstered his courage to climb up on the stage. Tonight he was in the mood for "Summer Wind," one of the many Sinatra gems he had spent hours rehearsing at home.

When Mike walked in off the street, there was a rather large woman with a beer in one hand and a microphone in the other making a painful attempt at singing "My Heart Will Go On." The last verse was a challenge for the most seasoned singer and required someone with an excellent range to hit the high notes. The woman on stage was not a gifted singer, and the last verse exposed her as someone with little talent. Beads of sweat rolled down her face, her eyes bulged, and the tendons in her neck looked ready to explode. She turned the operatic vocal crescendo that brings the song to its tragic finish into a spine-chilling war cry, three hundred pounds of raw flesh screamed into the microphone, "My heart will go onnnnnn!"

Mike sat down beside Charlie, who was laughing so hard he didn't notice his friend until Mike tapped him on the shoulder. Charlie wiped the tears from his eyes. The woman still stood on stage, traumatized by the emotional drain of her own performance.

"Mike!" Charlie said. "What are you doing here?"

"I was in the mood for some real entertainment."

"You came to the right place." Charlie took another look at the stage and broke into spasms of laughter.

"She's a whole lot of woman."

"THREEEEE hundred pounds of burning looove!" Charlie said in his best carnival barker voice. "It takes five men to hug her and ten men to lug her!"

"You should have stuck with the circus, Charlie."

"I would have, but I got busted, remember?"

"You were one of my first arrests," Mike said, signaling the bartender to bring Charlie a fresh draught.

"I was set up."

"You got off with a slap on the wrist." Mike laid a twenty on the counter for the bartender. "That put an end to your life of crime."

"Excuse me!" Charlie's voice filled with outrage; he didn't see himself as a criminal. "I sold nickel bags of third grade pot for the carney who hired me. That was for two months, and only two months! Life of crime, my ass. What's the real reason you're here?"

Mike lowered his voice, happy the stage had become silent for a moment. "I had a husband and wife visit me today. Their daughter's been missing for over a year."

"A runaway? Or did she leave with her boyfriend?"

"Small town girl comes to the big city with her best friend. They stay at a friend's house. That friend is wired to crack and turns tricks, and eventually the small town girl and her best friend are doing the same thing." Mike looked around the room as if searching for a familiar face. "She was down here working to support her habit."

"That's too bad. I hope the parents aren't staying up waiting for her," said Charlie. "They could wait a long, long time."

"What's that supposed to mean?"

"Working girls who go missing seldom come back alive, especially these days."

"What's different these days?"

"Somebody's out there, Mike. A killer, as in serial. The cops know all about it, but their shoes are nailed to the floor."

"What makes you say that?"

"Well, they took their own sweet time to issue that poster of the twenty missing women from the East Side, which means there's probably twenty more they don't even know about yet." Charlie knocked back his beer. "Just think about it for a second. All these women have disappeared in the last five years."

"It sounds like you're assuming all the women are dead."

"Missing for five years? You're the ex-cop; you figure it out." Charlie began to wonder if Mike had forgotten the life span of people on mean streets. He was thinking that Mike might be good for another round until the dreaded bass line that opened "These Boots are Made for Walking" boomed through the speakers, announcing another scary performance from Tina.

Tina was born Lionel Peacock in 1975 and discovered he was two-spirited during his adolescence. Now in her early thirties, she was thoroughly "girl" and strutted her stuff around like the bird that gave her the name. Tina was Lionel's new identity, and like Cher, one name was all she needed because in her mind, she was a star. Tonight, Tina was ready for the stage. Her wardrobe, an overstatement of bad taste, was a spectacle unto itself. The *coup de grace* was a leather mini skirt and white hooker boots that went up to her thighs, the Army & Navy version of what Julia Roberts wore in the movie *Pretty Woman*. Tina looked like a karaoke Marilyn Manson as she stepped up to the microphone and belted out the Nancy Sinatra classic, giving the chorus a new meaning.

These boots are made for walkin',
And that's just what they'll do.
One of these days, these boots
Are gonna to walk all over you.

When the song was over, the audience applauded generously, Tina smiled and waved wet kisses as she left the stage. A full house of bar patrons were saying silent prayers they remembered from childhood bibles, everyone frightened that Tina would choose to join them at their table. Charlie looked over at Mike and rolled his eyes back in disgust, then pulled a package of Drum tobacco from his coat pocket and turned his head toward the door as a hint to go outside for a smoke.

The traffic was loud and relentless, interrupted periodically by the screech of tires as drunks and junkies crossed the street daring drivers to splatter them all over the pavement from both directions. Such meetings of steel bulk with frail flesh and bone routinely tied up the seemingly endless parade of vehicles in a rush to go nowhere. Charlie pulled out a rollie and fired it up.

It had been six months since Mike had quit the filthy habit, but still he went through times like this when he could have killed for a cigarette. With his head turned away to avoid the smoke, he noticed the block had changed drastically over the last few years. The storefront windows of old shops that had been here as long as he could remember were now boarded up with "Out of Business" signs on their doors. Even the beautiful block-long Woodward's building, an historical piece of the landscape, had been sold to developers who were already pre-selling high-end condominiums.

"This whole block is up for sale." The anger in Mike's voice was unmistakable.

"Just a matter of time before this bar is sold." Charlie blew a cloud of smoke in the air.

"It doesn't bother you?" Mike sounded a bit irritated by Charlie's neutrality.

"Why should it?" Charlie responded. "The city wants to clean up the East End. Good fucking luck." Charlie let out a cynical laugh, but in his gut he knew the denizens of this part of the city were not here by choice. Most of them had nowhere else to go, which meant the city had a battle on its hands.

"The East End is a festered wart on the ass of the most beautiful city in the world," Mike said coldly. "An eyesore that would give all those foreign investors a bad impression of Vancouver during the Olympics."

"Exactly," said Charlie. "I mean, I do feel sorry for the old people living in these hotels. They will be evicted, and most of them will have nowhere to go."

"Most of them have no children to support them, either. These dismal rooms were supposed to be their retirement homes. Hotel owners are heartless bastards." Mike threw a glance at the Astoria Hotel down the street.

"Yeah, they are some sleazy fucks." Charlie flicked his butt out into traffic. "Do you have any idea how many of those slumlords have been caught cashing pension cheques for tenants who have already died? They're buried and gone, but no one bothers to report it."

"That's been going on forever," said Mike. "It's about as low as you can go. The real issue, Charlie, is time. City Hall let this garbage heap pile up for the last twenty years and never made any attempt to improve things. Now they have three years to make the worst skid row in North America disappear."

"Gotta be some kind of magic trick."

"I hear David Copperfield's coming to town," Mike said, and Charlie curled up a smile. Just then, a police cruiser pulled over a van right in front of them. Mike turned to Charlie. "What makes you so sure they won't get it done?"

"Because I'm part of the garbage they want to get rid of," Charlie said. "I live here, and I'm not moving."

Charlie was down here for the long haul; he had no other option. Mike knew it already, but this time he heard something more intense in Charlie's voice. Charlie put his tobacco pouch back in his pocket and turned to go back in the bar. He knew the implications, but like his neighbors, moving wasn't an option for him. Charlie pulled open the heavy door and made his way back into the depressing darkness of the bar with Mike close behind him. They sat down and returned to business.

"One more name I'd like to run by you. The only lead the family gave me was a woman: Candace Webber." Mike noticed a fresh round of draught the bartender had set down while they were gone, the price for holding their seats.

"Dandy Candy. She used to be down here," Charlie said. "Hung out at the Bourbon, usually with her biker friends."

"Are you kidding me?" Mike exclaimed, ashamed for a moment that he had doubted Charlie. "You know this woman?"

"I've never spoken to her; that's putting my life at risk. Candy's friends are known to be fond of knuckle surgery as a deterrent to anyone who gets too close to her."

"Bikers don't take kindly to anyone getting friendly with their women." Mike tried to conjure up an image of Charlie in a confrontation with half-pissed, paranoid, jealous bikers.

"She's no run-of-the-mill biker whore, man. Candy was moving a lot of crack on the street."

"The Angels were her supplier?"

"That's right, and when they wanted girls for parties, Candy knew where to find them."

"When was the last time you saw her?" Mike inquired.

"She never comes down here anymore. I heard she was running some porn site on the Internet."

"You got a name for the porn site?"

"No, but I know how you can find it." Charlie could hear the strains of "Summer Wind" coming from the stage. It was his cue. He stood up, took a quick look in the mirror behind the bartender, and started for the stage, proud as Pavarotti in his prime.

"Knock'em dead, Charlie," Mike said as Charlie stepped up to the microphone and started singing with his head tilted to one side like Sinatra, the microphone held tightly in his right hand. Charlie was in crooner's heaven. Everyone needs something sacred in their lives. Some find Jesus; some find love; Charlie found karaoke. For the few minutes he stood on stage, Charlie was living a dream that only he and Old Blue Eyes could truly understand. When he finished, the audience showed their approval with heartfelt applause. Charlie was a Sit & Bull favorite, and the regulars loved him.

"Don't quit your day job," Mike said, and pushed a beer in front of him.

"Let's see you get up there!" Charlie appreciated the applause, a wide smile lighting up his face.

"I was pulling your chain, Charlie. You were great." Mike raised his glass in a toast. "Frank would be proud."

"I'm just warming up," Charlie said with as much humility as he could muster. "I'm gonna do another one: 'Somewhere There is a Someone' by..."

"Dean Martin."

"He's the man."

"Was." Mike lifted his beer in respect for the departed. "Dino drank his last martini years ago; he never got over his son dying in that plane crash."

"What a shame!" A table in the corner gave Charlie a few thumbs up for his performance. "What was the movie Dean was in with The Duke?"

"*Rio Bravo.*"

"Right," Charlie said sadly. "I love that movie." His mood had altered to alcohol-induced sentimentality. "All the good ones are gone, and their shoes will never be filled."

"At a certain age, everyone makes that statement." Mike stood up to leave and dropped a ten spot on the table for the bartender. "Old heroes never die, Charlie. They just smell that way."

"What smells is the new crop of singers."

"We both agree on that one." Mike cased the room one more time before leaving. "One last thing… Candace Webber. If you can, help me track her down. Right now she's my only lead."

"If you're willing to stick around for awhile, we can go back to my office. I can show you her website."

"Thanks, Charlie. Whatever you got is more than I have now, which is nothing."

CHAPTER 5

Kim and Mona took turns refilling the pipe, and Bill sat at the table with a small plate filled with cocaine. He watched the girls with contempt as he snorted several lines then washed them down with a beer. Kim noticed he was not as relaxed as on her first visit. He seemed to be in a foul mood, and his indifference towards her had turned into a silent anger that was becoming more intense as he got drunk.

"I found out about your old man," he said, fixing Kim with a scornful stare.

"My father is dead."

"That's what happens to traitors."

"Why are you saying that about my father?" Kim was stung by the remark. Her anger was only tempered by her fear that Bill might get violent.

"It's true," he said. "Your old man was a fucking rat, and the Angels know how to deal with rats."

"I don't know what you're talking about."

"Sure you do. That rat bastard was your father."

"It's not true!" Kim stormed out of the living room. She hated him for what he had said, but she could think of no reply that would have done any good. She ran upstairs and closed the door to the washroom behind her; she wasn't going to give him the pleasure of watching her cry.

"Where do you think you're going?" He screamed from the foot of the stairs. "You get your fat fucking ass down here, right fucking now!"

Kim didn't reply. She would walk all the way back to town rather than have sex with that bastard.

"Why don't you give her a break?" Mona said, a cloud of crack smoke floating over her head. "She hardly knew her father."

"Shut up. If I want to hear you bark, I'll rattle your chain." Bill walked back into the kitchen and knocked back the rest of his beer.

Kim left the safety of the washroom, and if not for her hesitancy in going back downstairs, she might not have noticed that the door to the bedroom next to the bathroom was slightly ajar. Out of curiosity, she stuck her head inside the room. The bed was made and everything seemed in

25

order. She assumed it was the guest room. She noticed a box of clothes left in the corner near the window. She started to leave, but then stopped for a second look. The box was stuffed full of a ragged collection of dresses, skirts, and blouses of different sizes, and unless Roberts was a seasoned cross-dresser, the clothes didn't belong to him. Kim went through the box slowly, and about two thirds of the way to the bottom, she found a piece of clothing that stopped her cold: a Mötley Crüe T-shirt stained with dried blood.

Kim stood up quickly; her heart was pounding like a drum. The crack she'd just smoked ripped through her brain, distorting all linear thinking until slowly the box and its contents began to make sense. The clothes were all that remained of their former owners, the only reminder of their forgotten lives. Kim had no doubt that she and Mona would be his next victims. She could imagine her clothes on top of the pile. She went back into the washroom, splashed cold water on her face to get her head straight, and tried to calm down. Mona would somehow have to be alerted to the danger. Their only chance was to stay cool and try not to provoke him in any way. Once his pants were down, she and Mona would knock him out, steal his truck, and get the fuck out of here.

Kim moved to the top of the stairs. She was alarmed by the tone of the conversation wafting up in disconnected words from below. She made her way down the stairs, holding on to the banister. When she reached the vestibule at the bottom, she realized her imagination had not been playing tricks on her. The atmosphere in the living room was volatile. The first thing she heard clearly was Mona, who seemed to be blissfully unaware of the man she was dealing with.

"I don't like your fucking attitude," Mona said to Bill, who was standing right in front of her.

"Tough shit bitch!" He wasn't in the mood for no smartass remarks. "If you want the pipe refilled, you better shut the fuck up."

"Fuck you asshole!" Mona yelled. "I'm outta here." She stood up and was about to walk out the door when Bill sucker punched her. She collapsed in the middle of the floor, blood trickling from her nose.

"You ain't goin' nowhere," Bill growled. His fists were ready to punch her again. He hovered over Mona for a moment. She was lying on the floor, dazed by the blow, afraid he was going to lay a serious beating on her.

"Don't hit me! Please, I'll do whatever you say." Mona slowly pulled herself up off the floor as Kim retreated back upstairs.

"Fucking right you will." Bill walked into the kitchen, started opening drawers and swearing under his breath. Finally, he took out a hunting knife and held it in front of him so Mona couldn't mistake it for anything other than a weapon.

"You can put that away so I can do what I'm here for." Mona was hoping Kim was watching. She had the feeling this was going to end badly, no matter what she did or said.

"That's right bitch," Bill said, "because I could slit your throat right now and no one would know, let alone give a shit." He was filling the pipe as he spoke. He handed the pipe to Mona grudgingly and unbuckled his jeans. "Where the fuck is your friend?"

"Don't worry," Mona said, "She'll be back." Mona knew if she didn't take the knife away from him, he was going to kill her.

"Take another hit and then let's get down to business," Bill said. His jeans were piled up around his boots. He stretched the elastic on the front of his black shorts and gave Mona a look of anticipation.

"All right," Mona said, lighting the pipe before backing off a few steps to exhale the smoke. She offered him the pipe, but he sneered at it and turned away.

"Will you fucking hurry up!" He was beginning to feel awkward, standing in the middle of the room with his pants down.

"Last one," Mona said. Pretending she was going to take another hit, she held the pipe just inches away from her face and raised her voice to get Kim's attention. "Kimberly… we're waiting."

Bill looked back at the stairs and frowned. Just as he turned back to Mona, she threw the entire contents of the burning pipe into his eyes and ran towards the door. She thought of taking the road, but in her panic-stricken frame of mind she opted for the dark safety of the barn, hoping to escape through the open field beyond. This would prove to be a fatal mistake since the terrain was dark and unfamiliar and the chained dog who had witnessed her escape was waiting for his master to let him loose so he could bring her down. She would never make it; Bill and his dog would make sure of that.

"Cocksucker!!!" Bill screamed in pain, blinded for a few seconds. He stumbled to the sink and splashed cold water on his face; his eyes were on fire. He struggled to hoist his pants up to his waist, then he was out the door after Mona, clutching the knife in his right hand and screaming, "You wanna fuck with me you bitch?!?"

Hearing all the commotion, Kim inched her way down the stairs and stood at the doorway. She could see Bill running towards the barn his dog in front of him and Mona no more than ten steps ahead of them. The dog soon caught up to her, and as she shielded herself with her hands trying to stop him from biting her, Bill arrived with the knife clenched tightly in his hand and stabbed her repeatedly.

Kim ran out the door and down the driveway towards the main road. She heard loud, wretched screams from Mona and the sounds of a struggle, but the screams became weaker and weaker and until they died out altogether. Kim kept running, darkness all around her. She knew she was getting closer to the road because the light from the house had almost faded to nothing. It took her eyes a few moments to adjust before she actually noticed the outline of the gate. For a few moments, there was a stark silence. She felt her strength waning. She wanted to catch her breath, but suddenly the silence was broken by the scramble of four feet on the gravel road accompanied by a low guttural growl, the kind wolves emit when they are closing in for the kill.

Kim felt a last rush of adrenaline as the gate was now just ten feet away and the dog was closing in fast. She didn't want to look back, but she could hear it breathing heavily, the growls growing louder. Finally, she made it to the gate, stuck her hand through the wire mesh, and pulled the gate open in one quick motion. She passed through the hole quickly and slammed the gate shut behind her.

She saw the dog flying toward her, then heard the weight of its body crashing against the gate. It was a huge Doberman; its paws were clenched like a man's fists around the wire, mouth wide open for rejuvenating breath, time-sharpened teeth shining yellow-white in the darkness, froth and saliva rolling down sweat-drenched jowls. It had been cheated of its prey, and its anger had turned into rage. The dog tried to climb over the gate but was kept back by three rows of barbed wire at the top. Kim left the dog behind, its face flush against the wire mesh of the gate, frantic that it could pursue her no longer. It barked madly the further Kim disappeared into the night.

Kim ran along the pitch black road; no streetlights out in this crazy neck of the woods. She kept running until she couldn't hear the dog barking anymore and figured it was safe as she slowed down to a walk. Her heart was beating out of control, her lungs gasping for air, and her mind staggering in all directions at once, yet she would periodically jerk and shake as if reeling from shock treatment. She kept an eye on the road behind her, frightened that Bill would find her after he had finished with Mona; it was only a matter of time before the headlights of his truck would come down this same road after her. Kim thought for a second about what she should do. She could hide in the ditch and wait until sunrise when chances of a ride were better, but before she could think of anything else, she heard the sound of a car approaching in the distance.

CHAPTER 6

Mike fired up the Eldorado and headed towards the *Native Times* office. Charlie sat back in the passenger seat. It was a good night. He'd had his moment of karaoke glory, and now he was cruising down Hastings in a Caddy. "Life is good sometimes," Charlie thought out loud as they passed the hollowed out Woodward's Department Store and turned right on Cambie. They parked in front of a beautiful old building that had earned its heritage status on the strength of some turn-of-the-century bricklaying, and walked in through the arched open vestibule and huge double doors. The main floor was occupied by the Veteran's Society; a large poster of W.W. II hero Smokey Smith was centered in the street-side window. Charlie and Mike walked up one flight of marble stairs to the *Native Times* office on the second floor. Once inside, Charlie went over to his desk and turned on the computer, then invited Mike to pull up a chair. Mike was about to meet the infamous Candy Webber.

A blonde in her late twenties appeared on the computer screen, posing in front of a brand new Harley Davidson. Her upper body was tattooed and naked except for a black brassiere. She wore skin-tight leather pants and balanced precariously on Cinderella glass shoes with four-inch heels. Candy was every biker's wet dream, the perfect cover girl for a website. Her long curly blonde hair was her best feature, though ocean blue eyes highlighted her elongated face, and her bee-stung lips were reminiscent of Angelina Jolie's sexy pout. The shingle "CANDY & FRIENDS" floated above her head in bold letters. Loitering beneath the Harley in lower case, the single word "submit" invited all cyber wankers to enter the site.

"You wanna meet Candy or her friends?" Charlie asked, with a big grin.

"Let's start with Candy," Mike said as a photo collage of young women filled the screen and Charlie moved the cursor to select Candy herself. Her profile appeared above a gallery of pictures showing her in different costumes that ranged from schoolgirl to leather. She was clearly open-minded when it came to even the most adventurous sexual matters. She was also very clear about her own preference for a man who could take control, a real man, not just some pussy who thought being submissive meant showing his feminine side. According to the caption, the precise details of real and imaginary encounters could be discussed at length in the prurient security of the chat room. There was a fee for membership, of course, and clients had to sign up for a minimum of three months.

Charlie excused himself and walked away from the computer and past several other desks. Bundles of undistributed newspapers were stacked up against the back door, and pictures of politicians and Native leaders hung on the walls. Another room set aside for the art department was wired for sound, complete with computers, scanners, and printers. In one corner, there was a makeshift kitchen counter with a kettle, toaster, blender, electric frying pan, microwave oven, and cappuccino machine. Charlie went over to the portable fridge where he kept his beer in the bottom below the stash of assorted sliced meats and deli cheeses always there for late night sandwiches: pastrami, salami, roast beef, Gouda, Edam, Swiss, and good old Canadian Cheddar. The fridge was off-limits to everybody except the graveyard shift, which consisted of himself and Pontiac.

Charlie came back to his desk with two cans of beer and a few slices of cheese and stole another long look at Candy. "I figure the take is at least eighty large a month," Charlie said, handing a Kokanee to Mike. "She's laughing all the way to the bank."

"That's a lot of money for people who probably don't even know how to boot up a computer," Mike said, trying to figure out how bikers could have become so high tech, since most of them could barely read a newspaper.

"They hired some of the best programmers in town."

"Smart move," Mike said cynically. "But is this the real Candy, or has the make-up department worked a little cosmetic magic?"

"No, that's Candy alright," Charlie smirked. "She's actually hot, but in a biker moll kind of way."

"There's obviously a little gray matter between her ears," Mike admitted.

"Got that right. She's street smart; her real job is to find just the right girls and then keep them in line."

"Do you happen to know any of her friends?"

"Not really, but I'm on a first name basis with the bartender at the

Metro on Alexander Street, a few blocks north of the skids. Candy and her crew are regulars there. Mainly girls, but you can be sure her male friends are Hells Angels not wearing their colours."

"Nice work, Charlie!"

"Don't thank me until you speak to Pontiac."

"Pontiac? Pontiac knows Candy?"

"Pontiac knows everybody. He's done a few stories on her for the *Cyber News*."

"Really? Well, let's have a chat with super-freak. I haven't seen him in years."

"That could be a good thing," Charlie said to himself as he left the front office and walked towards the sales and writers room with Mike following him. They walked down the hallway into a large room filled small cubicles protected by dividers just large enough to accommodate one writer or salesman at a desk. This geographical density didn't seem to disturb Pontiac Dumont, who was leaning back in his chair resting his snakeskin cowboy boots on the blotter in the centre of his desk. His head was rocking slowly back and forth; he had his headphones on, and his eyes were closed.

Pontiac remained just as Mike remembered him, dark hair with red streaks, his face long and chiseled with a fine aquiline nose, his only jewelry a tiny silver tomahawk hanging from his left earlobe. Pontiac was wearing a Keith Secola & Wild Indians T-shirt. His right arm bore a tattoo of the famous Ottawa Chief Pontiac, and on his left arm the wind-blown bearded face of Métis hero Gabriel Dumont: buffalo hunter, warrior, and Louis Riel's general who did most of the fighting in the Northwest Rebellion. Pontiac was listening to the new Derek Miller CD on his iPod and never heard Charlie coming, not until Charlie stood right in front of him and yelled, "PONTIAC! YOU HAVE A VISITOR!"

"Wha... what?" Pontiac snapped out of his trance and was ready to give Charlie a piece of his mind for disturbing him when he spotted Mike. He took off his headphones and gave his old friend a smile.

"Mike the Mountie dude! I thought you retired." Pontiac's voice sounded like sandpaper scraped over concrete.

"My official title is Private Investigator."

"You're a gumshoe?" Pontiac wasn't sure he had heard right.

"That's right." Mike knew Pontiac wanted to know why. He would let

Charlie update him on what happened. "How's everything with you?"

"Still vertical; still virile." Pontiac dropped an empty beer can into a plastic bag tied to his desk drawer and looked at Mike with a trickster smile. "Maybe I could be your partner, you know, like Starsky and Hutch."

"Sorry, Pontiac. I work alone."

"How about I shave my head? People will think I'm Kojak or Bruce Willis."

"I wouldn't want to deprive the literary world of one of its only bright lights."

"It's a sacrifice I'm willing to make," replied Pontiac, now eye to eye with Mike. "You know, one for the team, the pair of us up against the evil forces of the world, making hell's half acre a safer place for the kids."

"Sounds good. Maybe we could turn it into a reality show."

"That would be rad dude."

"What can you tell me about Candy Webber?" Mike asked.

"I do know Miss Candy." Pontiac grimaced as he said her name. "She's got some nasty friends who enjoy hurting people they don't like, so you better have a good reason to make her acquaintance."

"It's a long story. I'm trying to find a woman who went missing, and Candy is the only person who might know if she's still alive."

"Good luck." Pontiac said cynically.

"She's the only lead I have."

"Then you got nothing, because even if she does know something about this missing girl, you wouldn't get it out of her with a crowbar."

"Maybe, but I'm willing to give it a shot." Mike tried to stay calm. "Charlie said Candy hangs out at a bar called The Metro."

"You try and get close to her at The Metro and her friends—we're talking Hells Angels here—they'll be on you like a school of piranhas." Pontiac gave Charlie the look, a silent reprimand for offering such bad advice.

"You got a better plan?" Mike asked with a touch of sarcasm.

"Ya mon, guaranteed to get you close to the Madame," Pontiac replied, the humor back in his voice. "Miss Candy and some of her friends are usually at the River Rock Casino in Richmond every Wednesday night. Candy's playing blackjack as we speak. The goon squad gets left behind when she gambles, which means you may approach her sweetness without the risk of being handicapped for life."

"Knowing you, I take it this information doesn't come second hand."

"I just happen to know one of the young ladies close to Candy. We were introduced many moons before she became a cyber porn queen."

"What about Candy?"

"She was in one of my stories on cyber sex." Pontiac opened the bottom left drawer of his desk and retrieved a hard copy of the *Cyber News*. "Candy loved it, and since then I've become one of her favorite people. Like many women of her generation, Candy thinks she's supermodel material and a movie career is right around the corner."

"Your kind of woman," Mike said facetiously.

"Ah yes." Pontiac smiled. "Beautiful women who dare to dream; I could listen to them all night."

Mike turned towards the window. He could see the lights from the Lion's Gate Bridge in the distance; a blue mist was settling over the mountains. Mike knew Pontiac's history of making promises he didn't always keep.

"Let me get this straight, we show up tonight at the Casino and Candy Webber will be there? You have no doubt?"

"Zero! She's a creature of habit, just like the rest of us. Tonight is girl's night out."

Pontiac took out his cell phone and started dialing. He smiled when the call was answered. "Am I speaking to Her Sweetness? It's your biographer, the one and only Pontiac. That's right. I'm headed towards the Casino right now, just checking to see if you're blackjacking tonight. You are? Perfecto! I will find you. Should be there in about forty minutes." Pontiac put his cell phone in his pocket and looked at Mike. "Ready to rock bro?"

"Alright, she's at the casino. I'm assuming there will be no problem if I come along with you?" Mike was a little suspicious of Pontiac's optimism; he had a history of winging it with mixed results.

"Straight up, dude. When we drift by the blackjack tables, the cyber vixens will be watching Candy lose her money." Pontiac raised his bony hands in the air as if he had just welcomed a guest onto his imaginary talk show. "I make the introductions. You're in film, currently working on a documentary."

"Let's get moving," Mike interrupted, not sure if he could be enough of a flake to be convincing. "Richmond is at least thirty minutes away. You can tell me what movies I'm supposed to have worked on in the car."

"Okay, partner." Pontiac stood up and gave Mike a high five.

"I appreciate you helping with the investigation," Mike said, "but we are not partners."

"Morningstar and Dumont!" Pontiac paused for a second, allowing the echo to leave the room. "Dude! You have to admit, that is powerful."

"Let's go, Pontiac. The clock is ticking." Mike shook hands with Charlie, thanked him for his help, and walked out of the *Native Times* office with Pontiac behind him.

Mona's body lay motionless on the ground outside the barn, her death the result of multiple stab wounds. Bill Roberts looked down at his victim, the bloodied knife in his hand. His dog Manson was barking wildly from the front gate; Roberts wasn't expecting anyone at this late hour. He went back towards the house, looking down the road to see if there was a vehicle parked in front of the gate; no headlights, all he could see was his dog barking. Sonavabitch… he realized the other one had got away. He ran inside and changed his clothes quickly then shoved a double deuce with a silencer into his coat pocket and left the house.

Roberts put Manson in the truck with him and headed down the road; his fear was the other hooker would seek help at the nearest farm less than a mile down the road. He put the headlights on bright, put his foot to the floor, and within minutes he was closing in on his neighbor's farm. He stopped in front of the mailbox and took a look down the driveway. No sign of life, which meant the girl was either still walking or someone had picked her up. He kept driving in the vain hope he might see her on the side of the road; no such luck. He went through a litany of curses until he hit Highway One, his headlights falling on a traffic sign that said New Westminster 47 kilometres.

She had been picked up, he guessed, probably by one of his neighbors.

It was a slim chance, but he might be able to catch her at the SkyTrain station. She would want to get back downtown, and he was betting any driver who picked her up was headed to New West. The woman had to be silenced before she had a chance to spill her guts to the police. Since she was a drug addict, Roberts hoped she might not be inclined to go to the cops immediately. These thoughts bounced around in his brain while he kept a close eye on the cars he passed on the highway, hoping that he might spot her in someone's passenger seat.

CHAPTER 7

Kim took her cell phone out of her purse and called her sister in Yaletown. She was hoping she could stay there for the night, but there was no answer, and she didn't leave a message. Kim watched the lights of New Westminster off in the distance. She had been picked up by a man in his late forties, dressed in work jeans and red flannel shirt. He was blue collar from the steel-toed boots on his feet to the BC Lions cap on his head. He smiled at Kim, his yellow teeth peeking through a scruffy beard, and introduced himself as Marvin Stewart.

"It's none of my business," he said, "but what the hell were you doing way out there in the middle of nowhere?" Marvin took a closer look at Kim. She couldn't be more than twenty or twenty-two, but he could tell she had street smarts.

"It's a long story; let's just say I missed my ride."

"Jesus, sounds like you got pissed off at your boyfriend, or maybe it's the other way around."

"I'd rather not talk about it," Kim replied, her face flushed by the flashing red lights of several police cruisers parked on the opposite side of the road.

"HMS Christ, it's a stop-check. Bulls and breathalyzers." Marvin slowed down to a safe 60 kilometres per hour, a few car lengths behind the Volvo station wagon in front of him. "If you've had more than one beer, it's game over. You're going downtown, and the car gets impounded."

"Are they going to stop us?" Kim wanted to take a chance and tell the police about Mona, but wondered if the men in blue would believe her. She was afraid the trained eye of the police would see the needle tracks, and once they knew she was a junkie, they would have no recourse but to lock her up until they found out what happened to Mona. She would have to come down in jail, and this was not the right time. Right now, she needed a point just to get through the night.

"Don't look like it; not this time. They're stopping all the poor fucks coming home from the hockey game. We're in the safe lane, thank fuckin' God. A breathalyzer is the last thing I wanna see right now."

"Have you been drinking?" Kim hoped to keep him talking about anything other than what she had been doing tonight.

"I've had a few, but that's all it takes. Zero tolerance. Kiss your driver's license goodbye. And if they catch you a second time, you're doing time. Believe me, I speak from experience!" Marvin slowed down as they drove past the line of cars in the opposite lane. Five cruisers and a paddy wagon were parked on the side of the highway and a steady stream of vehicles moved at a snail's pace. The line of lights stretched back into the darkness for at least a mile. Policemen pointed flashlights in drivers' faces; the lucky ones moved on, and the guilty were escorted to the paddy wagon.

"Are those people off to jail?" Kim asked.

"The Crowbar Hotel is where the poor bastards are headed," Marvin said, nodding his head. "I'm gonna have to stop for gas because right now I'm running on fumes, and running out of gas on this highway is no fun." He resumed a normal speed, as the police were behind him now, and breathed a sigh of relief. He lit up a Player's Light and rolled down his window.

"I'm going to the SkyTrain." Kim started to feel a bit safer. She still felt nauseous and was getting chills, but she no longer felt as if she was going to faint.

"No problem. There's a Texaco on Front Street. That's only two miles from the train station. You could hop a bus from there."

"Thank you. I don't know what I would have done if you hadn't picked me up."

"That's alright. I've been in one or two tight spots myself," Marvin replied, wheeling his El Camino into the Texaco and pulling up to the gas pumps.

Kim closed her eyes for a second and took a deep breath. She was safe; another half hour and she would be downtown. She would phone the police as soon as she got home. "I can get off here," she said.

"You take care of yourself." Marvin noticed for the first time that his passenger was wasted and possibly sick. He watched Kim struggle just to get the car door open, and when she stood up, she seemed to have great difficulty keeping her balance.

"Thanks again." Kim felt a twinge of vertigo. Her legs were like rubber. She smiled, looking back at Marvin as she walked slowly into the service station. She bought a can of Coke and drank it down quickly. The sugar rush gave her a little more focus, just enough to get her into to the women's washroom where the stench of urine brought on a heavy wave of nausea. Kim splashed some water on her face and stood up in front of the mirror; she didn't recognize the person looking back at her. She felt a flash of heat run up her spine, ending in a frightening dryness in her throat. She collapsed as close to the toilet bowl as possible and threw up.

Kim stumbled outside, gasping at the warm air filling her lungs. She needed to return the washroom key. As she came around the corner of the garage, she glanced toward the gas pumps and noticed the El Camino was gone. Several SUV's and a half-ton truck were parked at the pumps. She took a second look and recognized the black truck with the Harley logo; it belonged to Bill Roberts, and he was filling his tank. His dog was in the back with its front paws up on the tailgate. It wanted off its leash badly. Manson looked in her direction and started barking. Roberts stared hard toward the garage, but he couldn't see anyone; maybe there was another dog chained up in the back.

"Shut up, Manson! There's nothing there," Roberts yelled angrily, but the damn mutt didn't listen. Manson's barking grew louder, more vicious. Roberts returned the hose to the pump. The barking made him furious, mainly because the dog had ignored his command to shut up. He walked around to the back of the truck, grabbed the leash, and yanked Manson down onto his back, punching the dog in the ribs. "When I say shut up, I mean it!"

The dog winced and yelped in pain, then went silent for a few seconds until Bill got back in the truck. Manson began to whimper again, but when Roberts opened the door and stuck his head out, the dog ignored the pain and started growling again in the direction of the garage. Roberts uttered a few profanities as he took a box from under the seat; inside were several small tools laid out in a tray. He knew he was going to be pulled over at the first stop-check, and if the cops got nosy, they would search the truck and find the gun on him. He took the twenty-two out of his coat, removed the silencer and placed it under the tray, then locked the toolbox. He got out of the truck, which started the dog barking again while Roberts swaggered into the station with the box under his arm. He walked up to the attendant, and asked if his friend Jack was working.

"Jack doesn't start until midnight."

"Sonovabitch…" Roberts shook his head, feigning despair. "He's working the graveyard shift?"

"That's right."

"I've got some tools here that belong to him," Roberts said, as if Jack was his lifetime buddy, when really he only knew him from stopping at the garage. "Since he's coming in later, could I leave this here for him?"

"No problem."

"I appreciate your help." Roberts handed the attendant the box. "Tell Jack I'll give him a call around seven."

"Sure, bud, I'll let him know." The attendant glanced outside and saw the big Doberman in the back of the pick-up, scrambling and barking at the end of his leash. "Your dog, does he always bark like that?"

"He probably smells that watchdog you keep chained behind the garage."

"No dog back there anymore; he's been gone for months."

"I don't know what's going on then; my mutt never barks like that unless he's got a good reason."

"Christ, it could be skunks again. The stinking bastards never fail to come out this time of night to root through the garbage." The attendant put on a big toothy smile for the benefit of two customers walking through the door.

"My dog hates skunks!" Roberts seemed happy to put the matter to rest.

"That's probably the reason, then." The attendant turned away to deal with the customers paying for their gas purchases.

Bill Roberts was just about to leave when a tall, big-boned woman stormed through the door and dramatically dropped the keys to the women's bathroom on the counter. In a voice loud enough to be heard through the closed door and out at the gas pumps, she filed her complaint. "THE BATHROOM IS FILTHY!" she screeched, staring down contemptuously at the attendant. "Someone has thrown up in there. It's disgusting!"

The attendant tried to diffuse the situation. "The last woman to use it was just here a few minutes ago."

"Well, since she left the keys outside on the pavement, I don't think she will be cleaning up her mess!" The woman pursed her lips to dissipate her anger, then in her best schoolmarm voice, she popped the inevitable question, "Was she on drugs?"

"No sign of drugs," the attendant said defensively, not wanting to admit that the young lady had seemed more than a little bit lost.

"She probably hitched a ride and got dropped off here. Either way," said the big angry woman, "she's flown the coop and you, young man, must deal with this problem. Anyone from city hall happens to see that mess in there, your boss will be paying a big fine and you'll be looking for a job!" Whirling her large carcass around without waiting for a response, she marched like an elephant out the door.

The attendant breathed a sigh of relief as he watched her leave. "How in the fuck does she stuff herself into a car?" he muttered. His jaw tightened; the thought of cleaning up someone else's vomit made him angry. For a lousy seven dollars an hour, it just didn't feel right.

Roberts cracked a wry smile, thinking his trip may not have been for nothing after all. "This woman who puked in the washroom, was she a brunette wearing a light brown dress, running shoes?" he asked, in a calm but officious voice.

"I think she was, now that you mention it," the attendant recalled, not really thinking of the woman. The idea of cleaning the washroom was weighing him down.

Roberts was sure she was his girl and at this very moment she was probably not far away; that's why Manson was still barking. "I didn't pay much attention to her," Bill said casually, as if he was discussing the weather, "but when I drove up to the pumps, I thought I saw a woman in a brown dress walking down the street," he said, baiting the attendant into believing he didn't know who it was and why she had run away.

"I got no choice but to clean that shit up myself," the attendant sighed. "That fat cow will be calling the cops the second she gets home."

"She was blowing smoke. The cops are busy up the road pulling over drunks," Roberts assured him. "Who's she going to call in city hall at this time of night?"

"Who knows, but either way I'm stuck with getting it done myself."

The attendant was sadly resigned to his station in life at this particular flip of the calendar.

"Listen, I'll take that tool kit back now kid. You got enough on your plate at the present time. I'll just wait and give it to Jack myself."

"Sure." The attendant retrieved the kit from under the counter and gave it back to the still anonymous stranger.

"Thanks, partner!" Roberts gave him a half-baked grin and rushed out to his truck without even acknowledging Manson in the back, still frothing at the mouth. He fired up the pick-up and drove down 23rd Avenue towards the SkyTrain Station.

CHAPTER 8

Five minutes until the midnight hour and a few miles from the River Rock Casino, the Eldorado cruised down Oak Street while Pontiac tested Mike's knowledge as a director of indie films and well respected established Native actors. Mike needed to have their names stored in his brain along with the films that made them famous.

Pontiac quizzed him, "What actors were in the remake of *Bury My Heart At Wounded Knee?*"

"Adam Beach, Gordon Tootoosis, and Wes Studi," Mike answered.

"You're cooking with gas, dude!" Pontiac said, convinced that Mike would pull this off, no problem. "Candy loves Adam Beach, so tell me which Clint Eastwood movie was he in and what character did he portray?"

"*Flags of Our Fathers*! Adam plays the original Native American war hero Ira Hayes, made famous in that great song by Johnny Cash. You're the musician. You should know the song!" Mike made a layman's attempt at singing the refrain:

> *Call him Drunken Ira Hayes*
> *It don't matter anymore*
> *Not that whiskey drinkin' Indian*
> *Or the Marine who went to war*

"Cool. You're getting the drift," Pontiac said, smiling as the Caddy turned the corner and the Red Rock Casino came into view. "Remember! You are working on a documentary right now about missing Native women, so you should be able to question Candy about Carrie without arousing suspicion."

"That's real good, Pontiac! And what am I doing while you're looking for Candy and her friends?"

"Having a martini at The Geisha. I should be able to convince the ladies to join you at the bar later."

The moment they walked in the door of the casino, Pontiac went looking for Candy while Mike made his way to the restaurant and sat down at the bar. He ordered a Singapore Sling. There was music from a recent James Bond flick in the background. The wall traditionally reserved for a barroom mirror now boasted an identical pair of flat 57-inch high-definition television screens, both showing James winning $50 million at a poker table. Mike could see Pontiac over in the corner where several blackjack tables were up and running. Pontiac was surrounded by a gaggle of beautiful young women whose body language implied someone was winning big time.

"The girl's on fire!" said Pontiac, raising his martini high in a victory toast while Candy pulled in a big circle of chips. "You're at five large, sister, don't push your luck!"

"I'm cool, honey." Candy took the advice politely and returned a row of chips to the betting circle. "Thanks for caring."

"Tough love."

"Shove it where the sun don't shine," she said with a smile. Then she picked up her scotch and leaned over to look down upon the card.

Pontiac turned to his old friend Betty who had been following the game hoping her boss would not lose all that money. "Close your eyes," he whispered in her ear, "and think positive for Candy."

The players stood silent in their positions at the table in respect of international gaming protocol. Nobody moved an inch or spoke a word until Candy asked the dealer, "What's your name sweetheart?"

"Mai Ling."

"Nice to make your acquaintance. My name's Candy."

"You are very lucky."

"Luck's got nothing to do with it. By the way, I'll stand." With only a queen and a nine, Candy was pushing her luck, but it didn't matter; she was on a roll. Candy waited for Mai Ling to play her hand. Mai Ling's first card the Jack of Spades, second a six of Diamonds and then the heartbreaker: a ten of Hearts. Mai Ling was at 26 and busted. Candy breathed a sigh of relief as a large stack of chips was pushed in her direction.

"You can open your eyes now," Candy said without taking her eyes off of the dealer. She could tell Mai Ling was not happy with the outcome. Tough tacos you geisha bitch, Candy thought to herself, because I'm just warming up.

"I don't believe it!" Pontiac exclaimed. As if their presence had been crucial to the win, Pontiac gave Betty a big hug. In her late twenties, Betty was a busty brunette stripper cum cyber-queen poured into a tight pink turtleneck that gave prominence to her cleavage. Her dark brown hair, cut short in waves, framed a long face with sleepy, deep gray eyes. Her lower lip seemed a bit out of proportion but added to the sensuality of her face. She spoke in a soft but measured tone that she had cultivated in order to do her job.

"Wow! Look at all those chips!" Betty thought there must be six months worth of salary on the table.

"You can relax; this is my last hand," Candy said to Betty, then pointed her finger at Pontiac, "Not a word from you!" She pushed all of her chips, a value of eight thousand dollars, into the circle. Mai Ling looked around, hoping there was a floor manager observing the action. Candy's first card was the King of Diamonds. She held her breath; her face became as still as a sleeping baby's. She waited for the second card with the countenance of the Sphinx. Devoid of emotion, she finished her scotch as Mai Ling placed the Ace of Hearts on top of her King for a perfect 21. Blackjack! Candy laughed excitedly.

Mai Ling gave Candy a contemptuous smile and proceeded to deal. The three of Spades was her first card, then an eight of Clubs, and what should have been her last card, a four of Diamonds. Mai Ling forced a smile, this time suppressing her fear of losing. There were already three cards on the table, but it wasn't enough to beat this arrogant white-trash woman. Mai Ling needed twenty-one, or she'd be the loser. She stared at the deck hoping for a miracle, and finally pulled the fourth card: a ten of Clubs; she was busted. Mai Ling pushed a small mountain of chips towards Candy who was sporting a big smile. She gave the dealer a wink before putting the chips into a casino basket and walking away from the table. Her female posse, along with Pontiac, followed behind her. In Candy's world, everything was perfect at this very moment.

Mike was reading the entertainment schedule in the restaurant and was happily surprised to see that Redbone was playing the main ballroom Saturday night. He went to one of their concerts when he was seventeen and could still remember all the lyrics to "Come And Get Your Love." Perhaps Theresa would be interested in seeing one of the few Native bands to ever sell 20 million albums. He noticed the players coming from the casino: Candy with a shopping basket full of gambling chips, and Pontiac arm in arm with a mystery brunette, the three of them laughing and talking as they made their way to the restaurant. Candy was close to six feet tall, and she reminded Mike of Courtney Love, beautiful but trashy. Her streaked blonde hair was pulled back in a ponytail, showing off her piercing blue eyes and a killer smile. She was wearing expensive clothes, but on Candy everything looked as if it had been dragged out of some back alley bin and belonged on an original Sally Ann blowing a second-hand trombone like it was the hose-end of a crack pipe.

On the big screen, Bond was now in Venice. Mike ordered a second Sling and the hostess made sure Candy and company were seated in the centre aisle. When the bartender finally returned with his drink, Mike noticed Pontiac making his way over to the bar.

"Dude, the vixens are waiting," Pontiac said.

"You told them about the documentary?"

"No, I stretched your contribution to the movies we discussed. It's cool. Candy can't wait to meet you." Pontiac waited for Mike to finish his drink and then ushered him over to the winner's table.

"One of my oldest and dearest friends, ladies. Mike, I want you to meet Betty, and over here, the winner is... Miss CANDY!" Pontiac was doing his best Pat Sajack from *Wheel of Fortune* pointing at the full basket of chips on Candy's lap.

"Betty, nice meeting you, and Candy, I see you have the basket of goodies."

"The real goodies are underneath the basket honey."

"I will keep that in mind." Mike smiled at Candy. The "chance" encounter was starting well, he thought to himself.

"To our blackjack queen!" Pontiac said, lifting his glass of champagne.

"Every dog has her day!" Candy filled her glass with bubbly. "Betty, would you be a sweetheart and cash these chips for me?"

Betty finished her drink and picked up the basket. "No problem! Should I tell him big bills only?"

"You got it."

"You're gonna need someone to ride shotgun with all that cash," Pontiac said as he stood up to follow Betty, realizing this was Mike's best shot at being alone with Candy.

"You're my hero, Pontiac!" Candy blew him a kiss. "And if you see Donna and Chantal, tell them to join us!"

"I'll be back in a flash with the cash and the babes."

"So Mike, you and Pontiac... what's the connection?"

"Years ago, we worked together on a college newspaper." Mike said nonchalantly, hoping he dodged the bullet as long as Pontiac hadn't come up with an entirely different story. "Pontiac was also playing in his own band at the time. Buffalo Soldiers I think they were called."

"And you're still friends?" Candy gave him a lopsided smile. "What I mean is, Pontiac doesn't really give a shit about anything anymore."

"Let's just say his ship came in, but at the time Pontiac was waiting at the train station," Mike said as he looked around to make sure his friend was not within earshot. "The offers have never stopped coming; they have always been there. He's been published in *Rolling Stone* and in *Guitar Player*. Problem is, Pontiac only works six months of the year; the other six, he's on tour."

"He's insane," Candy cut in, letting out spasms of laughter.

"He's a limited edition, that's for sure."

"Dare I ask what you're working on now?" Candy moved closer to Mike and whispered, "Or is it a big secret?"

"Not really. It's my own project," he said, matter-of-factly.

"You're making an indie flick?"

"A documentary."

"Cool." She moved her elbow onto the table and rested her cheek in her palm, inches away from Mike's face. "Are you going to tell me what it's about, or do I have to wait until the champagne kicks in?"

"It's about the missing women from the Downtown East Side. You might have seen a poster offering a reward for info on them."

"Is that right?" Candy mused, the humor gone from her voice. "I happened to know some of the women that are on that poster."

"You're kidding me."

"I've been around the block, Mike. I was a dancer for six years," she said with a hint of sadness, hoping he understood that "dancer" was just a polite term for stripper. "I knew girls who lost everything and ended up on the street."

"Would you be willing to talk about those women in front of a camera?"

"You want me to be in your documentary?"

"If you're willing to talk about the women you knew, yeah." Mike lowered his hook, let the line go limp, and looked long and hard at her body language for a sinker. Candy looked interested, which meant she was now ready for real bait.

"Honey, I can tell you all you need to know about those women and more, and there are a few women that aren't even on that poster. The police are dumb as a post when it comes to what goes on in the East Side."

Mike gave Candy a list of some of the people he said had already been interviewed. She sat back in her chair, list in one hand, bottle of champagne in the other, and immediately began to comment on two girls she had worked with at The Glass Cage. Melanie Peters was an A-list peeler on the circuit, taking home three to five large a week before she turned into a crackhead and ended up working the low stroll on Powell and Cordova. Candy spoke of her in the past tense, insinuating that the woman was already history. She slipped in a tinted version of her own background to distinguish herself from the poster girls. Candy didn't go down the same road her friends had taken. She had lofty ambitions of her own that resulted in a website that was turning into a goldmine.

Mike was visibly impressed. He told Candy an interview with her was exactly what he needed. He pulled out another short list and handed it to Candy. These were names of young women who were not yet on the police department's poster but had overdosed on drugs; the name "Susan Wabigon" was on this unofficial death list.

There was no reaction for a few moments, then Candy's face hardened, and she placed the bottle back on the table as she prepared to tell Mike about Susan. They had practically grown up together. Susan was like her younger sister; she'd stayed at Candy's apartment when she first came to Vancouver. Susie wasn't a bad kid, but she started walking on the wild side until eventually she ended up in a Calgary rehab.

"Susie was in Edmonton when I spoke to her last, and two days later she was dead… overdosed." Candy took a napkin from the table and blew her nose as politely as she could.

"It is tragic. She and so many others, so young." Mike pretended to know her story when all he really knew was what the George family had told him.

"Susie's best friend—Carrie I think her name was—got hooked up with some weird people," Candy said.

"Her friend gave her the drugs?" Mike queried.

"No, that bitch was in Calgary."

"Is Carrie alive?" Mike asked calmly.

"I'm sure she is. Last I heard her she was in Winnipeg with The Blade."

"Why don't we leave Susan out of the mix?" Mike intervened, trying to keep the conversation calm. At least Carrie was still alive. He finished his champagne with a satisfied silence just as his interest was peaking, a silence Candy translated as a direct result of her sensuality and her hot body. These two attributes she knew added up to a seductive charm most men were powerless to resist.

"The women you mentioned," Mike said, "the ones you knew personally, they are crucial to the project, but I can't offer you any money. It's a documentary; it has to be as real and true as we can make it. But I really need for you to speak, to talk about yourself and any other women who can no longer speak for themselves. So, I'll cut to the chase. I would really appreciate an interview on tape, so we can get the details right."

"Honey, I'm there," Candy agreed. The dark cloud dissipated above her beautiful head, and the lopsided smile returned to make her face just that little bit more interesting.

CHAPTER 9

Mike sat in the Eldorado waiting for Pontiac to say goodnight to Candy and her friends. She had been worth the wait. At any rate, he finally had something like a real lead, or at least a hint of one. Candy had given him the name of Carrie's pimp or her boyfriend; it was hard to tell these days, when everything was about money. They called him The Blade, apparently, and it was not the name his mother had chosen for him, but since he was probably a biker, this was normal. Nicknames for bikers usually defined their criminal specialty. "The Blade" indicated that this person was handy with a knife, maybe for killing, maybe for torture. If this was the case, there was a pretty good chance the Winnipeg police would have a file on him. The alternative was to set up another meeting with Candy, feed her more bullshit on the documentary, and maybe she would give up The Blade's real name; then again, she might never bring it up again, and pushing her about Susan's death could arouse suspicion.

Mike's musings were interrupted by Pontiac, who appeared right out of nowhere, shaping up from the shadows of the parking lot. He opened the door of the Caddy and, without a word, fell exhausted into his seat. The performance had taken its toll; he was completely drained, but relieved that the charade was over.

"Candy loved you. I mean it, dude," Pontiac rested his head on the leather seat, looking out the window before he turned to Mike to finish his question, "but why did you ask her to be in your bogus documentary?"

"I had no choice. She was so close to telling me everything about Carrie's boyfriend, I wanted to keep her talking, and all I had to offer was a fictional part and fifteen minutes of fame in a non-existent independent film." Mike knew he had opened a can of worms, but this was after all a fishing expedition, and the prize was worth the risk.

"Did she tell you anything about Carrie?"

"Almost. I can't be sure until I go to Winnipeg." Mike weighed his words carefully. "A nickname was all she had, but it could be good enough in this case."

"You're tripping on me dude. What'd she say?"

"Candy told me Carrie had a boyfriend. She was sure Carrie was still with him," Mike said, turning on to the Oak Street Bridge.

"Does the boyfriend have a name?"

"The Blade."

"Dude, I know at least six guitar players with that nickname."

"I know it's not much to go on, but I also know he lives in Winnipeg."

"Cool, but can the police find someone with only a nickname?"

"Sometimes," Mike said. "If he's a biker and has a record, his alias will come up and so will his real name." Mike was being optimistic. Candy had not said The Blade was a biker, yet she spoke about him as only an insider could.

"Should I be booking a flight to the Peg?" asked Pontiac.

Mike didn't answer immediately. He was grateful to Pontiac for setting up the meeting with Candy. "I appreciate everything you've done so far, my friend, but Winnipeg is another kettle of fish. I don't want to put you at risk."

"I'm a big boy, Mike, and I'm from Winnipeg for Chrissake! I have friends in the North End who might even know this so-called Blade."

"Are you sure? We're headed towards biker central, buddy. Things could get rough." Mike knew he could use the help. He had never been to Winnipeg for more than a few days. He needed someone who knew the streets better than he did, and he was aware that Winnipeg was more than just the notorious corner of Portage and Main.

"I'll try and stay out of the line of fire, bro. I'm looking at it now from a different angle. The editorial perspective! There's a story here; a big one if we find Carrie." Pontiac sat up straight. The Caddy moved gracefully over the Oak Street Bridge, and he could see the neon rainbow that was downtown Vancouver.

"I'll book the flights when I get home." This was Mike's way of saying Pontiac was in and had better be ready when the bullets started flying.

"Cool, let's get it done, bro. I could be in the Peg tomorrow."

"You will be," Mike said optimistically. I have to make a stop in Calgary, but we'll meet up tomorrow night." Mike felt a rush of adrenaline. It had been a long night and now the door had finally opened onto some real progress; he wasn't staggering around blindly anymore.

Kim had hidden behind the garage after she spotted Roberts at the gas tanks. She ran down an alley, not sure how far she was from the SkyTrain station. When she stopped to catch her breath, she took a cautionary look back toward the garage. From her vantage point, she could see people filling up their gas tanks, but to her horror she saw that Roberts' truck had disappeared. She felt weak. The night had already drained her of any reserve of strength, and she wasn't sure if Roberts had been tipped off by the cashier or if he had simply filled his truck with gas and gone home. Why didn't she get out of the car at the stop-check and tell the police what happened at Roberts' house? There was nothing she could do about it now.

Thoughts of Mona flooded her brain. Kim could still hear her screams and tried not to think of what Mona's final minutes on Earth were like; she fought back the tears and started walking. The alley pavement was uneven and riddled with potholes. On both sides, rows of houses were separated by steel fences topped off with razor wire like some refugee camp. She nearly fell down twice before she gave a thought to picking up the pace. Kim started gathering speed, moving along blindly. All she could hear was the muffled sound of her shoes slapping the asphalt, which was soon drowned out by the roar of a motor getting louder as it moved closer and closer. Within seconds, two headlights flooded the alley as a vehicle stopped right in front of her, the glare making it impossible to see.

Kim froze, blinded by the light, paralyzed by an overwhelming fear. It must be that sick bastard, she thought, When the vehicle got closer, however, Kim saw the yellow taxi light on the roof of the car and breathed a sigh of relief so deep that she almost fainted. She had begun to accept that all her bad choices had finally added up to one last ride to the graveyard.

The driver realized he had startled her and rolled down his window to apologize. "I'm so sorry. I did not mean to frighten yourself. Do you need a ride?"

"I thought you were someone else." Kim opened the door and fell into the back seat. "I'm headed for the SkyTrain."

"We are very close."

"How long will it take?" Kim was still trying to catch her breath. She wanted to tell him that she was being followed by a killer, but he would likely think she was mental, so she just kept her mouth shut.

"Six minutes. That is very short time you know." The driver had thick dark hair with streaks of white; his tanned face was slightly lined and furrowed with a prominent nose and a friendly smile. He methodically turned on the meter, backed out of the alley, and drove down Ottawa Street, turning left on Lougheed Highway.

Kim slouched low in the seat. She could see the lights of the SkyTrain in the distance, and she could feel and hear her own heartbeat. Fucking Roberts had followed her in hope of killing her, and she knew he wouldn't stop until the job was done. As the cab pulled up to the station entrance of the SkyTrain, Kim asked the driver, "How much will it be?"

"Only five dollars," he replied, wheeling the taxi into the right lane. "Do you have a ticket or a train pass? Because I could drop you off at the side entrance, and you can avoid the line-up and catch your train."

"I do have a pass." She handed him a fin with a toonie tucked inside and waited until he had parked the car in front of the terminal before she got out.

"Six minutes. Did I not tell you?" The driver smiled brightly at Kim and put the money in the pocket of his silk vest.

The SkyTrain terminal was a sprawling three-storey concrete monument to rapid transit and fast food. The main floor had Starbucks, McDonalds, and Tim Hortons concessions along with smoke shops. The second floor was alive with people; twenty-five thousand went through the building every day. The police had set up a special unit to patrol all the terminals at night, still the muggings and drug-related crimes persisted. Kim took out her cell phone and called her boyfriend Frankie. She wanted him to meet her at a hotel a block away from the Terminal Avenue train stop. The phone kept ringing until finally he picked up.

"What's up?" he asked.

"Red flag. Meet me at the American Hotel. I'll be there in 15 minutes." Red flag was their password in case of extreme emergency; life and death situations, like when the cops were on their way to break down the door.

"Awright." Frankie uttered the word very slowly, as if he had been on the nod. There was a long pause, then the line went dead. Kim's cell phone battery had run out.

Kim kept walking towards the stairway that led to the trains, picking up speed as she moved closer to her freedom. She gave a fleeting glance toward the ticket booth on the first floor and stopped dead in her tracks. Approaching the second floor was Roberts. Kim turned quickly so he wouldn't see her and ran towards the stairs. She didn't spot the Chinese gang coming down the stairs until she was only a few feet away from them.

"Where are you going bitch?" Danny Liao gave Kim a straight arm to the forehead and knocked her backwards onto her heels. She picked herself up and started pleading with him.

"It's an emergency! Let me through!"

"You want to walk through the ranks bitch? You say please!" A collective round of laughter arose from the lesser members, as Danny looked down at Kim with a brutish grin.

"Please, it's a matter of life and death." Kim, afraid to look behind her in case Roberts was closing in.

Danny Liao was enjoying his little game. He gave Kim another push, to the approval of the gang. "You ain't going nowhere bitch!" These words were barely out of his mouth when suddenly a security guard's fist caught him on the side of the head and he crumbled to the floor. Within a few minutes, the gang was surrounded by four more burly guards with taser guns drawn. They were ordered to lie face down on the floor while one of the guards checked each of them for weapons. In the meantime, Kim escaped up the stairs towards a waiting train. When she made it through the door to the ramp, she could see the last of the passengers getting on board.

Bill Roberts had followed a hunch and parked his truck outside the terminal. When he didn't spot Kim among the arrivals, he went in and bought a ticket. Hordes of people were coming and going. Roberts searched the crowd for Kim while he made his way up the escalator to the second floor. He moved cautiously through the crowd, not sure if he had missed her coming in the building; his last hope rested on her waiting for the train.

Roberts looked towards the top floor where a wave of arrivals were pushing and shoving their way towards the few exits as one huge writhing body. He spotted the Chinese gang on the stairs before he saw Kim. A smile creased his face instantaneously as he watched her in the altercation with the gang members. He began to close in on her and was only fifty feet away when the security guards moved in. All he could do was watch as she climbed the stairs and headed for the departing trains.

Roberts made his way to the top of stairs, just in time to see Kim approach the open door of a train. The crowd had thinned out; most of them were already on board. Small line-ups were being swallowed up by the automatic double doors as the train was seconds away from departure. He moved in closer, slipping his left hand into the pocket of his coat, where he could feel the cold grip of his twenty-two. Kim was no more than fifteen yards away, but people were slipping in and out of his line of fire, ruining his concentration and any chance of getting in the perfect shot.

Roberts started running after her with the idea of unloading a few rounds in her back before she could make it inside the train. He pulled out the gun. He was now in full flight, closing in on her but not close enough to get a clear shot. The last of the lineup had moved quickly inside the train; only Kim and a few straggling passengers rushed to get on before the doors closed. At the precise moment Kim stepped on board, Roberts brought the pistol up with military speed and precision and emptied three rounds at Kim's head just as the door slammed shut behind her and the train started moving. Roberts never looked back. He put the double deuce back in his pocket, walked calmly to the exit, and rushed out of the building to the parking lot.

CHAPTER 10

Bullets shattered the window in train door, and glass flew in all directions, shards lodging in the ceiling. Screams rang through the train car and out onto the platform. The train screeched to a halt when someone pulled the emergency cord. Kim dropped flat on the floor. She knew instinctively those bullets had been meant for her; what she didn't know was that two had missed her by a bare fraction of an inch. The last passenger to enter as the door was closing wasn't so lucky. He caught a bullet in his left arm and was taken to the Royal Columbian Hospital. When the train started moving again, fear hung in the air until the station was far behind them. The passengers, still in shock, stared at the decimated door as a transit cop, gun in his right hand, made his way down the length of the train looking for anything suspicious.

Kim rose to her feet and moved away from the confusion, walking up the car until she found an empty seat. She glanced out the window, comforted by the changing landscape, and closed her eyes in an attempt to erase from her mind what had just happened. Pain ripped through her body in a terrible combination of early withdrawal symptoms, physical trauma, and fatigue. Yet all this was overshadowed by her brush with death. She slipped into a light sleep, the train now running smoothly at full speed, miles away from the station. Roberts was left behind. His ugly image had finally vanished from her subconscious.

And now, even in such a light sleep Kim's dreams carried her back to her childhood, to a life so utterly different from her present existence that everything about it seemed out of place; nothing made any sense. Like most children born into relative comfort, she grew up thinking that her world would never change. She had no reason to worry about the future. She was unaware that her father was a member of the Hells Angels or that the house they lived in, the car, the boat, everything was a result of her father's significant role in the burgeoning cocaine trade.

Kim's childhood had been an idyllic time spent in a typical suburban house in Port Moody. Her best friend Lana lived on the same block. Her parents Ray and Sharon were both originally from Winnipeg and had plenty of Native relatives on the reserve they grew up in, but that half of the family history was left behind, and Ray never spoke about the cousins he never invited to his home. The children knew almost nothing about their own heritage, and their parents never tried to connect with their past. In the Lower Mainland during her youth, everything seemed utterly normal to Kim. Her father never allowed his business inside the house, and although her mother wasn't quite as subtle about hiding her drug habit, the children were too young to suspect her secret.

When she was twelve years old, Kim's world fell apart. She was in the schoolyard with Lana watching the boys play soccer when her name was announced over the loud speakers; she was to report to the principal's office. Kim was afraid something had happened to her sister. She ran all the way to the office only to find Karla sitting in a chair, head bent over, tears rolling down her face. Kim's mother was in the worst shape; she kept screaming at a policeman for some kind of an explanation.

Kim stood at the door, aware that something terrible had happened, thinking maybe her brother Kevin had been in an accident. Constable Darcy Halverson smiled at Kim as he walked her outside to have a talk while his partner stayed with her hysterical mother. Halverson had been with the Port Moody Police for two decades, but all his years of experience hadn't prepared him for what he had to do now. They sat together in his cruiser parked by the soccer field on the street parallel to the schoolyard. Kim stared vacantly at the kids playing soccer, silently hoping she might not have to hear whatever it was that had happened.

"What grade are you in Kim?" The policeman asked in a friendly voice, trying to soften the blow.

"Seven," she replied, her stare still fixed on the game.

"Sounds like you must have jumped a grade."

"Grade two."

"That means you are a smart little girl." Halverson smiled at Kim and put his hand on her shoulder. "You probably already figured out that something's not right here."

"What happened to my brother?" Kim turned to face the policeman and held her eyes on him, waiting for an answer.

"Your brother is fine, Kim."

"He wasn't in an accident?" For a second, she felt a great sense of relief, but unfortunately the officer hadn't finished his answer.

"No, Kevin is safe." Halverson paused, and took a deep breath. "Your father was in an accident, and unfortunately he didn't survive." Halverson couldn't believe the words came out so easily. He looked down to check her reaction, but Kim showed no immediate emotion, except perhaps total disbelief.

"My father is dead?"

"I'm afraid so," he said.

Tears began to trickle down Kim's face. She tried to look away, but the emotional pain short-circuited her motor skills; she could only bring her hands up to her eyes to stem the increasing flood of tears. Immediately, she wanted to know where her father was. She had never seen a dead person, but she knew for certain that she needed to see her father. She asked the officer, "It was an accident?"

"I can't discuss the details with you Kim." Halverson felt helpless. This little girl's life had just been turned upside down, and he could only watch her fight off the tears.

Kim wouldn't find out until much later that her father had been murdered. Three men had entered their house in Port Moody just before noon and calmly emptied their shotguns into Ray Lawrence, then left him lying face down in a pool of blood. The police suspected Sharon's life was in danger also, as she was privy to her husband's business dealings, and as a result the family was put under police protection. The days that followed were hazy; Kim was not allowed to return to her home or to attend her father's funeral. Instead, the family was sent 2,000 miles away to a small town called Port Frank in southern Ontario, just a two-hour drive from London and six hours from Toronto.

On a street lined with identical red brick houses, they lived in a small three-room bungalow with neither a front lawn nor a back yard. The house was as old and nondescript as all the other houses on all the streets in the sleepy little town. It was completely different than their old home, and with the emotional trauma of the father's death hanging over them, the family settled in reluctantly, strangers in a strange town.

Sharon, who even under normal circumstances would have had great difficulty with the task of raising three children alone, was almost completely immobilized by grief over her husband's murder. She was still in a state of shock. Sharon had cultivated a moderate cocaine habit over the years, and without her husband to intervene, she quickly went from user to abuser. The kids were left entirely on their own, and eventually the officer monitoring the family's protection found out that Kim, her sister, and her brother were not attending school. Sharon's questionable behavior in front of the children—not to mention the lack of food in the fridge and total negligence on every level of parenting—resulted in an investigation by the Ministry of Social Services. Shortly thereafter, the children and their mother were returned to British Columbia where upon arrival Sharon was judged unfit to care for her children. Kim and her siblings were placed in foster homes.

By this time, Kim was fourteen, her body changing from girl to woman. She had lost the high-spirited side of her personality that seemed always to carry her through the bad times. She had been forced by events to realize that she had to accept what happened, not understanding why her destiny was in someone else's hands. Her foster parents, Lester and Judith Brown, were not a happy couple. It wasn't simply because Judith was unable to have children of her own. The couple had never been sexually compatible, and as the years went by, Lester lusted after young girls and found satisfaction in massage parlors. It wasn't long before he began sneaking into Kim's room, using her to satisfy his own repressed sexual frustrations. Lester would wait until Judith was out of the house shopping or meeting with friends, then he would find Kim and rape her. He often stuffed a pair of her own underwear in her mouth, in case she decided to scream. The entire disgusting coupling was all over and done with in a matter of minutes.

On the rare occasion when Kim mustered the courage to resist, Lester simply threatened to replace her with her younger sister Karla. He was by no means averse to physical violence; more than once, he warned Kim what would happen if she ever told his wife. After being abused for an entire year, Kim didn't have to tell. Judith could no longer ignore the obvious signs of sexual abuse; her own feelings of guilt were so great that she felt compelled to go to the police. Kim and her sister were immediately returned to their mother, who had only recently completed three months in a drug rehabilitation centre and was—at least for the time being—clean and sober and back on her feet.

The SkyTrain floated down the electrified tracks stopping at one station after another, slowly shaking Kim from her bad memories. She heard someone's voice saying, "Excuse me miss, I must speak with you. It's about the shooting." A uniformed Transit Officer stood over her as she came out of her sleep. He noticed there were still particles of glass on Kim's shoulder, lodged in the material of her coat.

"Yesss… " Kim replied, still half conscious.

"You were standing by the door when the shooting occurred?" The guard was tempted to shake her, just to check for some sign of life. "Can you hear me, Miss? Miss?"

"I'm fine!" Kim opened her eyes. The guard's blurred face appeared before her.

"What I need Miss, is your name and phone number, in case the police might need you as a witness."

"Do you have a pen?" Kim could tell him right now who the shooter was, but she doubted the guard would be convinced, and in any case, he was not the real police.

He handed her a pen. "There you go."

Kim wrote down her cell number and gave it back to him.

"Thank you, Miss… Lawrence? You still have some glass on your shoulder." The guard took out a small lint brush from his pocket and meticulously brushed the glass particles into a napkin he held in his left hand, and when he was finished, he walked away in silence.

Theresa fell asleep listening to one of her favorite CDs: *The Canyon Trilogy* performed by R. Carlos Nakai. Native flute music had a peculiar way of creating the perfect ambience for sleeping. She didn't hear Mike come in the door. He stood there for a few moments, his eyes adapting to the darkness; the only light came from a streetlight that was several houses down the block. He could see her now, her face flush against the pillow. The subtle light gave only an outline of her form, but like a picture he had stared at a million times, her face was locked in his memory. He undressed slowly in an attempt not to wake Theresa, then crawled in beside her, adjusting to the warmth of her body. It was only seconds before she turned around instinctively and laid her head on his chest.

"Michael," she said in a whisper, part of her still in dreamland.

"I'm sorry. I didn't want to wake you."

"I'm just glad you're safe." She gave him a kiss. "What happened to keep you out so late?"

"I was at the casino in Richmond tonight with Pontiac." His voice was barely audible as he spoke directly in Theresa's ear. "Candice Webber just happens to be a friend of Pontiac's. She was at the casino, and since she knew Susan Wabigon, she remembered Carrie's boyfriend."

"Really?" Theresa's eyes opened wide, as if she had just regained consciousness. "Does she know where he lives?"

"Last seen in Winnipeg."

"What about Carrie?"

"Chances are, she's with him."

"She's alive." Theresa sat up, not sure if she had heard right.

"I believe she might be among the living, but there is one problem," Mike said in the calmest of voices.

"She's alive! What's the problem?"

"All I have is a nickname: The Blade."

"Wouldn't Jimmy know who it was?"

"I've already e-mailed him," Mike said remorsefully. In the old days, he would have simply called Jimmy at four in the morning. Today, he felt compelled to wait for a digital reply.

Theresa took in a deep breath; for a moment she held a slim hope that she could call Carrie's parents and tell them the good news. "How will you find him if that's all you have?"

"I can start by showing up in Winnipeg, then hope for the best."

"You should wait to hear from Jimmy before making any decisions," Theresa said, showing a look of concern. She was from Winnipeg, and the gang problems there were of a very serious nature.

CHAPTER 11

Bill Roberts wasted no time getting out of the parking lot; he knew at least one of the three bullets he fired at Kim had hit someone standing in front of the train door. He was sure he had hit the hooker; chances were pretty good she was dead. He took a right on Lougheed and drove down a side street until he spotted a public garbage bin in the parking lot of a Royal Bank. He parked the truck down the block and took the silencer off the gun, rolled the twenty-two in a copy of the Jehovah's Witness rag *The Watchtower* that someone had left in his truck, and slipped everything into a brown paper bag. He looked up and down the street when he left his truck, and when he was certain no one had seen him, he casually walked through the parking lot and flipped the package into the open dumpster.

Evening traffic had thinned out by the time he headed home, and he felt a sense of relief when he saw the police had vacated their stop-check positions. Roberts was fairly confident that this strange night was about over, and he smiled as he cruised down the empty road toward his place. He had taken some risks back at the SkyTrain, but it had also triggered some familiar old feelings; the rush of taking someone out in a public place was a powerful fix. He was left now to deal with the other hooker's body, which would take the rest of the night. Roberts could picture removing her skull and placing it with the rest of his trophies.

He pulled into the lane and turned the radio on to hear the news, in the vain hope they would report the death of a junkie hooker at the SkyTrain station, but there was nothing about the shooting on the news yet. He would just have to wait until morning. Manson was happy to finally be off his leash, so Roberts gave the dog time to run off some pent-up energy while he took his own time walking back to the house. His adrenaline was still pumping from the shooting, and he wasn't used to that kind of action anymore. It had been a long time, maybe too long. He was over the hill, and some people assumed he had lost his touch, but right now he didn't think so.

The house he had bought twelve years ago had not changed much since he moved in. It was a roomy two-storey with four bedrooms. Some of the shingles on the roof had been replaced and the veranda had been repainted, but that was the extent of the upkeep. The only remnant of the working farm this place had once been was the stable that now housed a collection of motorcycles along with a large inventory of tools.

Roberts had a cordial if distant relationship with his neighbors. There had been friendly exchanges over the years, and he was on a first name basis with some of them, but he avoided any close social interaction. He showed up for funerals and weddings, paid his respects the widowed and bereft, and always gave generous gifts to the bride and groom so as not to be known as a miser. He never invited anyone to his home, however. What went on behind his closed doors remained his business alone. His neighbors seemed to have learned to accept these boundaries and for the most part respected his space. Without arousing questions about his past, he had simply given the impression of a successful businessman who retired early on the strength of wise investments. He was now free to pursue and enjoy his one true passion, the world of vintage motorcycles.

It was a clever ruse, far, far from the truth, a mirage he had created to avoid arousing even the subtlest hint of suspicion. Oddly, he had only been arrested once in all his forty-seven years of psychotic behavior, and that was in Marguerita Island along the Venezuelan coast. He had bought his way out of trouble, leaving no record of the charge. Roberts was, at last count, responsible for the deaths of more than fifty people—even more if you counted the women buried in the hard black clay of the fields behind his barn, frozen stiff.

Bill Roberts grew up in Montreal during the fifties when the city was filled with promise. French Canadians had found their folk hero in Maurice "The Rocket" Richard, soon to become a martyr after being suspended from playing hockey with *Les Canadiens*. Jazz clubs had sprung up throughout the city, and a young Oscar Peterson was establishing himself as one of the world's premier jazz piano innovators. Bill lived in the East End, in a working class neighborhood that had become a breeding ground for young men with criminal tendencies. He could barely remember his mother; she died when he was four. His father Wilfred, a burly longshoreman well known in the local bars, had never spent much time with his son. Wilfred never spoke about personal matters; the closest his son would ever get were his drunken rants about his shitty job and all the assholes he spent eight hours a day with sweating out barely enough money to keep his family alive.

Bill's father remarried a year after his wife's death, which created resentment in the young boy who felt he was finally getting close to his father and now had to share him with some gold digging tramp. For so long, it had been just the two of them trying to survive, which created a small but cherished bond for a child who would never be the recipient of real parental love. Martha James was twenty-three, much younger than Wilfred, and she had never really considered the responsibility that came with raising a five-year-old boy. Martha was a waitress at *Le Bon Poulet*, a restaurant on St. Catherine Street, and she usually worked nights, which gave her a ready excuse to postpone or ignore all the duties that came with motherhood. As the years went by, Bill and his stepmother would neither become accidentally attached nor were they forced in any emotional way to drift together for the illusion of looking like a family. Martha made no effort at all to endear herself to Wilfred's son, who for some reason she had found repulsive from their very first encounter. She could sense a repressed evil inside the boy that was waiting to manifest itself. She hated being close to him and loathed the thought of showing any kind of affection towards her stepson.

Wilfred made no attempt to bring his wife and son together, and eventually it was too late; the emotional gap between Martha and Bill became as wide as the Grand Canyon. The father's drinking became the cause of frequent quarrels, and these became more intense as the boy got older. Violence became a natural part of the hostile exchanges that dominated communication in the house. Martha began to stay home, unable to work because of a black eye or a swollen lip. Appearances at least had to be kept up, if nothing else. She could never even begin to stand up to Wilfred's horrible temper; she simply rolled over in response to his increasingly savage cruelty. But when Wilfred was out, Martha unloaded her own pent-up anger on his son. On this basis, Bill developed for his stepmother a seething hatred that could be soothed only by revenge.

One hot July afternoon in 1958, the family was on the road in their '53 Ford two-door sedan, headed out for a weekend in the Eastern Townships. Wilfred pointed to a cottage in serious disrepair sitting by a lake, a derelict shack in which some manic-depressive was rumored to have killed three of his wives in sequence to collect on their insurance policies. The crime had been in all the newspapers, even *Hello Police*, and the man was where he belonged: in jail for life without parole.

Wilfred laughed at the audacity of the crime, but his son wanted to read the articles on the murders. Bill wanted to understand the method in the man's madness and what tools and tactics he had used to kill the women. For the rest of the trip, he sat in the back seat with his feet on the drive-shaft hump, fantasizing about strangling his stepmother. He could feel a rush at the mere thought of his hands wrapped around her throat as she gasped for air. In his mind, he would laugh at her while she begged for her life as he squeezed until death shut her up forever.

When he was sixteen, Bill left home and ran with a gang that robbed beer stores and pizza joints; they were street punks in an era distinguished by switchblades and brass knuckles. He worked out every day and had become a big boy, built like a halfback: six two and a hundred and eighty-five pounds with tree trunks for legs and arms that resembled coiled rope. He had a mean streak that made him lethal in a street fight, an obvious asset to any gang he was with. At age nineteen, he was wheel man for a friend who shot down a gambler indebted to the Dubois mob. Jacques Knight, the shooter, made his bones with the Cotroni mob before he joined the Dubois family. Jacques was a puppeteer; he held the other end of the strings attached to a group of heavies known as the Last Chance, shadow puppets who settled scores for the family. Knight's modus operandi was to keep his crew anonymous so the enemy never knew who was coming after them.

Knight decided to hire Bill Roberts, whom he later referred to as his killing prodigy, primarily on the strength of the methodical manner in which he stalked his victims, but also for the brutality with which he came down on the prey once he decided the time was right. Under Jacques Knight's orders, Roberts was responsible for the deaths of eighteen men by the end of the '60s, until the Dubois family began their slow decline after a former bodyguard turned informer. When one of the Dubois brothers ended up in jail, Knight decided it was time to leave, and he took his puppet show with him. He cut a deal with the Diablos and the Last Chance crew became the bikers' new enforcers.

Roberts' reputation grew accordingly and overnight. The word on the street was that Bill Roberts was the real McCoy, a cold hearted killer who enjoyed his work. What threatened to blow his cover happened at a private party with the leaders of the pack in attendance. As always, there were plenty of women ready to please the biker bosses. Bill Roberts had taken Linda Myles to bed, and in the chaos that continued unabated until the early hours of the morning, no one heard Linda's screams. The next day, they found her body; her throat had been slit with a razor blade. The remains were quietly disposed of, no questions asked. It was a biker party. Shit happened, and people knew when to shut the fuck up if they valued their lives. However, the unfortunate incident had not gone unnoticed by the colours that mattered.

This wasn't the first time it happened. Women who went home with Bill were sometimes never seen again. Among those who knew him, no one dared criticize him for fear of "disappearing" themselves. Jacques Knight had already spoken to Roberts about this problem, but Roberts dismissed the incidents as payback for stupid women's clumsy attempts to steal from him. The stories made no sense, and Roberts was not a good liar, especially when he was under interrogation and Jacques Knight was the Grand Inquisitor. Knight had every right to be cautious about Roberts' behavior. The bodies were beginning to make certain Diablos a little nervous. Their world was a violent one, but murder was a matter of revenge in defence of honor or in order to silence a rat. A kill had to be approved by committee. Roberts' stupid habit of killing women for kink was not tolerated. The bikers who gave the orders had concluded Bill Roberts was a borderline serial killer and the police would eventually come looking for him, but for the time being his reputation prevented them from taking any disciplinary action. There was a confrontation with their arch rivals (the Roc Machine) looming, and they needed Roberts. He was a warrior; he was the equalizer, the one who made the difference in a fight where losers ended up in shallow graves in the remote Quebec countryside.

When the war with the Roc Machine finally broke out, Jacques Knight was one of its first casualties, and the crew chose Roberts as their new leader. They set out to find the men who had murdered the boss. Roberts suspected a gang called The Renegades (who worked for the Roc Machine) was responsible for the hit. Bill had the two men who killed Jacques Knight kidnapped and brought to a farm near the small town of Hawkesbury, a hundred miles south of Montreal. His treatment of Claude Lachapelle and Ronnie Greenspan showed just how sadistic his tactics could be.

In the late afternoon, Roberts had both men stripped naked and whipped, then he took a red hot branding iron and pressed it against Lachapelle's head, burning through hair, skin, and into the bones of his skull. Lachapelle crumpled to the floor, the pain so excruciating that death would have been an act of mercy. The smell of burning flesh spread through the room, and Greenspan watched in horror as his partner lay motionless and nearly comatose, knowing that he was next and his fate could be worse. He cringed when Roberts dragged the unconscious Lachapelle up from the floor and put a rope around his neck, lifting him slowly until his body was stretched erect, held up by the tightened rope. Greenspan gave Roberts the names of the gang members who gave the order and where they lived; in return, Roberts bypassed the torture and put two bullets in the back of his head. Roberts then drenched both victims in battery acid and hung their bodies in front of the Renegades clubhouse. Their mutilated bodies were found by the horror stricken Renegades, the victims' faces unrecognizable because the battery acid turned them into ghoulish Frankensteins.

The story spread through the ranks of the biker community like wildfire, and Roberts became one of the most feared men within the rank and file. He now had free rein to build his own crew. One of his new recruits was a young Columbian, Sebastian Garcia, whose reputation with a knife had earned him the nickname "The Blade." Bill was impressed by the man's intelligence and his connections with the Columbian cartels and eventually made Sebastian second in command.

Roberts had by now developed both a reputation and a bankroll, but it was not yet enough for his own needs. His psychotic nature was best satisfied when his victims were women. Since rising to power, he had gone on a killing spree, and to celebrate his success he started collecting body parts from his female victims and storing the trophies in his freezer. This eccentricity reflected the sadistic pride that came with his new position, for in his power-drunk mind he had become invincible. He tossed caution out the window and soon lost all inhibitions about the women he killed. One day at a biker picnic after a long day of barbecue, beer, and cocaine, Bill Roberts was introduced to Helen Paquette, a tall blonde looker who had been the girlfriend of several bikers over the years. He drove back to Montreal with her, listening all the way to her loud and lewd re-telling of his murderous exploits, as if her own enunciation of the gory details turned her on until she couldn't wait to get under the sheets with him herself. After that evening, neither hide nor hair of horny Helen was ever seen again.

Eventually, there was an outcry from several members who felt Roberts had crossed the line, and a meeting was set up between top leaders and the head of the Last Chance crew. They made their case very clear: Roberts would take a long holiday and let things cool down. The police were starting to ask questions, and if a disgruntled biker ever turned informer, Roberts would be arrested and it would put all of them in danger. In the meantime, Sebastian would handle Roberts' duties until he returned. Roberts knew right away that he had no alternative but to accept the conditions, so he booked a flight for Marguerita Island. He left Montreal without realizing he might never return; his stay on Marguerita threatened to make his "leave of absence" a permanent one.

On the island, his killing pattern continued, until finally one woman escaped from his cottage alive and told the police of her violent confrontation with Señor Roberts. The police arrested him, and only because of Sebastian's intervention was he able to escape and not end his life rotting in a Venezuelan jail.

CHAPTER 12

Kim walked away from the SkyTrain trembling in fear. She didn't expect Roberts to be waiting for her again quite yet, but she knew intuitively that he would be downtown before the night was over. She descended the concrete stairs that led to Main Street, avoiding eye contact with everyone that walked by her, moving through the crowd until she was close to the American Hotel where Frankie was waiting. She crossed the street, slightly less paranoid when she saw Frankie standing at the hotel entrance. Kim fell into his arms and broke down in tears, trying to explain what happened to Mona. She blubbered to Frankie about a fucking psycho named Roberts who tried to kill her getting on the SkyTrain.

Together, they walked back to Frankie's apartment on East Pender, a small one bedroom in a three-storey building that was in such disrepair that its only tenants were hookers and drug addicts. Inside, there was a mattress on the floor next to a table and chair rescued from the garbage in the alley out back. Kim searched the sparsely furnished room. "Take everything you need," she said, "because you can't come back."

"Why would he come here?" Frankie asked, as he gathered up some clothes and packed his shaving kit.

"He knows people downtown. They will tell him we live together, and he will make this place his first stop."

"Well, I don't want to be here when he shows up," Frankie spoke casually, not sure if this psycho would kill him, too, but not wanting to find out the hard way.

"We could stay with Margo on the North Shore," Kim decided. "He wouldn't find us there." Kim took the point of down Frankie had hidden in the freezer and went into the washroom.

"She don't live there anymore. She's on the island." Frankie watched as Kim began rocking back and forth, sitting on the john after taking the needle out of her arm. She came back into the front room looking disoriented; her eyes glazed over, but at least the pain was on hold for a while.

"When did she move?" Kim asked.

"I don't know. I met her boyfriend last week. He just came back to pick up some of their clothes. He found a job in Duncan, and Margo left with him."

"I think I have enough cash for a hotel room." Kim checked her purse to make sure she still had the money Roberts gave her.

"Hotels don't let you in the front door unless you've got a credit card," Frankie said. Now Kim looked ready to panic. Frankie put his arm around her. "It's gonna be okay. Maybe you can stay with your sister tonight. C'mon, I'll give you a ride."

"What about you?"

"Your sister hates me. Don't worry. I can take care of myself." Frankie picked up his suitcase and walked towards the door.

Kim's sister's place was the only alternative left, although she had become very unfriendly since she started working at that fancy escort service. Kim really had no other choice. It would buy her some time, and time is free when you're on the on the run. In the end, though, time is a killer... the best in the business.

Kim's sister, Karla Lawrence, had an apartment in Yaletown in one of the many tall buildings that had risen like huge concrete erections during the last decade, turning a neighborhood once famous for warehouses and other interesting old buildings into an urban forest of overpriced condos and apartments. Restaurants in Yaletown catered to the so-called sophisticated palate, and there was plenty of overpriced office space available upstairs for Asian entrepreneurs making millions from their Internet companies.

Kim's sister reluctantly opened the door to apartment 2203 and was surprised to see just how much like a homeless junkie hooker her black sheep sister had really become. Kim told her sister the events of the evening, but Karla just rolled her eyes in disgust. In her pathetic family, someone was always in some kind of trouble; now her sister escapes death by a thread and quite likely has led a serial killer to her front door.

"Karla, can I use your phone? My cell is dead."

"I don't want you calling the police from here," Karla said tightly.

"Karla, what is wrong with you? Mona is dead! The police have to know." Kim was not feeling at all welcome. She felt as if she should turn around and go right back out the door.

"You are so stupid, Kim. The police will want you to come down and give them a statement." Karla took a long look at the physical condition her sister was in. Kim was just like their mother, a terminal addict with only one thing on her agenda: getting stoned out of her mind.

"You won't even show up, will you? That is what you normally do, isn't it?" Karla never gave Kim a chance to answer. "So, what do you think will happen? The police will trace the call, which means they will show up at my front door. I don't want them knowing where I live or what I do for a living. Can you understand what I'm saying?"

"Yes, and don't talk to me as if I'm some kind of moron." Kim's sister was a professional escort working for Midnight Foxes, and it wasn't unusual for escorts to look down on women who worked the streets, to think of them as trash in comparison to their own more respectable professional economic pursuits. "I will go down and give the police a statement. I just don't want to do it tonight."

"I don't care what you do," Karla said, waving her hands in the air. "One thing's for sure, you are not calling the police from here."

"Don't you have a cell phone?" Kim asked.

"I do, but you are not using it." Karla rolled her eyes again. Was her sister mental or had the drugs so ravaged her brain that she could not have a rational thought? "You want to call the cops, use the pay phone down the street."

"Are you serious?" Kim realized her sister was in one of her moods and putting up a fight would only aggravate the situation.

"Kim? Have you not been listening?" Karla spoke without emotion, "I am serious. Call from the pay phone or don't call at all."

"Karla, I don't want to go back out there! I'm afraid! You don't know what it was like. I'll call the police tomorrow."

"I hope you don't think you're staying here."

"Why are you being such a bitch?" Kim was unable to understand her sister's cruelty. "I just need a place to stay, only for tonight."

"You are not staying here!" Karla looked at her sister, imagining what the neighbors would think if they saw her.

"I can't go downtown; he's looking for me. Can't you understand what's happening? He killed Mona. Now he wants to kill me! Where do you think I should stay tonight?"

"In the ditch for all I care," Karla said coldly.

"Alright." Kim felt tears welling up in her eyes, and in a thoroughly beaten voice that made her sound like a little girl, she forced out one last plea. "Can I at least call Earl? He's my social worker. He'll pick me up."

"Go ahead. Just make sure he's here in the next half hour or you will be waiting outside," Karla said as she turned her back on her sister and walked into the bedroom, an unsubtle hint that the conversation was over.

Kim dialed the phone number slowly, silently hoping Earl would answer. He finally picked up on the fourth ring, and she tried to tell him what had happened but broke down in tears in the middle of it. She gave him her sister's address, and Earl told her not to worry; he would be there in twenty minutes. She gathered up her clothes, went to the washroom, and splashed cold water on her face until the cobwebs cleared, then made her way to the door.

"Do me a favor," said her sister, "and don't call me next time you get into trouble." Karla appeared from her room, her short hair neatly coiffed and her purple lipstick impeccably applied, now dressed in a black Armani dress and a pearl necklace, just to remind her sister which one of them was the failure in the family.

"Don't worry!" Kim ignored Karla. "It won't happen again."

"Famous last words. Next time I'm not opening the door."

Kim just kept walking; her suitcase felt lighter, and she heard the door slam behind her before she even made it to the elevator. "Goodbye Karla," she said to herself, as the elevator doors sealed shut.

Bill took his time wandering through his living room, checking for anything left behind by the two hookers. He found nothing, so he went down into the basement, which was filled with boxes of musty, moldy, old clothes piled among discarded and dismantled furniture. Under a single bare light bulb dangling precariously from a frayed cord in the ceiling was an old yellowed enamel freezer whose once white paint had chipped off in large chunks, revealing the grey undercoating beneath. He maneuvered himself slowly around stacks of boxes until he stood directly in front of the freezer. He smiled in anticipation as he unlocked it. Bill always felt the same rush when he rediscovered his victims.

He held the freezer door open with both hands above his head; a blue-tinged skull stared back at him, the eyes like frozen marbles caught in an eternal expression of terminal terror. Beside the skull, four severed hands were neatly tied together in matching pairs with their long fingers curled as if ready to coax music from a piano. Two headless bodies stretched out in ghastly repose on the very bottom of the icy interior. Bill smiled to himself, then took one last look and closed the freezer door. He would soon need to make some room for another skull. His eyes felt better now, although there was still a mild burning sensation around the edges. He walked upstairs feeling like a vampire after a blood feast, ready to deal with the woman whose corpse now lay hidden in the stable.

There were only a few hours left before sunrise, so he went back to the kitchen and poured himself a shot of tequila, which he took down slowly to let his brain clear. He would never sleep until the body had been disposed of and he was damn sure there were no traces left behind. The alcohol coursed through his veins like a weak fix, but it did the trick and had the necessary calming effect. He went into the living room and turned on the television, surfing the channels until he found a news station. He saw footage of an accident scene. An SUV was wrapped around a telephone post, the paramedics were carrying someone on a stretcher, and a motorcycle with a bent frame and the twisted body of a rider lay prone on the street. Bill turned up the volume as the accident scene was replaced by the image of a reporter standing in front of a SkyTrain station. Several transit cops stood behind him, and an ambulance siren sounded in the background.

"There has been a shooting tonight at the New Westminster SkyTrain station." A newsman with a perfect haircut and a navy blue suit seemed filled with outrage as he turned toward the SkyTrain entrance. "One man has been taken to hospital in serious condition, and two women are being treated for shock. Police have no suspects, but they believe the shooting may have been gang-related. We will update you with more information at our next newsbreak. And now, back to Helen with today's weather."

Roberts' mood had just taken a wild swing towards nasty. That hooker was still alive, and the stranger who just happened to be in the wrong place at the wrong time was in intensive care. He felt anger rising up like black bile in his throat, heartburn coming on, all because that slut was still breathing. She was more than likely talking to the police right now. To top it all, some poor bastard was going to croak because he had the misfortune to be standing right behind that bitch. It wasn't just a sense of failure; Roberts loathed sloppy workmanship of any kind, and this was just pure unadulterated incompetence. Maybe he was losing it, or maybe the bitch was just lucky. In the old days, he would have shot one of his own underlings for fucking up a hit. This was going to turn out bad; he could feel it in his gut. She had to be dealt with, but he couldn't risk another attempt because the police would be waiting for him.

The irony was, this woman's father had been an easy kill. That hooker daughter of his must have horseshoes up her ass, Bill thought, but luck has a short run with junkies. If he couldn't take her out, he knew someone who could: a specialist in eliminating undesirables who had worked for him before. Roberts picked up the phone and dialed the number. On the fourth ring, the voice mail cut in. "Sebastian can't take your call… leave your name and number." Roberts was disappointed that he was forced to speak to a machine.

CHAPTER 13

Theresa got up at the crack of dawn and made a Spanish omelette for her husband, served along with Maple Leaf sausages, rye toast, a quart of pure Florida orange juice, and several cups of steaming hot coffee. It was going to be a busy day of travel, and on the plane, he'd only get a stale croissant and java that tasted like the sludge that comes out of an oil filter. She wanted to be together with him alone the last few hours before his flight. Their rare times apart were usually no more than a few days in a row, but this time Mike would be gone for more than a week. "How long will you stay in Calgary?" she asked.

"I'll land at 9:30 a.m., spend time with Dennis Anderson who is in charge of the rehab, find out what he can tell me about Carrie, make it back to the airport to board a 6:30 flight for Winnipeg and arrive there at around 9:30 tonight," Mike said, a cup of java in his hand, savoring the satisfaction of warmth and abundance that went with a perfect breakfast prepared by the woman he loves. It was at times like this that he realized how lucky he was to have found Theresa.

"Will Pontiac pick you up at the airport?"

"Maybe. If not, I will see him at the hotel the next day."

"You be careful, Michael. In my heart of hearts I can feel something good is going to come from this trip, but I am so worried about you." She leaned over and gave him a gentle kiss on the cheek.

"You, worried about me?" Mike smiled at her. If she only knew the danger he had dealt with when he wore a real badge. "I appreciate the sentiment, but remember, when I'm on the job, I'm tougher than old King Kong and meaner than a junkyard dog." Mike pulled her head against his shoulder, the smell of her hair and the warm smooth softness of her skin made him happy to be alive.

"All right tough guy, you call me every night so I'll know you're not hurt or something terrible has happened to you."

"Worst case, I come up empty handed and The Blade has moved and no one knows where Carrie is anymore." Mike was always skeptical of leads. The ones with the greatest promise fell flattest so often that he had lost count, and that made him hesitant to put much faith in the first big break they'd gotten on this case. He was suspicious of Candy Webber's story, especially after she had knocked back a bottle of champagne.

"Stop it, Michael. I know you will find her." Theresa lifted her head from his shoulder and looked him in the eye. "Trust a woman's intuition; it's always right."

"Thank you," he said. "I want to believe in your intuition, but my native instincts tell me to beware of quicksand."

"There is no quicksand in Winnipeg." Theresa let out a soft laugh.

"Maybe not natural quicksand, but plenty of man-made stuff. When you're looking for a missing person there is quicksand everywhere."

"Mary called me yesterday. When I told her you were going to Calgary and Winnipeg, she started asking questions, wanting to know why and when are you leaving and if you are on her daughter's trail."

"You told her nothing?" Mike had kept little contact with the George family since they had come to him with the case, mostly because he didn't want to sow false seeds of hope, nor did he want to get emotionally involved with the parents. The moment he found Carrie, he would call, and not until then.

"Not a word Michael. I mentioned you were simply talking to people at the rehab, hoping to find some friend or acquaintance of Carrie's who might have some helpful information."

"Perfect. I want you to stop talking to Mary altogether until I return."

"I promise. But I can't stop her from calling me."

"Put a message on your voice-mail that you're working late. Trust me; it will be better this way. I'll know within a few days if we can track Carrie's boyfriend." Mike checked his watch. It was time to leave for the airport. He finished his coffee, savoring the moment, because one thing was certain, he'd be watching the late show alone for the next week.

Addicts stood at the stainless steel counter, empty food trays pressed like battle shields against their chests, men ranging in age from nineteen to fifty, disoriented, suffering. One after the other they inched methodically, thoughtlessly, toward their warm reward for having survived another night of fighting their demons. It was a simple breakfast of scrambled eggs, sausages, and toast doled out by one of their own who would soon be ready to return to the world outside. The rag tag army dispersed with their meals to scattered tables. Some gathered again in groups or pairs to banter and talk; others sat alone, licking their wounds in silence. Mike watched the awkward dance from the corridor above, waiting outside the office of the senior counselor of Saratoga Rehab so he could discuss Carrie George and the time she had spent here.

"Mr. Morningstar, you picked a busy day to drop in," Dennis Anderson said, putting his phone down. He had a long slender face, a polished bald head with sad gray eyes, and a bulbous nose, the legacy of his drinking years. He had spent more than half of his forty-six years working in the Calgary centre counseling men and women dealing with drug addiction.

"I won't take up much of your time," Mike said.

"How can I help you?"

"I'm a private investigator. The George family has retained my services to help find their daughter." Mike hated telling people he was a private dick. The years of carrying a badge and receiving immediate respect made it difficult to admit he was no longer a real cop.

"You mean Carrie George?"

"That's right," Mike answered. "She was last seen in here."

Anderson looked down at the addicts in the cafeteria below, attempting to appear aloof, disinterested, but his face showed signs of concern. "I remember her, and Susan... she died a few weeks after she left here." He paused for a second, reflecting on the tragic circumstances of Susan's death. "I'll go on the record right now. Her death was no accident."

"I believe the RCMP has reopened the investigation." Mike noted a quickening in the counselor's pulse as he tried to suppress the anger that was obvious in his eyes.

"I've spoken to one of them, but I can't remember his name." Anderson leaned over his desk. His face was flushed, the lines in his neck tightening into a knot. "I believe that it was upon my insistence that they actually decided to take another look at the evidence."

"Why would anyone go back out after kicking the habit?" asked Mike. "It makes no sense." Even after all the years of dealing with druggies, Mike was still unable to understand the doper mentality.

"Because in a perverse way it's the only life they will ever know." Anderson paused briefly. "You know, Mike, I was a full-fledged alcoholic myself. I've been there. Getting clean is only half of the problem, the easy half. Staying straight is the hard part. That's the mountain every addict has to keep climbing for the rest of his life, or at least until he's worn it down into a molehill. I talk to recovering addicts every day in here; the older ones usually already have serious health issues, and unless they clean up totally, a good percentage of them will die when they get back to the streets." Anderson finally had his anger back under control. It seemed to Mike that it was more for dramatic effect than anything else, but Anderson had made his point.

"It's a foregone conclusion then, is that it?" Mike said. "For a lot of these people, it's already too late by the time they bite the bullet."

"Yes. The biggest obstacle to recovery only disappears when a person can truly resist the poison that put them in rehab in the first place, and believe me, it's a daily battle for every one of them. Nobody's immune. The tiniest slip or misstep can prove deadly."

For some reason, Anderson was irritating Mike more and more with every word he spoke and every move he made. Mike ignored the intellectual redundancy and returned the conversation to its original intent. "Then, you don't think Susan had a slip?"

"No, I don't. There is always the chance, though. The younger the addict, the higher the percentage of recovery, women especially. Susan was never a full-blown junkie, and her recovery seemed as complete as we ever see when she left here." Anderson opened a drawer to his right, pulled out a manila envelope, and placed it on his desk. "A slip would have meant her doing crack because of some emotional crisis, but she never would have done a speedball. Susan was around long enough to know the danger. Someone must have been with her the night she overdosed, and that person gave her the fatal injection. Find that person, and you have the killer."

"Who would have wanted to kill Susan?"

"I don't know. You can appreciate that our conversations were confidential, but Susan never mentioned feeling threatened or that she was in any kind of danger."

"What about friends?" Mike asked. "Did anyone visit her while she was here?"

"We don't encourage visitors while the addict is in early withdrawal. There were a few women who came once or twice; former co-workers, if you know what I mean. That was about it. I doubt if she wanted anyone to see her in that condition."

"What about Carrie?"

"I was never able to get as close to Carrie as I was with Susan. Carrie was really overwhelmed with guilt. She felt she had betrayed her family and her friends; she was recovered but still very hesitant about returning home." Anderson was visibly straining to remember. Carrie may be alive and kicking, but she had left less of a concrete impression on him. Susan's death had made her the more prominent person in his mind, and it had remained that way since.

"Did Carrie's parents ever visit her?"

"No. I doubt if they knew she was here for most of her stay, because when she finally did call them, her father sent money for a flight back home. She had the same visitors as Susan, except for one male friend who came to see Carrie just before she and Susan left the centre. I recall he was well dressed and older than Carrie, but I was never sure if he was her boyfriend or simply a friend."

"You were never introduced?" Mike's interest was piqued, but the description didn't fit the biker persona he had in mind.

"We met briefly for a group picture before the girls checked out. Said nothing more than hello and goodbye." Anderson took a Polaroid picture from the envelope and handed it to Mike.

Mike thanked him. The photo was slightly out of focus, but there was no mistaking Carrie George. She wasn't smiling like Susan and Dennis, who both gave the impression of sharing an inside joke. Another staff woman and Carrie's male friend who looked to be in his mid-thirties and respectable were also smiling, but Carrie was clearly not in a celebratory mood. Her friend looked Spanish. Bronzed skin, black hair, a goatee, and a single gold cross earring. He was strictly business, judging from his wardrobe. He could have easily been a pimp, but he was definitely not a card carrying Hells Angel. Mike took the photograph with him when he left. It was the only clue the trip to rehab had produced. The stranger in the picture had aroused his curiosity. Time to find out if the stranger had a criminal record. Mike would e-mail a copy of the photo to Jimmy Secola and another to Richard Beaulieu, his friend on the Winnipeg police force.

Kim sat in a cubicle with a table and chairs so old they could have been built in the last century. Across from her, Constable Judy Larch took down Kim's story about Mona's murder. When Constable Larch questioned Kim about her relationship to Mona and why they went out to this guy's place anyway, Kim rolled up the sleeve of her blouse so Larch could see the tracks on her arm and told the New Westminster police officer that she and Mona worked the streets together for the same reason.

"Have you ever been arrested?" Larch asked.

"Yes, once for possession and prostitution, and once for attempted manslaughter." Kim felt a twinge of anger. She was here to report a murder. A psychopath was on the loose out there, and this cop was more interested in the ancient past than in Kim's clearly dangerous present and immediate future.

"Any time spent incarcerated?" Larch asked in the flat robotic voice of someone who would spend most of her life asking redundant questions in little rooms.

"A few weeks for possession, then I was released."

"Nothing for attempted manslaughter?" Larch looked up from her laptop, just to make sure Kim wasn't lying.

"The charges were stayed because it was self-defence. My mother's boyfriend tried to rape me."

"Do you have any family other than your mother?"

"A younger sister and a brother. My father's dead." Kim paused for a second, trying desperately to hold back the tears. "I have a son; his name is Clarence. He was adopted last year."

"He was taken away by social services?" Constable Larch exhaled in a huff and pursed her lips in outrage. How such women were allowed to procreate remained a mystery to her.

"Yes," Kim said quietly.

"Were you still a heroin addict when this happened?"

"No. I had cleaned up during my pregnancy."

"That was thoughtful of you," Larch said curtly. "If you were clean, why was your baby taken away from you?"

"Frankie, my boyfriend, is my son's father," Kim explained. "He always came by on Friday mornings to visit. It gave me time to go shopping and take care of little things because I stayed with my son 24/7. Frankie was still using, but he never did anything inside my apartment. One Friday, I came home and he was fixing in the washroom, and before I could convince him to leave, a social worker knocked on my door."

"And why did you return to working the streets?" Larch's voice was filled with contempt.

"I relapsed." Kim was growing tired of the cop's patronizing treatment. "Look, I'm not here to talk about my problems. I'm here to report a murder. There's a psycho out there killing women! His name is Bill Roberts."

"Your friend has not been reported missing," said the constable, in a voice as cold as ice. "You were smoking crack with her. You are both heroin addicts living off prostitution. All this is going in my report. Another officer will decide what action should be taken. Now, can we continue?"

"No! I've said everything, and if more women are being killed by Roberts, the blood is on your hands! Yours and all the other cops who don't give a shit how many women are found dead!" Kim stood up, her face flushed with anger, and walked out of the room, down the hallway, and out through the main doors. The warm, fresh air calmed her down. Her anger subsided just a bit, enough to remind her that she was right. Mona's killer was still on the streets somewhere looking for her, and the police weren't laying any rubber to leave the station. There were no sirens screaming. They were in no great hurry to arrest anyone.

CHAPTER 14

No one could have guessed that the New Westminster Police would question Kim's story, but their rationale for not taking it at face value was simple and perfectly logical in an old-fashioned conservative detachment. For starters, they imagined themselves to be the Scotland Yard of the Lower Mainland. Mona had never been reported missing in the first place, and not even Kim really knew for certain what had happened to her. The police had no justification for visiting Roberts' house with a search warrant. The best Kim could hope for was to speak to the RCMP officer Harold Jenkins later in the week, and that left Roberts free to do as he pleased, for the time being. This news had never reached Frankie, who had not been in touch with Kim.

Frankie slept in his old Buick for two days straight while Kim was holed up with her social worker waiting to be interviewed by the cops. Once Kim had given her statement about the SkyTrain shooting, Frankie fully expected Roberts would be arrested and locked up right away and the nightmare would be over. Then he could resume his life without fear of that psychopath showing up at his front door in the middle of the night. Right now, though, his most urgent need was to get back into his apartment building to pick up his welfare check. Frankie needed to score, and score quick, because he was already getting dope-sick.

Early withdrawal came down on him like a ton of bricks, a combination of symptoms giving him chills and violent sweats. Waves of heat rose up through his spine igniting flash fires in his aching skull; every joint in his body was dried out and painfully arthritic. The dry heaves caused him to retch and try to force himself to vomit, but there was nothing in his stomach to throw up. He was dangerously dehydrated. The muscles in his abdomen had tied themselves in a knot, his esophagus felt like it was going to burst open, and the ulcer in the pit of his stomach felt as if someone was turning a corkscrew into it.

It was midnight when Frankie drove by his apartment. He cruised past once and then down the street to make sure Roberts wasn't waiting for him. There was no sign of the black half-ton truck with Harley logos painted on the doors, and Frankie breathed a sigh of relief. He parked the Buick on East Pender and walked over to the Carnegie Centre. Outside on the notorious corner of Main and Hastings, or "Pain and Wastings" as it was known to the locals, the usual crowd of chronic pill poppers and crackheads were looking for anything to bring them up, or down. They mumbled to themselves and periodically screamed out loud at phantom dealers. Here and there, the ones with a bit of beggared or borrowed cash filled their paperless prescriptions from the local street pharmacists who huddled in around this central location for the bottom-feeding drug trade.

Traffic came and went in all four directions of the compass, but for the barely ambulatory pedestrians that tried minute to minute and hour after hour from sun up to sun down to stay vertical long enough to score, this precise dot on the map was really the end of the road. Everything from Percocet to Oxycontin (better known as "hillbilly heroin") was available at a drastically inflated price, of course. It was a low-life entrepreneurial paradise where the market shifted from buyer to seller in an instant. If a small time dealer was a friend of a friend, you could score for the going price, provided you were lucky enough to find your drug of choice. If you couldn't find the pill of your dreams, you settled for something else that brought similar results. Frankie dropped his last ten bucks on a Dilaudid. If it was good enough for terminal cancer patients, it was good enough for him.

All was quiet on Gore Street. The steps up to the front doors of First United Church were end to end full of homeless women trying to get a bit of sleep under a big blue plastic tarp that somebody had been competent enough to hang from a few nails pounded into the eaves. The women huddled under it, waiting for the rain that was supposed to start falling during the night. Chivalry lived among those who bedded down in filthy Sally Ann blankets and bedrolls on the outer periphery of the church entrance. Frankie passed by on the way to his apartment and made his way through the alley so he could enter his building by the back door.

By now, Roberts had to be sitting in an interrogation room with a couple of cops firing questions at him. Frankie unlocked the back door and walked in towards the mail room off to one side near the main doors. The sound of televisions turned up too loud added to the mess in his head. The smells of fried onions filled the hallway as usual. At least there was no one around to interfere with his mission. He unlocked his mailbox, always amazed that he had never lost that little key. A stack of flyers and other junk mail nearly filled the small cubicle, but right on top of all that disposable paper, there it was: the brown government envelopes that contained his and Kim's income assistance cheques. Frankie smiled, feeling a sense of relief, and he was about to put the envelope in his pocket when he heard a dog growling behind him. He turned around and there was a huge black Doberman straining at its leash, no more than twelve inches and a half a second away from ripping him apart. At the other end of the leash, barely holding Manson back, was Bill Roberts in a long black raincoat.

"Call your dog back, man!"

"Not until you answer a few questions, Frankie." Roberts walked around Frankie, keeping the dog in check but saying nothing. He stared at the cheques Frankie held in his hand.

"What you want to know?" Frankie's voice was cracking under the stress of this unexpected encounter.

"Where is your friend Kim?" The words flowed slow and deliberate from Roberts' mouth; a wrong answer and Manson would have his prize.

"I haven't seen her for a week. She checked into a rehab on the North Shore." Frankie tried not to look at Manson, but he knew the dog was poised to attack, jaws stretched and ready, every muscle tensed.

"When did you last speak to her?"

"Today. She called me from rehab."

"Give me your cell phone!" demanded Roberts.

Frankie took his cell from his pocket with shaking hand and gave it to him. The rehab number appeared on the screen, and Roberts dialed. Someone picked up on the second ring.

"I realize how late it is ma'am," Bill said calmly, "but this is an emergency. I must speak to Kim... Kim Lawrence. I believe she checked in today." There was a long pause. Roberts kept staring at Frankie with an expression of caged anger on his face. "She doesn't arrive until tomorrow? Okay. Thank you. I'll call back in the morning." Roberts returned the cell phone to Frankie and asked him if he knew where Kim might be, since she wasn't due at the rehab until tomorrow. Frankie stammered that he didn't know; she might be with Earl, her social worker. Earl probably wanted her to stay with him just to make sure she stayed clean and showed up at rehab.

"I have Earl's cell number if you want it." Frankie offered. He was getting real loose with the information. Frankie was begging for his life. Roberts took a bankbook and a pen from his pocket and handed it to Frankie.

"Write down the number."

"Sure thing." Frankie scribbled it down and gave the bankbook back.

"Very good," Roberts said, showing a hint of a smile, "but there is one more favor I must ask of you, Frankie."

"Anything, man."

"The cheques you have in your hand, there…" He was right in Frankie's face now. "You hold on to them as tight as you can!"

"No problem." Frankie's fist tightened until the envelopes were locked in his right hand.

"Perfect." Roberts let out a muffled laugh and then without warning he snatched the envelopes from Frankie's hand. They ripped in half, leaving Frankie clutching tightly two useless scraps of government paper.

"If I find Kim, I'll return your cheques." Roberts held the torn envelopes in the air above Frankie's head, baiting him. Frankie was stunned silent. Roberts slipped his half of the torn envelopes in his coat pocket.

"Don't worry man; Kim will be there." Frankie was on the verge of a meltdown as he watched his only chance of scoring disappear. He was broke again, and the Dilaudid would only do him a few hours at the most.

"Good. We have an understanding, then." Bill Roberts smiled and turned towards the door, as if he was finally leaving. He threw Frankie a contemptuous parting glance, the pathetic junkie willing to pimp his girlfriend, steal her welfare cheque, and then give her safe place away. Frankie had no fucking right to live, and he was no good to him anymore anyway. He loosened his grip on the leash and let Manson loose. The Doberman went after Frankie like a hyena after dead meat, attacking with the kind of ferocity reserved for someone guilty of trespassing on his turf. Frankie screamed in agony as Manson tore off a piece of his arm before going for the jugular, ripping Frankie's neck and throat to shreds.

Roberts finally pulled the beast off before somebody happened by to check their mail. Frankie lay in the corner where Manson had dragged him, spurting blood onto the carpet, his left leg jerking involuntarily. Junk mail was strewn around the room like fallen leaves scattered by a great gust of wind. The man and his dog prepared to leave. Roberts opened the door and jerked Manson's leash to get him to follow. The door sucked shut after them, leaving a kind of breathless vacuum where they had been.

Roberts walked to his truck parked up the block and drove away trying to think up a plan to silence Kim once she arrived at the rehab centre. She would definitely rat him out once she had detoxed. That's what people do at AA meetings, tell their stories to people who were once as fucked as they are. That couldn't happen; she couldn't be given that opportunity. The nurses would give her methadone to ease the withdrawal symptoms. The tough days spent agonizing in bed while the heroin left her body would take up at least a week.

There wasn't much time, but the plan could still work if the right person was responsible for it's success. Sebastian would find a way, Bill had no doubts. The man was a trained hunter; the hooker would never leave rehab alive. Roberts drove down Main, turned onto Hastings, then went down a block and took a left on Gore. He needed to relax; he needed a woman. He cruised the low stroll for a few blocks and finally spotted a lady of the night in a fashionable blue raincoat. He pulled over to take a closer look.

Sally Louie smiled at Roberts as the truck window came down slowly. Her body language, the fake smile, the slow movement of her eyes as she weaved back and forth on her leather pumps, it all spelled junkie hooker. "Looking for someone to rock your world honey?" Sally's tongue danced over her upper lip, as she tried to keep her balance.

"Get in sweetheart."

"Ooh! Someone wants to play!" She got in the truck quickly, sat back in the seat, unbuttoned her coat, and showed off her long legs before she moved closer to Roberts and placed her hand between his thighs.

"How much?" he asked.

"Depends on what turns you on."

"Full service," he said, pulling away from the curb.

"If we do it in the truck it's a hundred. But if you want to come to my room where we can relax and have a good time, how about one-fifty?"

Roberts raised his eyebrows, knowing she was highballing him. It was close to one-thirty in the morning, the slow time for women working the street. She would be lucky to get forty bucks for a blowjob. "I'll give you three hundred," he promised, "if you come to my place. I have some grade-A Mexican heroin and some rock. You can help yourself."

"Where's your home?"

"New West."

"That's a forty minute drive from here. I'd rather you came to my room."

Roberts guessed why she wanted him in her room. She probably had a friend who lived next door and was ready to rip him off. "Three hundred and all the drugs you want, but it has to be my place." Roberts stopped at a red light and pulled out a wad of hundred dollar bills from his coat pocket.

"Can you pay me now?"

"I'll give you a hundred now, then the rest when we get there."

"Alright!" She agreed and put her hand out. Roberts pulled a bill from the wad and handed it to her. "You're not lying about the drugs are you?"

"The best smack you will ever do. Take my word." Roberts was on East Broadway now, approaching the city limits. Sally had seen the wad. She wasn't worried anymore. She figured if she could get high and pocket three bills, it was going to be a good night after all.

CHAPTER 15

Pontiac was sitting with his old friend and former bandmate Josh Wheaton in the front row at the Blue Angel, Winnipeg's premier blues bar. The opening act, Sliding Clyde Roulette, had just finished his set, and the main act was getting ready to come on. Johnny Winter didn't look all that healthy and had to be helped onstage. As an albino with a history of health problems who was now well into his sixties, it was a miracle of sorts that he was still standing at all, let alone playing the guitar. He had titled one of his albums *Alive and Well*, an inside joke about his rather precarious relationship with his health. His fans were behind him, all anyone in the audience cared about was that he could still play that Gibson guitar he was plugging into his Fender Pro-Reverb amp and that he could still belt out the classic blues songs that established him as one of the last living blues legends.

Johnny opened with "Highway 61," the Dylan gem that he had fashioned into his own, then segued into "Good Morning Little Schoolgirl" before slowing it down with the Ray Charles classic "Drown In My Own Tears." A wave of applause erupted from the audience as the song finished, and Johnny thanked them in a raspy, whispery voice that hinted at just how fragile his constitution was. The band then settled into a medley of old country blues tunes inspired by Sonny Terry and Brownie McGee. When the set was over, Johnny told the faithful that he would return after he imbibed the proper libations and slowly made his way back to the dressing room.

"He's still the man," Pontiac said, thinking back thirty years ago to the first time he had seem Johnny Winter perform. "Life takes its toll, though. Johnny's one of the last survivors since Stevie Ray Vaughn died."

"Don't forget Buddy Guy and Clapton are still touring," Josh said, finishing his beer. He was in his mid-forties and quite fit for his age, though his hair was shorter now and his face a little rounder. He had played bass for Pontiac's band The Buffalo Soldiers, but that was long ago. He stopped playing professionally when the band broke up and had opened his own booking agency.

"That's all good. Those dudes are heavy players," said Pontiac, "but Johnny is still the man."

Josh gave a little headshake. "So what brings you back to the Peg? You haven't been here in what, twelve years?"

"I felt a need to reconnect. You know, get in touch with my roots." Pontiac scanned the crowd, noticing the biker crew over in the corner wearing their colours, most of them Hells Angels.

"Spare me the bullshit!"

"Straight up, dude. I'm helping a friend."

"What's your friend's name? Maybe I know him."

"Negative. He's from the coast; never been in the Peg."

"Jesus, Pontiac, what's his name?" Josh was growing impatient with the cat and mouse game that was vintage Pontiac.

"Mike Morningstar. He's a retired cop," Pontiac said in a low voice. "He's trying to find a girl gone missing. Her boyfriend, who could be a biker, was last seen here in town."

"You figured I would know his name?"

"Well, if anybody would have heard of this dude, it would be you."

"Thanks for the vote of confidence," Josh smiled. He had been booking bands for the last twenty years and had provided plenty of entertainment for bikers' picnics and private parties. He knew the pecking order of most bike gangs in the city simply by his professional association.

Pontiac gave him a short history of Carrie George and the nickname of his only lead: a biker called The Blade. "Does the name ring any bells?"

"No," Josh replied without a pause. "Never heard of him. All the bikers I know have real handles. The nickname shit is something they pick up in jail."

"It's all I have, man." Pontiac hadn't expected a miracle, but Josh's reply had just reminded him that he was looking for a needle in a haystack.

"I can give you a list of peeler bars where you might find him," Josh said. "One dude who might know this guy is our old buddy, Jerry Fleming."

"The piano man," Pontiac smiled. Josh was starting to scare up old ghosts. "He's still playing?"

"He's with a Chinese guitar player, another one of your former associates, Johnny 'Too Bad' Wong; they play for a lot of biker parties," Josh said matter-of-factly. "He would know if this guy is local."

"Where do we find him?" Pontiac was hoping it wasn't tonight.

"Are you up for some Chinese chow?"

"You're kidding me!" Pontiac shook his head in disbelief. Jerry was a bit on the strange side, but still an excellent piano player with a great set of pipes. "Jerry's playing in a Chinese restaurant?"

"That's right. We can catch his last set if we leave now."

Pontiac let out a deep breath. He was going to miss Johnny Winter, just so he could catch a lounge lizard playing for Chinese diners chewing on their Peking duck.

They left the bar, and Josh got behind the wheel of a Mercedes 260 SL, silver gray with black leather seats, the radio was pumping out "Reeling in the Years" by Steely Dan as they drove down Portage Avenue. Pontiac felt a little more in the zone now that he noticed a few of the taverns he used to play in were still standing, though many others had simply disappeared into thin air. The drive down memory lane brought back flashbacks of special nights that every musician lives over again when he's back on his home turf. Pontiac remembered nights when everything was in sync and the band he was on stage with was ready to conquer the world. Such feelings belonged in the past, but somehow they were always waiting for the right moment to resurface, a reminder that the clock was still ticking and nothing had really changed except his address. "Tomorrow, we will row faster," Fitzgerald had mused, but even he, the drunken scribe, knew from personal experience there were no happy endings in real life.

Pontiac asked Josh about why he'd never left, what made him stay when the thrill had been gone a long time ago. Josh replied without taking his eyes off the road; things had simply fallen into place on their own. The business made money, he got married—Jesus, that was twenty years ago. Now his oldest son was in Toronto and his daughter was in her second year of university. Josh could never leave Winnipeg; he had Métis blood in his veins, and the prairies would always be his home. Pontiac didn't say anything, but he felt a pang of jealousy that it seemed so easy for some people to find a nest and settle into it for good.

The Tokyo Rose belonged in Vegas with it's gaudy neon sign out front and the strings of lights running up and down the walls and fake pillars at the entrance. Pontiac asked Josh if there was a chance they would be refused at the door because of a dress code. Josh assured him there were no worries; Jerry would put in the fix. And sure enough, both men were escorted by the Maitre'd to a coveted table in the corner near the band, which was really just a duo with Jerry on keyboards and Johnny Wong on guitar. Jerry immediately directed a surprised and friendly stare at Pontiac and Josh.

"Ladies and gentlemen," Jerry announced, "we have been blessed by the presence of a legend in our midst! Please give it up folks for my old buddy, Pontiac Rasta Dumont!" He sounded like he was announcing a WWF wrestling match. There was a sprinkle of applause as Pontiac acknowledged his status by standing up and raising his right hand, and before he could sit back down, Jerry and Johnny tore into Barry Manilow's signature tune:

> *Her name was Lola, she was a showgirl*
> *With yellow feathers in her hair and a dress cut down to there*
> *She would merengue and do the cha-cha*
> *And while she tried to be a star, Tony always tended bar*
> *Across a crowded floor, they worked from 8 'til 4*
> *They were young and they had each other*
> *Who could ask for more?*

Drinks with little tropical umbrellas to shade their ice chips arrived unannounced at their table along with pot stickers, spring rolls, and menus. Pontiac took a closer look around the rather large restaurant. It was spread out over two floors, and every table was full, not an empty chair in the house. The Chinese loved their lounge lizards. The band finished its tribute to Barry Manilow and took a break. Johnny leaned his guitar up against his amplifier. Jerry Fleming, all two hundred pounds of him poured into white pants and a tux jacket with a keyboard stitched into the wide seventies lapel, came over and sat down at the table.

"Pontiac, my man! What brings you to the city of broken dreams?" Jerry thrust a meaty palm towards Pontiac who was thinking how much Jerry reminded him of Fats Domino.

"It's a long story, bro. I'm trying to help out an old friend."

Jerry nodded slowly and smiled. He was a Mohawk from Brantford who had first come to Winnipeg as a member of Pontiac's band, The Buffalo Soldiers, in the mid-seventies. "It's good to see you man."

"Mutual dude! I like the suit, but Manilow? What's that about?" Pontiac wanted to ask Jerry who had threatened him, because he could think of no other reason for doing a cover of any song made infamous by the King of Lounge Lizards himself.

"Check it out, man! Barry is the big egg roll in Hong Kong. Bigger than Elvis, the Stones, U-2, The Beatles, or even Marvin Gaye."

"Say it ain't so, dude!" Pontiac was often at odds with the musical aspirations and ambitions of the generation coming up behind him. He understood that age had shaped his musical tastes and that now there was no turning back. "Barry Manilow bigger than Marvin Gaye? I don't think so."

"Seriously, Barry is the man in Hong Kong. If I was to sing 'Mandy' next set, half the audience would be in tears." Jerry puckered his lips, and sunk his big head into his shoulders in an expression of dismay. No, he didn't understand it either, but that wasn't going to stop him from taking their money.

A man in a light green silk suit appeared from out of nowhere and placed a crisp thousand dollar bill on the table in front of Jerry. He was in his mid-thirties, slim and tall with a gold earring hanging from his left ear, black hair cut short, brown eyes, and a goatee. In a lilting English dialect tinged with a Spanish accent he said, "Amigo, my name is Sebastian. Can you play some reggae?" His eyes rested on Jerry, the star of the show. "I spend a lot of time in Jamaica. Even partied with Peter Tosh once or twice. I'd like my friends here to hear some good reggae."

"No problemo. Next set we could do a little Marley, some Tosh, and maybe Toots & the Maytals," Jerry replied with a big smile.

"Gracias!" Sebastian pointed his index finger towards Pontiac. "My friends tell me this man is an excellent singer."

"They're correct, and you can be sure I will do my best to get him to sit in with the band." Jerry stood up and gave Sebastian high five. He placed the money inside his tux pocket, then he took out five crisp one hundred dollar bills and gave them to Pontiac.

"What's going down?" Pontiac stared at the money in front of him, not sure if he wanted any part of this deal. He didn't feel much like singing.

"The man wants to hear some reggae. Five songs should do it. Works out to a hundred dollars a song." Jerry turned towards the small stage, realizing he needed to get a look at his list to see if he even had five reggae songs in his repertoire anymore.

"Why am I singing with you Jerry?" Pontiac had never sung with anything under a five-piece band. "Because some dude's throwing cash around like it's monopoly money?"

"That's right, man. You have in your hand five hundred reasons to sing with us tonight." Jerry moved a little closer to Pontiac and in a much lower register said, "If the man asks me to sing 'Happy Birthday' in Cantonese, that's what he's gonna hear, and it's not just about the money. I'll let my agent man fill you in on what I'm talking about." Jerry gave Josh a look that said tell this fool who Norm Kwan is while he's still healthy.

Josh caught on. "What Jerry is trying to say, Pontiac, is that our pal Sebastian is a friend of Norm Kwan, the owner of the restaurant."

"Well, if that's the case…" Pontiac unceremoniously put the cash in his shirt pocket. "We be jammin in the key of dough, mon!"

Johnny "Too Bad" Wong brought Pontiac one of his guitars, a white Fender Stratocaster. The three musicians quickly went over a proposed set until everyone finally agreed upon the order. The first song was the Peter Tosh version of "Johnny B. Goode." Pontiac was no further than the middle of the first verse when couples came pouring out of the upstairs lounge where Kwan was having his private party. The space down in front of the stage reserved for dancing was soon as crowded as a liquor store on New Year's Eve. Sebastian himself was on the dance floor surrounded by beautiful young women.

Pontiac didn't notice at first, but as the mood slowed down during Marley's classic ballad "No Woman No Cry," he caught a glimpse of Sebastian's dancing partner. He tried to remember where he had seen this beautiful Native woman before, but it wasn't until the song ended and she stood alone on the floor giving Pontiac a perfect view that he finally realized he was staring right at Carrie George.

CHAPTER 16

Since Mona had not been reported missing by her family, the New Westminster Police had brushed Kim's story off for lack of hard evidence. The file was passed on to the RCMP where Harold Jenkins had his own reasons to be interested in conducting an investigation. He was part of a special task force the Mounties had recently set up to deal with missing women. Any case that even hinted at violence against a woman was given serious attention. Jenkins had been around the block in terms of police work; he had done time with the drug squad and had worked vice for many years. Serial killers were new territory, but take a misogynist with a vicious taste for inflicting pain on women, then add a diet of alcohol and drugs and kinky sex and you get the kind of suspect Jenkins was now tracking. He had set up a meeting with Kim Lawrence, despite all the disinterest expressed by the New West Police and even other members of his own team.

His office was on the second floor of the RCMP headquarters, a fair sized room, but not large enough for Harold. There were files all over a table in the corner of the room where a fax machine and Xerox copier sat beside each other along with a cappuccino machine. Pictures of Harold hung on the wall, one of him receiving an award, another one of him standing guard in front of the Queen Mother. His prized Apple laptop computer fought for space on his desk, which was cluttered with forms and newspapers. In two chairs facing his desk, Kim and her social worker Earl were uncomfortably waiting for the inquisition to begin.

"This wasn't the first time you were picked up by this man?" he asked.

"I went to his house once before," Kim replied softly.

"What happened?" Jenkins noticed the tracks on her arms.

"He gave me some rock. I gave him what he wanted, that was it." Kim was looking the worse for wear, and Earl placed a supportive hand on her shoulder. After her humiliating session with the unsympathetic Constable Larch, Kim was beginning to hope that she might have finally found a sympathetic ear in the big Mountie.

"Was it your idea to bring Mona?"

"No." Kim felt the sting of accusation, as if whatever had happened to Mona was her fault. "He wanted two girls. I suggested Mona because I knew she was in the bar at the time."

Jenkins put his pencil down. He had been monitoring Kim's body language for any signs of anxiety or distress. So far, nothing had registered that might lead him to dismiss the authenticity of Kim's story.

"There was nothing unusual about his behavior, nothing that made you suspicious?"

"He started getting weird with me, saying my father was a traitor and had gotten what he deserved."

"He knew your father?" Jenkins asked incredulously.

"I don't think so. He probably heard it from some Hells Angel."

"Your father was involved with them."

"My father was a member of the Hells Angels, yes," Kim affirmed. "He was killed by someone in a gang, but I was never told why."

"How did he know your father?" Jenkins was curious to find out if there was a connection between Roberts and bikers.

"I don't know. Roberts never mentioned anything the first time I was there. How he would have known is weird, unless he spoke to someone who knew my mother. She has a lot of friends who are bikers."

"Do you think Roberts is a biker?"

"I don't know. He told me he repaired motorcycles, but I have friends who have been to his club and they told me the place was packed with bikers."

"That's interesting. Did he ever get violent with you?"

"No, but by the time we got to the house, he was becoming very aggressive."

"How did you respond?"

"I didn't. He was snorting coke. I was afraid he would get more insulting if I called him on it, so I told him I had to go to the washroom and went upstairs." Kim was becoming unsettled about what Roberts had said about her father.

"Was he giving Mona a hard time?"

"I don't know how it started. I was upstairs in the washroom. When I came out, I could hear their voices."

"Did you go back downstairs?"

"Not right away. There's a room beside the washroom, and I happened to look in there. I noticed a box of women's clothes and started rummaging around. Then, I found a T-shirt with dried blood on it, and that's when I got worried. I could hear Mona and him yelling at each other. I listened from the top of the stairs. I saw Mona throw the pipe in his face, then she ran outside. Roberts followed her."

"Did you see what happened out there?"

Kim took a while to answer. She had blocked out Mona's last moments along with the fear and feelings of helplessness she experienced when she ended up running for her own life. "I ran down the road," she said, "and I could hear Mona screaming like she was being stabbed or something. There was a dog chasing after me." Kim broke down in tears, unable to continue.

"All right. No more questions." Jenkins placed several sheets of blank paper in front of her. "Here's a pen. You just write down everything you can remember from that night. I'll get you a fresh cup of coffee, and if you need to smoke just step outside."

Kim took the opportunity to soothe herself with a cigarette, and Jenkins tilted his head toward the door as she left, signaling Earl to go with her. Jenkins wasn't sure what Earl's role was in all this; he had introduced himself as a social worker and a friend, which was wide open for interpretation. Still, Jenkins had no desire to wade too deep into Kim's private life. She wasn't quite a crack whore, but she was definitely wired to heroin, a situation that was not considered a fertile breeding ground for the truth. Then again, he didn't really doubt the validity of her story. It rolled too freely off her tongue despite her distress, which was clearly genuine, and there were too many details for her story to be entirely fabricated.

Unfortunately, Jenkins wasn't yet able to find a proper address for Mona Yellowbird, and since no one had reported her missing it was a no-brainer: no body, no crime. He very much wanted to believe Kim, but without concrete proof and nothing but her word, he would have a hard time convincing his superiors to sign for the search warrant he needed in order to pay a visit to William Roberts. What truly piqued his interest in the case was this bloodied clothing Kim had mentioned. That was the kind of evidence that opened up possibilities. There may have been several women murdered at Roberts' house.

Kim was busy writing when Jenkins returned. He placed a tray of donuts and a cup of coffee in front of her, and she gave him a quick smile as she helped herself to the coffee. She seemed more relaxed, like telling the story had relieved some pressure. When Jenkins asked her if she was ready to resume the interview, she simply started talking again, beginning where she had left off. Now, however, she was laboring and it was only with great difficulty that she put together a description of what happened at the SkyTrain.

"Are you saying that Roberts followed you straight to the SkyTrain?"

"My ride left me off at the service station, and when I came out of the washroom, there he was at the pumps."

"Did he spot you?"

"No, I ran through the alleys until a cabbie picked me up. I had no idea he would show up at the SkyTrain."

"But you saw him at the station?" Jenkins was now much more attentive. He knew psychopaths lured their victims to a selected location. Murder in a public place is not their modus operandi. Targeting someone at a crowded SkyTrain station would not have been an option unless the shooter was a professional killer.

"I'm not sure if he saw me." Kim flashed back to the exact moment she had seen Roberts at the station. "I thought I was safe, until the bullets came through the train door."

"Did you report this to the transit cop on the train?"

"I spoke to him and he took down my phone number and address. I didn't tell him I thought the bullets were meant for me, though."

"What's your home address Kim?" Jenkins had a hunch that Roberts would come looking for her to make sure there were no witnesses to Mona's murder.

"I've been living with my boyfriend on East Pender, but today I'm checking into a rehab centre on the North Shore." Kim turned to Earl for support. She still wasn't sure if this was the right decision.

"Your boyfriend, he's still on Pender?"

"No, Roberts could show up there looking for me. Frankie's staying with friends now. He won't go back home until you've arrested Roberts."

Jenkins breathed a sigh of relief. He would call his old friend Kevin Chandler, a sergeant with Vancouver Police, and ask him to check out the apartment, maybe speak to a few of the tenants, just in case Roberts had been around. His main concern now was that Kim could not be safe at all in a rehab centre, especially if Roberts was a trained killer. The rehab would be a carnival shooting gallery. Kim would be better off in jail.

"I'm not so sure we can count on his being arrested immediately," Jenkins pointed out. "Your evidence is powerful Kim, but Mona has yet to be declared missing by one of her family, and we have no hard evidence, no body, no murder weapon, no other witnesses."

"You're not going to arrest him?" Kim couldn't believe it. She had been living in terror since that awful night, and she needed to feel safe again; the fear was wearing her down. She had to know that the psycho who killed her friend wouldn't have the opportunity to track and kill her, too.

"He will be arrested, Kim," Jenkins reassured her. "There is no doubt in my mind, but it will have to be done according to the proper protocols. We need something to help us secure a search warrant."

"What do you mean?" Kim's voice was broken by renewed terrors. "That bastard killed Mona, and he will kill me if he's not arrested!"

"Kim, no one is going to hurt you. I'll make sure of that. In the meantime, I can promise you that I will do everything possible to put this William Roberts behind bars as quickly as possible, and for as long as possible… for the rest of his life." Still, Jenkins knew he could no more guarantee an immediate arrest than he could a sure-fire conviction and life imprisonment.

"What if he shows up at rehab?" Kim dropped her chin to her chest in utter despair, contemplating the reality of the next few days ahead of her. She felt betrayed. Her friend was dead, and Roberts was still out there calculating his next psychotic move. At first, Jenkins had seemed different than the other cops she had encountered. Why couldn't he see the danger she was in? Why wasn't this killer being hunted down? She couldn't help thinking that if the suspect was a Native man there would be no protocols to follow; they would find an excuse one way or the other to bring him in. If he was an Indian, he would be in jail already.

"Listen to me Kim! Nothing is going to happen to you!" Jenkins promised. "I will visit you every day while you're in the centre, and if anything seems in the least bit suspicious, you will be moved to a safe house right away." Jenkins shared her concern about safety since his understanding of Roberts had taken on a larger dimension. In fact, what Kim needed was police protection until Roberts was behind bars, but without something more to go on he could never convince anyone else of that. He had to conjure a way to make the arrest on what they already had, which really amounted to nothing more than the statement from an arguably less than credible source.

"How long before he's under arrest?" Kim's question suggested that she was having second thoughts about showing up at rehab after all.

"We need Mona's family to declare her missing, then I can get a search warrant to check out Roberts' house. If we find Mona's body or other evidence, we can arrest him for murder, and you won't have to worry about him anymore."

Bill Roberts stood by the open window of his bedroom, stripped down to his briefs. Sweat rolled down his face, and he was breathing heavily as if he had just finished a workout, which was close to truth. He had lowered himself to fucking yet another low-life, drug-addled hooker. She had tried to lure him to her apartment, but Roberts saw through her ploy to rip him off. Now he would have the last laugh, because the real party was about to begin. It was times like this when he felt in total control. His mind drifted unfettered; all thoughts of repressed anger disappeared. Lying on the bed was Sally Louie, his latest hooker, picked up just a few nights ago. She was handcuffed to the headboard, and her legs were splayed, chained to the foot of the bed. Sally didn't complain about any of this because a metal ball gag was tied around her head.

Roberts breathed in deeply, then left the bedroom and followed the hallway to the living room. There on the coffee table was a gram of Mexican heroin—not the light brown smack that was sold on the street, but a bright canary yellow powder that was ten times more powerful.

"You like to get high Sally?" Roberts was back, taunting her as he held up a syringe filled with yellow smack. Sally had already fixed once today and was slightly comatose. She fought to keep her eyes open. She couldn't remember being cuffed and chained, but what little consciousness she had left registered fear, and rightly so. Her eyes were crisscrossing, but she finally caught a glimpse of Roberts and the syringe. She couldn't speak, but she tried to move her head. Roberts laughed and leaned over to tighten the ball gag in her mouth.

"This is your lucky day," he said, "You will get higher than you have ever been in your life. Your friends would die to get so stoned, and perhaps someday they will." Roberts looked down at Sally and smiled. "But only you, Sally, will know what it's like to be so high you'd need a stepladder to scratch your ass." Roberts giggled himself into a gurgling laugh that got louder as he closed in on Sally with the syringe. "Lucky, lucky Sally. And does a low-life hooker who likes ripping off her customers deserve such treatment? Of course she does," he said, answering his own question. "Perhaps if you had shown some respect I wouldn't have to punish you, but you reap what you sow, you mindless slut." He found an unspoiled vein in her left arm and pushed the needle in, blood filling the syringe as he drew the plunger back. Sally's eyes fluttered shut as the smack entered her system.

CHAPTER 17

It was a good thing Pontiac was a professional musician, because music was pretty much the last thing on his mind throughout the entire set. Pontiac had to keep right on singing while he watched Carrie leave the dance floor and walk up the stairs with Sebastian by her side. When the song was over, Pontiac walked off the stage and informed Josh what had just happened.

"It was her, I swear, and she's sitting up there right now with mister moneybags!" Pontiac said, trying to contain his excitement.

"Just cool it! This table has ears," Josh said, as he waved goodbye to Jerry who was talking to a group of women in front of the stage.

"I'm not leaving until I see her one more time."

"Wrong, we're leaving now," Josh urged. "Right fucking now."

"Chill out, dude!" Pontiac took one more glance upstairs, still no sign of Carrie. He followed Josh towards the exit, but instead of going down the stairs which led outside, Pontiac made a U-turn and walked upstairs, smack into the middle of Norm Kwan's private party. His first impression was that he had just entered the Playboy Mansion. The room was filled with well-tailored Asian men surrounded by attractive young women, and large round tables were piled high with food and drink. Pontiac saw Sebastian right away and walked up to his table, which caught Sebastian off guard. It took a few seconds for him to identify Pontiac, but when he did, he simply laughed it off.

"I just wanted to tell you, it's the first time I've ever played with this band. Things were a little loose." Pontiac was all smiles, trying to be cool. Two older Chinese men were sitting with Sebastian, along with young women whose task it was to keep the old geezers entertained.

"Excellent! You were excellent," Sebastian assured him. "You must play at the Tokyo Rose with your own band." Sebastian held a glass of champagne in his right hand, and a young Asian woman stood behind him, massaging his shoulders.

"Cool." Pontiac was about to suggest that Josh could handle the booking when another young woman sat down. She was not Asian but Native, with long shiny black hair that fell straight down her back. She was wearing a light brown chiffon dress that hugged her body. When she glanced around the room, Pontiac noticed her eyes weren't really registering what was happening around her. "My agent will call Mr. Kwan," he said.

"Excellent," Sebastian replied, and in a gesture of friendship, he introduced his female companions. "I want you to meet my friends, Señor Pontiac. Nikki here is from Hong Kong, and this is Carrie." Pontiac smiled at Nikki and offered a hand to Carrie.

"Are you a Métis?" Carrie asked.

"I am and proud of it." Pontiac turned to one side so Carrie could see the Gabriel Dumont tattoo on his arm.

"Very nice," she said.

"Louis Riels' right hand man. He escaped the hangman's noose and lived to ride with Buffalo Bill's Wild West show. Along with Sitting Bull and Wild Bill Hickok."

"You're a wonderful singer, Pontiac. Sebastian knows a lot about reggae."

"He put in the request." Pontiac turned toward Sebastian, who seemed to be growing impatient listening to them talk about some folk hero he'd never heard of.

"I want you to know how much I love reggae," Sebastian said, flashing his big smile. "You seem to have a passion for the music, so you will comprehend what I am saying. I would love for you and your band to play here soon. I will make all the necessary arrangements." He sealed the deal with a handshake and said he would draw up the contract later. Pontiac agreed and said goodbye to Carrie as he walked away.

Josh had stayed outside waiting in the Mercedes, a little hot under the collar, afraid that Pontiac might be dragging him into a quagmire that could cost him a lot. At the very least, Josh's dealings with Norman Kwan had already been jeopardized, if not his own life. He was shocked when he heard what Pontiac had just done.

"All right, you found your girl. Congratulations," Josh said. "But if you think you can just walk up to her and snatch her away from one of Kwan's henchmen, forget it! I suggest you call your cop friend and let him take it from here."

"It was totally cool, bro. The dude's gonna book my band. And

Carrie, she looked wasted, but she's alive!" Pontiac slapped the dashboard in celebration. "I gotta call Mike. He will freak the fuck out." Pontiac turned away from Josh and looked out the window at nothing for a few seconds. He could see the entrance to the Tokyo Rose, but no one was leaving the party yet.

"Then tell him to bring his own wheels, because if you intend to follow her, I'm outta here." Josh handed Pontiac his cell phone. "Look Pontiac, I can tell you where most of the women at Kwan's party came from, including Carrie."

"You mean they weren't girlfriends?" Pontiac replied sarcastically while dialing Mike's number. "I hope he's in town by now." Pontiac was keen to deliver his bit of information.

Mike had been in Winnipeg since 9:30 that evening. The original plan was for Pontiac to show up at the airport, but when Mike wasn't able to reach him, he checked into the Radisson Hotel on his own. He had spent a restless, frustrating two hours on the plane trying to piece together Dennis Anderson's statements on what had happened to Susan Wabigon. There was no doubt in his mind that Susan had been murdered, but the RCMP had yet to come to the same conclusion and lay charges. Mike had fallen asleep thinking about the mystery man in the photograph. Was he just a friend or maybe a john? There was the remote possibility that he was in fact The Blade. If appearances meant anything, the guy didn't look like a biker. Mike was in a deep sleep when the phone rang, and before his own half-baked theories had time to enter his head, the utter shock of Pontiac's news hit him like a sledgehammer.

"Mike... Dude, you are not going to believe who I saw tonight. Carrie... Carrie George! The Tokyo Rose on Portage and Riel. Park on the north side across the street. I'll be waiting in a grey Mercedes."

A short while later, Pontiac spotted Mike's rented Pontiac Grand Am coming down the street. He watched as Mike parked and walked over to the Mercedes with a Tim Hortons coffee in his hand. Pontiac went through the introductions and gave a brief history of the night's events, starting at the restaurant. Mike smiled at Pontiac when he explained the encounter with Carrie. He couldn't wait to get in there and see for himself, but Josh had been waiting patiently for an opportunity to interrupt without seeming rude. He decided to appeal to Mike's sense of logic.

"Look," Josh said, "there is no point in following this party just to find out where they're going. I know where the party's going. It's moving to a very predictable location, and we have no official invitation."

"Explain, dude." Pontiac said as two limos pulled up to the entrance of The Tokyo Rose.

"Kwan always starts his parties in the restaurant, then invites everyone over to his house, or should I say mansion."

"Kwan is a rich man," Mike said, noticing a group of well-dressed diners filing out of the restaurant and approaching the limos. "Does the restaurant really bring in the kind of cash it costs to throw this sort of party?"

"No, although the Rose does very well. Kwan's money comes from the Triads. And speak of the devil, there he is getting into the limo." Josh then subtly drew Mike's attention to the short, stocky Asian man in a three-piece suit. Kwan and a brood of beautiful young women all disappeared inside the first limo, followed by his business associates. More and more people kept streaming out of the restaurant; some headed for the second limo, others to their own vehicles parked further up the street. Among the group getting into the second limo were Carrie George and Sebastian.

"There's our girl, Mike." Pontiac pointed in her direction.

"I see her." Mike had envisioned finding her in some deadbeat crack house where he would courageously stumble over the bodies of used up pipeheads to rescue her anorexic bonerack from the prison of the hose pipe and return her triumphantly to her parents like a suitcase lost by an apologetic airline. Now the whole thing had become much more complicated. Carrie George appeared to be a working girl whose current employer was affiliated with one of the most murderous mobs of organized crime: the Triads. The question now was whether she was here of her own free will or under duress. Had she been ordered to do what she was told, lest she end up like her friend Susan?

"Who is the man directly behind her?" Mike asked.

"He's the reggae freak who paid a thousand dollars to hear me sing Bob Marley," Pontiac told him.

"Was he on crack?"

"No, dude. He loves reggae."

"I'm sure he does." Mike had seen the man before and very recently. "So Josh, what do you propose we do since you don't think we should tail the limos?"

"Well, if you have any doubts, we can take a different route and drive by the house. I guarantee the limos will be parked in the driveway." They all watched as the first two limos drove away and two more pulled up in front of the pillars.

"I believe you, Josh." Mike was taking note of the fact that Pontiac had, in his inimitable way, put some pressure on Josh's friendship. "I take it the guests and their women stay at the mansion all night?"

"Into the early hours of the morning at least." Josh gave the impression he had attended one of Kwan's parties in the past. "The men are shuttled back to their hotels, and the girls are sent home."

"So, what are the chances of waiting until sunrise to tail Carrie?" Mike asked.

"Zero! The mansion is in the most posh neighborhood in the city. You can't just park on the street without being noticed by Kwan's goons."

"What do you suggest?" Pontiac broke in. He was beginning to feel a bit left out, and started listening closer for a place to enter the conversation. After all, it was he who had found Carrie in the first place.

"All these women at the party, including Carrie, they all work at Kwan's peeler joints or massage parlors or his escort agencies. One of the women I spotted on the dance floor tonight works at the Silver Slipper; that's a peeler joint on Mackenzie Avenue. Lila... she's a wannabe singer. Every time I go there she hands me her band's CD. So, maybe tomorrow I drop in and mention I saw her at the Tokyo Rose. She might tell me where the pretty Native woman works."

"That's a rather large favor, Josh, and you're putting yourself at risk," Mike said.

"Don't worry. There's no real danger. She's just a dancer who turns tricks. I can also give you a list of some of the select massage parlors Carrie might work in," Josh offered. "You could check them out tomorrow yourself, Mike, and Pontiac could visit the peeler bars."

Mike thought for a moment. "It's a good plan," he said, "and it's been a good night. Pontiac found Carrie alive and well. There is no point in asking for trouble this early in the game."

Mike and Pontiac walked to Mike's rental car and drove back to the hotel. It was four-thirty in the morning. Mike's mind was racing at the possibilities that had opened up in a matter of a few hours, but he had a feeling the hard work was just beginning. They stopped at a McDonald's drive-through on Pontiac's insistence; his adrenaline was used up and he needed sustenance. A fish burger and fries would do the trick.

If Carrie was working in one of Kwan's brothels, they would find her quick and easy enough, but what would their next move have to be? Winnipeg had just turned into a very expensive chessboard, and if Carrie George was Mike's queen, he needed to make the best of his pawns. The Triad was certainly not to be taken lightly, and the Chinese were notoriously good at games like chess. They loved to gamble, too. And some liked to hurt people. He would need to place a call to his contact on the Winnipeg police force, Richard Beaulieu, to find out how the local cops were dealing with Norm Kwan.

Mike asked Pontiac about the connection between Sebastian and Carrie. Pontiac didn't think there was anything beyond business. The dude was surrounded by an army of women, which meant he's a big man with the Chinese mob. Carrie just happened to be one of those women. Mike took out the picture Dennis Anderson had given him and handed it to Pontiac.

"This is too freaky, dude." Pontiac stared at the photo of Sebastian standing beside Carrie and Susan along with some official-looking dude. "Where was this taken?"

"Calgary. Sebastian visited Carrie just before she left rehab."

"He's the man with the deep pockets who loves reggae," Pontiac said, trying to make the connection that Mike had figured was obvious.

"I'm willing to bet he's also The Blade."

"Get outta town. He's too cool to be a biker."

"Candy never said The Blade was a biker. We simply assumed he was because of her past."

"So, he's not Carrie's boyfriend. He's her pimp?" Pontiac shook his head in disgust.

"That's right. Was Sebastian talking to Norm Kwan when you were upstairs?"

"I wouldn't know who Norm was if he shit in my hand." Pontiac handed Mike back the picture. "Sebastian was sitting with some heavy looking dudes, but I don't think any of them was Kwan.

CHAPTER 18

When Harold Jenkins showed up in room 201 of the Royal Columbian Hospital, Jeff Walker was asleep, his left arm in a cast held up by a wire tied to a metal stand that stood beside the bed. The nurse spoke softly to him, as if she were speaking to a child, and finally Jeff stared out of medicated eyes and registered a brief moment shock, as if he didn't know where he was until the he saw the cast. The expression of forced acceptance on his face slowly turned into a visible state of depression.

"You have a visitor Jeff. He's with the RCMP." The nurse backed away so Officer Jenkins could approach the patient.

"Harold Jenkins is my name, Jeff. Do you feel up to talking about what happened?" He spoke in a low a register, as he had muted his voice following the nurse's manner.

"I've already told the cop who was here yesterday what happened. I'm not a gang member, and I have no idea why someone shot me, unless he was some kind of lunatic." Jeff's voice rose by a few decibels as he spoke, and his eyes filled with anger.

"I believe you," Harold assured him. The nurse who had been monitoring the conversation brought in a chair so the officer could sit bedside. Harold appreciated the gesture.

"Jesus, I'm sorry," Jeff corrected himself. "The policeman who was here yesterday, he kept asking me about gangs. I know nothing about gangs, but he wouldn't listen to me."

"I doubt if the he knew what was really happening," Harold said. "I think you got hit by a stray bullet. You were simply in the wrong place at the wrong time."

Jeff seemed relieved, but confused. "Are you saying I wasn't the target?"

"That's why I'm here." Harold sat back and looked around the room. "I need to ask you a few questions that might help me identify the shooter."

"I didn't see him officer," Jeff said, biting his lip to squash his anger before it resurfaced. "I was trying to get on the train, then it felt like someone hit my arm with a baseball bat. I didn't think it was a bullet until I saw the blood gushing down my sleeve."

Harold lowered his head. This wasn't the first time he had spoken to an innocent bystander in the hospital; at least Jeff was alive. "When you were approaching the SkyTrain door, could you see the people who were getting on the train?" He noticed the blank expression on Jeff's face. "The people who were immediately in front of you before the door closed, could you see them?"

Jeff was fatigued and clearly frustrated that his memory was betraying him. "I was running towards the door; there were two women getting on just before the door closed."

"I want you to take your time, Jeff. Is there anything you can remember about the women you saw?"

"The woman who got in as the door closed looked Native. She had brown hair pulled back in a bun. She was young, and so was the Asian woman in front of her."

"Really? That's very good. Obviously your memory hasn't been affected by the shooting." Harold looked back at the nurse, who smiled approvingly. "The woman with the brown hair, was she short or tall?"

"She wasn't real short; maybe five foot four, but definitely not tall." Jeff closed his eyes, and let his head fall back on the pillow. "She was slim and could have been wearing sneakers."

Harold smiled, grateful that Jeff was trying hard. "I've got a photograph I want you to see." He took out his cell phone, brought up Kim's picture, and handed the cell phone to Jeff.

"That's her!" Jeff exclaimed, unable to contain his surprise. "She was the woman in front of me."

"You a hundred percent sure?"

"Totally. It's her."

"Thank you Jeff," Harold said. "One more thing, three shots were fired from a twenty-two handgun. Did you hear the sound of gunfire before you were shot?"

"No, I was running for the train. There was the usual crowd noise, but nothing that sounded like a gunshot. That's what freaked me out. I was shot, no warning, not even the sound of gun. I had no idea where it came from."

"The shooter must have used a silencer," Harold said as a different impression of his suspect was beginning to take seed in his mind. He handed Jeff his card. "I want you to call me when you check out of the hospital."

"No prob, officer. Do you have a suspect?"

"Let's just say I am gathering information right now." Harold stood up and returned the chair to the nurse. As he left, he took a last look at Jeff Walker, who now seemed a little more comfortable with his fate, and said, "I appreciate your help."

There is collection of smells in every hospital that gives a hospital building, no matter how modern, a sterile ambience. That, combined with the incarcerated state many of the patients suffer through, made these interviews painful for Harold. He wanted hospital security to post a man in front of Jeff's room, but really he needed to get out of the hospital, even just for a few minutes of fresh air. He would have his office call the hospital and work out the security.

Harold took his time driving out of the parking lot. The lot was filling up. It crossed his mind that all the people leaving their cars could be visiting family or relatives who might never come home. It wasn't a pleasant thought, but hospitals had that effect on him. He was happy with Jeff's testimony because it confirmed Kim's story. Roberts had followed her to the SkyTrain station and tried to kill her. The rest of her story was probably equally factual, which meant Mona Yellowbird was dead.

Harold wanted to call the head of the task force. Captain Hawkins would want to hear the news, and his first questions would likely be "where is the body?" and "is there a witness who can identify Roberts as the shooter in the SkyTrain incident?" The answers: no body and no witness, only Kim's story, and that would not get him the search warrant he needed in order to visit Roberts' house. Harold couldn't figure why Roberts had followed Kim to the SkyTrain station. The attempt to murder Kim in a public place without worrying about the risk meant Roberts was either mentally challenged or he was a professional killer, and since only pros use silencers, he could be a trained assassin.

Harold was on Main Street just a few blocks from the Vancouver Police Station before he realized there wasn't enough time to call his boss. He decided to check in with his buddy Kevin Chandler, since he was close by.

Harold parked and went up to Chandler's office on the third floor, which had a perfect view of the Carnegie Centre right across the street.

"What's cooking, Kevin?"

"Something you might be interested in. Mona's boyfriend has reported her missing."

"Her boyfriend? What about the parents?"

"We've reached them. No one has seen Mona for the past week, and since her welfare cheque is still sitting in her boyfriend's mailbox, the consensus is something must have happened to her."

"You're a pal, Kevin. Now we can get that warrant," Harold said. William Roberts was about to receive an unwanted visitor.

"One more corpse you should know about," Kevin said. "Frankie Morin was killed in his apartment building two days ago. Cause of death: a dog attacked him in the hallway of his apartment."

"When did you find him?"

"Yesterday morning. Apparently, someone tried to steal his welfare cheques. No suspects so far, and no one in the building owns a dog."

"What makes you think it was a robbery?" Harold could not imagine Roberts stealing a welfare cheque; it didn't fit the profile.

"Frankie was found in front of mailboxes, clutching half his torn cheques. He wouldn't give them up, and it cost him his life."

"You've been set up," Harold said, giving no further explanation. "I might have your prime suspect. What you need to do, Kevin, is speak to forensics and find out if they can tell what breed of dog did the damage."

"I could use a few more details, forensics will want to know why I'm poking my nose into their investigation."

"I have a witness to a murder. Frankie Morin was her boyfriend, which is why I asked you to speak to some of the tenants from his apartment. My suspect owns a vicious dog, and I have a feeling it was his dog that killed Frankie. "

"Alright. That should get me some quick results."

"One more thing. You need to get a cruiser over to the rehab on the North Shore, immediately." Harold took out his cell phone, called the centre, and asked for Kim. There was a long pause. When the receptionist came back on the line, she explained that Kim was attending an AA meeting and couldn't be disturbed. Harold told her he was with the RCMP and Kim's life was in danger; the police were on the way, and if a man came to visit Kim he was to be denied entry.

William Roberts was driving home from Vancouver. He considered visiting the rehab centre where Kim was staying, but he scrapped the idea because someone would obviously see him and remember him. Roberts realized he would have to hire a hitter just as Sebastian called from Winnipeg.

"Sebastian, what a pleasant surprise! I was just thinking of you," Roberts said, happy to hear from him. Sebastian apologized for not calling him sooner, but he'd been very busy as usual. He wanted to know if Roberts needed his services.

"I have a problem that must be dealt with immediately," Roberts said with a sense of urgency. There was no need to explain the reason; the message was clear. Sebastian told his old boss not to worry. He planned to be in Vancouver in a week, and they could discuss the details when he arrived.

"A driver will be waiting for you. His name is Johnny, most people call him The Greek. He'll take you to your hotel, and when are ready, come visit me." Roberts felt relieved that his problem with Kim was about to disappear.

CHAPTER 19

The Chinese receptionist was dressed like a Catholic schoolgirl. The small frame of her body fit snugly inside a white blouse unbuttoned at the top and tucked into a very blue, very short tartan skirt. Mike Morningstar followed her into the main room where several other young women, most of them of Asian descent, were watching television and stuffing their mouths full of hot buttered Orville Redenbacher. The receptionist motioned toward them, "Verrrry beautiful girls!" She had learned her lines well, but these three words were quite likely the extent of her English vocabulary.

Mike smiled awkwardly, leaning closer to the young woman in the deep blue tartan. "I was hoping to see the blond you've got in your advertisement," he said. "I was told she was working today."

"Sharice?" asked the receptionist in a bird-like voice. "She come latah!"

The other girls were engrossed in a Jackie Chan movie, sporadically erupting into hysterical laughter. When they noticed Mike, several began gesturing seductively for him to join them on the soft and ample couch. Mike showed great resolve and politely declined, promising to return later, then allowed the young receptionist to book him for nine-thirty. It was an appointment he had no intention of keeping, but he smiled at the harem nevertheless as he left the third massage parlor he'd visited that afternoon. He drove down Riel Street and turned up Market Square, looking for the cheating part of town. Within a few minutes, he was there, right smack dab in the mad middle of The Strip, as horny businessmen liked to call it. The sky is the limit there, until it starts falling. There is a old Chinese saying: "Women hold up half the sky." So, if their hands are pressed into pleasing johns, then the sky is bound to take a tumble.

Along the street, plate glass pawn shop windows offered everything from chainsaws to diamond rings as a backdrop to the parade of working girls strutting by in thigh-high boots, the bushy collars on their goatskin coats turned up against the frigid air. Mike parked the rented Pontiac Grand Am directly in front of Pandora's Box, a biker joint lit up in neon that boasted cold beer and hot babes. He took his time checking out the women working the street before paying ten bucks to get past the burly bouncer at the door.

Mike sat down at the bar, watching a woman work the stage. She wore a pink nurse's uniform with a little pink hat and black-rimmed reading glasses, to remind the men seated up close that nurses and strippers can read after all. In a moment most of her clothes were gone, and she was strutting around topless, showing off her surgically enhanced cleavage. Only her skirt was left, and she let it slip slowly down over the longest legs in the West until it lay crumpled on the stage with her blouse and coat. She was a sight to see leaning on that pole, as she gave her pretty little hat a nudge to the right. As she shook and shimmied, she jiggled her library spectacles down to the end of her nose where they stopped to rest, just as cute as a button.

Mike watched the bar patrons in the front row, most of them looked like gang members. The hoods and sneakers crowd mixed in with several tables of bikers wearing their colours. Near the stage, everyone's attention was on Miss Alicia, the naughty nurse next door, but in the back of the bar, young women from the oldest profession were hustling customers at their tables. They tried to get lost among the strippers and waitresses, but sooner or later their leather and fishnet wardrobes gave them away. Mike searched their faces trying to find anything that reminded him of Carrie, but nothing so far. Many of the women were in their late twenties, with hardened faces that no plastic surgeon could fix. Their expressions were sleazy, not seductive, and most of them looked wired to the tits, begging for a fix. Unfortunately, no one even remotely reminded him of Carrie George.

The bartender finally brought Mike a beer in a frosted glass, but before he could pick it up, a large hand attached to a tattooed arm pushed the beer back to the barkeep and a gruff voice said, "Lawmen ain't allowed in this bar." The heavyset man wore a black leather vest over a T-shirt that read "Liquor in the Front and Poker in the Back" and a multitude of tattoos crawled up both his over-sized arms. Carney Bill was an ex-con, six-foot-two and counting, with a mean disposition and a beard that went down to his chest.

"We don't want any trouble here." The bartender started to return the beer to Mike, but he reconsidered and held it as ransom.

"House rules!" Carney Bill wasn't talking to the bartender anymore. He was standing three feet away from Mike, giving him the prison eyeball. "I put in six years at La Ronge because of this sonavabitch!"

"Are you a police officer?" The bartender asked with a degree of indifference usually reserved for under-age punk drinkers.

"Retired," Mike said, hoping to put it to rest. The bartender looked relieved Mike didn't shove a search warrant in his face.

"You must have packed it in early... unless you fucked up and was told to leave." The bartender was siding with Carney Bill, who was waiting for a sign to let loose.

"Considering that someone in your position must have a real understanding of what 'fucked up' truly means, I hate to disappoint you." Mike hadn't raised his voice, but there was enough malice in the delivery to make his point. "I retired, asshole, and that's as much as a loser like you needs to know."

The bartender made little effort to hide a contemptuous smile as he emptied Mike's beer on the bar and said, "When the bulls show up here with a search warrant, I have no choice but to let 'em in." The yellow liquid oozed dangerously close to Mike's elbow. "But, like Carney Bill said, house rules: no cops or ex cops."

Mike stood up slowly, took out a fiver, and laid it on the bar. "That's for the beer." The bartender stood silent, staring at the blue face of the Queen floating in the beer puddle. Mike didn't wait for a reply. He started toward the door, anticipating the hefty biker was about to sucker punch him. Mike turned quickly and brought his elbow flush against Carney Bill's throat, staggering him. Carney Bill fell backwards against the wall, gasping for air. Mike followed with a right, this time with his body behind the punch, which landed on the left side of the biker's nose. Inside the big man's brain, the light switch turned off, and Carney Bill crumpled to the floor, blood dripping down his face.

The bartender looked around for help and started shouting. In two quick steps, Mike returned to the bar and grabbed the mouthy bartender by his shirt collar, landed a few right hooks to the side of his head, then shoved the bartender's face into the spilled beer on the bar, turned and moved quickly towards the exit. The crowd was alerted now, and a low rumble of disgruntled voices went through the room as the bouncers rushed towards the action and the patrons strained their necks to see what was happening at the bar. Mike was only three steps from freedom when the doorman tried to stop him. He reacted instinctually from his days the RCMP, taking out his wallet to flash his badge, which unfortunately at this particular time didn't exist. The doorman froze for a few seconds thinking Mike was a cop, just enough time for Mike to ram the heel of his left cowboy boot into the doorman's rib cage, sending him reeling through the door.

Mike Morningstar could hear the disappointed grunting of the mob behind him as he left. He was in the Grand Am before the horde of bikers that emerged from Pandora's Box could cause him trouble. He drove back to the hotel with his eyes in the rear view mirror to see if they were stupid enough to follow him. Mike filed a mental note to self: do not return to Pandora's Box. He wasn't sure anymore that he was on the right trail. From Pontiac's description, most of the women he'd seen with Carrie wouldn't be found in a peeler bar or a massage parlor. They were on a higher level, women meant to entertain Triad members. Mike wanted to speak with Josh and let him know the strategy wasn't working. He needed to find out where Kwan kept his chosen women.

Later that afternoon, Mike got a call back from one of the escort agencies he'd contacted earlier in the morning. The woman on the phone said her name was Carrie... Carrie Ann. Her voice had a nice rhythm, one that gave away her age. Mike estimated she was somewhere between nineteen and twenty. She asked if he liked Winnipeg, and he wanted to tell her how "friendly" the people were at Pandora's Box, but he let it slide. He'd seen her picture on the agency website, and she definitely held a fleeting resemblance to Carrie George. He asked her, "Are you from Winnipeg?"

"No, I just moved here last year," she said in a silky tone. "I'm from Regina."

"Really? I've been there. Nice town." After only a couple of questions, it was clear she was not the Carrie he was looking for, and he needed a plausible excuse to end the conversation.

"When did you want to get together?" she asked.

"I was hoping around five, but I'm stuck with a meeting, could I call you around seven?" he asked, lying through his teeth.

"Excellent. I will be finished by then… at the gym."

"Seven it is." Another dead end appointment he wouldn't keep. He didn't really lie because he was actually meeting Richard Beaulieu at a restaurant at six o'clock. Mike had worked with the Winnipeg detective years ago, and they had remained friends. When Mike had called from Calgary and e-mailed the picture of Carrie and Sebastian, he hadn't expected anything much, but after last night he wanted to know everything about Sebastian and what his connection was with Carrie. Mike parked the Grand Am across the street from the restaurant and took another call, this time from Jimmy Secola. The RCMP had a breakthrough on Susan Wabigon's death; a convict up for parole told the warden at the Kent Penitentiary he had information about what happened to Susan, and he was willing to trade what he knew for a lesser sentence. Jimmy was just waiting for the brass to give him the okay so he could set up a meeting with the convict.

The Ratatouille was a few blocks from the police station, and the menu was French Canadian inspired. All the delicacies were available, from *pate chinois* to their infamous poutine (a jumbo serving of fries with cheese and gravy, available in a variety of flavours). The place was practically empty when Mike arrived, but within minutes a heavy-set man in his late fifties stood by his table.

"Richard!" Mike got up to shake his hand. "Been a long time." Ten years ago, Mike had helped Richard Beaulieu catch James Hart, a bank robber the cops had been chasing for a year.

"Nice to see you again, Mike." Richard was dressed in a brown suit that was slightly wrinkled, and he wasn't wearing a tie. His large frame hadn't seen a gym for years, but it didn't seem to bother him. His grey hair was combed back on his massive head, his face had rounded with age, and there were bags under his eyes. He put a manila envelope on the table, and said to Mike, "If you had waited another year, we would be discussing this case on a golf course."

"Thinking about retirement?" Mike asked.

"That's right," Richard signaled the waitress. "Anyway Mike, you found your girl."

"My friend did. It was a stroke of luck, but it's going take more than luck to bring her home. We have to figure a way to rescue her without anyone getting hurt."

"Have you found out where she lives?"

"I know she's working in one of Kwan's massage parlors or escort services. I've spent all morning checking out leads, but no Carrie."

"I might be able to help. Most escort services need a license from the city to stay in business. I could make a few phone calls and circulate the picture."

"That would save me a lot of time." Mike stared at the menu in his hand. His earlier altercation had made him lose his appetite. "I don't know what hold this Sebastian has on Carrie or how difficult it will be to rescue her. That is, if she wants to be rescued."

"I know most of the Asian women who work for Kwan are on a short leash. If Carrie was at Kwan's party, then she is one of his favorites. I'm referring to the women who keep the Triad bosses happy." Richard was speaking from experience. The Triads survived in secrecy; even the call girls who serviced the upper echelon had to be women they trusted.

"I believe she is under Sebastian's control, but I don't know enough about him to make the connection."

"Well, the picture you sent me from Calgary has produced some interesting results." Beaulieu picked up the envelope, took out a mug shot, and placed it on the table.

"The man has a file?"

"He does, but it's rather sketchy. We received most of the information from the Montreal Police. His name is Sebastian Garcia, a.k.a. The Blade. He was charged with murder in 1994, but all charges were dropped, and he has never been arrested since. In fact, Jean Larose, who is in charge of a special unit that keeps tabs on the biker gangs, was sure Sebastian had left the country. Larose told me the unit suspected Sebastian was with a special group of assassins who worked for biker gangs."

"Garcia. Which country is he from?"

"Columbia. He came to Montreal in the eighties."

"And he's never been charged for anything since '94?"

"No. Larose was surprised he was even in Winnipeg; he thought Sebastian was in South America."

"That's it. He's a biker suspected of murder who now works for the Triads, and nobody knows what he's been doing for the last ten years." Mike felt let down. How could Sebastian be in Beaulieu's back yard and still slip through legal cracks while working with the Triads?

"There's not much I can do," Richard said. "He's under Norm Kwan's umbrella, which makes it even more difficult. We have put a watch on him since we received the file, but he has been here for a very short period of time. If you hadn't brought him to our attention, he would have flown right under the radar."

"I've a feeling that's how he works. If he's smart enough to work for the Triads, this man must have the connections they need to expand into Canada."

"Since he's not Asian, he would have to be someone they trust, and surrounding himself with the kind women who satisfy the needs of Norm Kwan's associates would mean he's really in tight with Kwan."

"I have no doubts Carrie can be rescued, but I have a feeling it's not going to happen without crossing swords with Sebastian," said Mike.

"You're probably right," Richard said, trying to decide which special would be least fattening, "but the good news is that Sebastian just boarded a plane for Vancouver."

CHAPTER 20

Sebastian forced himself to drink the cheap Canadian wine the stewardess brought. He had planned his visit to Vancouver meticulously: dinner with William to discuss his "problem," then a meeting with Candy to look over her website, and then he'd catch a late flight to Hong Kong. The only potential snag could be William, who had similar problems in Montreal and in South America. The last time Sebastian had interceded on his behalf was on Marguerita Island, and it had taken a substantial amount of cash to keep the guy out of a Venezuelan jail.

The images that crowded Sebastian's brain as he stared out the window were ugly: mutilated bodies of women in a common shallow gravesite in glossy photographs taken by the local police. The police assumed a serial killer was loose on Marguerita Island, but they had no clues until one night an off-duty officer picked up a woman who had been beaten and tortured. Carla Santos was wounded and bleeding when she was found, but later at the hospital she was able to tell them it was the tourist, Señor William Roberts, who had tortured her. When the local police raided his beach cottage, they found body parts in the refrigerator and a drunken coke-addled Roberts in the bedroom. He took a bullet in his right leg before they were able to cuff him.

At the time, Roberts was in serious trouble. The police had dragged him from the hospital a few days after his arrest and thrown him in jail where he languished in pain, just long enough for gangrene to set in. The heat was unbearable in the tiny cell. Under the cast on his leg, the gunshot wound had begun to fester almost immediately because of careless cleansing, and after the first week, he would have been dead if the police hadn't dropped the charges. Sebastian arrived and saved his life, negotiating his release at a cost of 100,000 American dollars, which converted into fifty million Venezuelan bolivars. The chief of the local detachment and his four subordinates became millionaires overnight. Sebastian only had to escort Roberts off the island himself and promise in writing that the loco would never set foot on Venezuelan territory again.

Sebastian and William were on a boat that same night, headed for Columbia. There, they spent a couple of months in Bogotá waiting for Roberts' leg to heal enough so they could move on to Medellin, where Sebastian set up cocaine deals between the Diablos and the cartels. Roberts remained in a foul mood for most of the trip, and Sebastian never missed an opportunity to remind him just why they were traveling together in this abominable heat in the first place, and Roberts' free pass out of Venezuelan prison had to be paid for somehow. It was Sebastian who had suggested then that Roberts not return to Montreal but rather to Vancouver, as far from Montreal as possible.

Despite the Marguerita mix up, William Roberts remained Sebastian's silent partner, receiving a yearly percentage of the profits from drug deals and from the Last Chance contracts. For almost a decade, everything had been smooth. Roberts remained anonymous while the police had arrested most of the Diablos kingpins. In fact, he had thrived and prospered without attracting any attention, and luckily, his name was never brought up during the biker trials. Sebastian had profited even more by the arrangement, and soon found a way of ingratiating himself to the Triads and bringing the members of Last Chance with him.

Bill Roberts stood behind the bar of his private club, about a mile from the farmhouse where it offered complete seclusion for its patrons and could remain open until the wee hours of the morning. There was nothing special about the place. It was a gutted one-storey house converted into one large room in which 150 people could sit comfortably. Built by the previous owner, Roberts simply carried on the tradition and kept counting the coin. It was a bona fide booze can, available to anyone in the loop from the Hells Angels to the local ol' timers hockey team. The mayor and a good portion of the city council had all been in the club at one time or another, and the local police department even held a private party there a month or two ago. The place wasn't usually open during the week, but Roberts had made an exception tonight for a group of Angels in from Nanaimo celebrating their anniversary. When Sebastian took a seat at the bar, Roberts' attention was glued to the television; he was watching a soccer match between France and Brazil.

"Tequila. Make it a double."

Roberts turned slowly away from the game and registered pure shock when he saw the Columbian sitting at the bar. "Sebastian!" he exclaimed, giving him a firm handshake and smiling broadly. There was a marked contrast between the two men. Roberts was a big man with wide shoulders that supported a large bald head. He looked comfortable in his jeans and denim shirt. Sebastian was tall and slim, his face long, and his hair and beard perfectly groomed. He was dressed impeccably in a long grey overcoat.

"Gracias," said Sebastian. "We should speak in private, William. But first, the tequila."

"Coming up!" Roberts filled a short glass with Cuervo and handed it to Sebastian. "We can talk in my office."

In the back room, sitting across from each other at a desk covered with invoices and ledgers, Roberts told Sebastian the whole story of what had happened to Mona and the subsequent shooting at the SkyTrain. On top of that, Frankie's death was unavoidable. He was a low-life junkie anyway; no real loss. The real target was in a rehab centre.

"This woman has to disappear," Roberts emphasized, "before she gets a chance to speak to the police."

"William... we agreed no more trouble with women, and now here we are again. She's a junkie in a rehab centre. I'd call that a sitting duck, no?"

Roberts took out a pair of Cuban cigars, handing one across the table and then lighting his own. "If I'm lucky, she's waiting for her methadone treatment to start before talking to the cops."

"Perhaps she's already told her story and they don't believe her." Sebastian made himself comfortable. "Have the police questioned you about the dead woman?"

"No, nothing. Not even a phone call."

"Excellent. Then let's eliminate the problem. Dead people don't talk to the police, and they make very bad witnesses." Sebastian smiled and took a long slow hit from his cigar. It was business as usual with William, who leaned back in is chair, his bald head reflecting the light from the bare lightbulb hanging above the desk. The lack of emotion on his face and the razor-edged stare in his steel blue eyes told Sebastian everything he needed to know for the present moment.

Pontiac sat inside the Silver Slipper. He'd been to the Red Zone and Georgina's International without finding Carrie, but there were worse ways to waste a few hours than watching a parade of beautiful women work the pole. When he heard himself humming a few bars of "Nice Work If You Can Get It" as back up to some of the more sophisticated routines the women had perfected, it gave him a new sense of respect for the peeler profession. The Slipper was the best of the clubs he had visited so far; even the waitresses were drop dead gorgeous. Most of the clientele were stockbrokers and dot-com geeks, but the dancers were the real deal: a collection of former playboy centerfolds and porn stars. The supporting cast was the usual Miss Nude Japan, Miss Nude Australia, Miss Nude Sweden, and every Miss Nude country in the world that has hosted the bogus naked beauty contest no one has ever witnessed.

"Pontiac, any luck today?" Josh showed up in a navy blue suit, black silk shirt, and red silk tie, carrying a patent leather briefcase filled with contracts. He was strictly business today, which made him fit right in with the clientele of the Silver Slipper.

"Not so far," Pontiac replied, "but this is more the kind of room we might find her in."

"I doubt it. This place is legit, man, no working girls allowed. Some of the dancers freelance, but if management finds out, the dancer is history." Josh had barely finished his sentence when a petite young woman of Asian descent wearing silver-grey shorts, brown suede boots, and a black T-shirt with a sliver slipper embroidered on the front stood at the table.

"Check out the stranger," she said, and gave Josh a little pout, trying to lay a guilt trip on him for not showing up at the Slipper for the last four months.

"Lila! My little songbird! I saw you last night at the Tokyo Rose."

"My God, you were there?" she gasped. Josh was the last person Lila wanted to meet at the Rose. She was a singer, not some Triad whore, but like any of the girls working here, she couldn't afford to turn down the invite.

"I was front row with my friend Pontiac here who was sitting in with the band."

"That was you?" Lila placed her small smooth hand on Pontiac's shoulder. "You have a great voice; so close to Marley."

"Thank you." Pontiac had met many people like Lila in his line of work, women who wanted to be singers or musicians, who weren't even half bad and were pretty enough to get respect without doing anything.

"Is it true? Your band will be playing at the Rose?" she asked.

"The dude who asked to hear some reggae mentioned he wanted my band to play, yeah." Pontiac said in a tired voice, insinuating it wasn't a major deal for him.

"I would love to see you guys, but right now I should be taking your order." Lila turned around to face Josh, who smiled up at her.

"A Mojito for Pontiac and a Heineken for me."

"Menus? Or is it liquid lunch today?"

"Right now, lunch is not an option," Josh said. He was paying through his nose and every other orifice in his body for last night's debauchery. Lila gave him a warm smile, implying that she understood, and walked back to the bar to fill the order.

"She's a sweetheart." Pontiac's stare was still fixed on her profile, which showed another side of her beautifully well-rounded presence.

"Smart to boot," Josh added. "Unfortunately, as a singer she's more Yoko than Blondie, and one Yoko is more than this world will ever need."

"You think she knows where Carrie's working?" asked Pontiac.

"Lila has eyes in the back of her head. If she doesn't know, she can point you in the right direction." Josh watched her exchange small talk with the other waitresses at the bar, then she lifted her tray of drinks and walked towards their table.

"I spoke to Mike," Pontiac said. "Nothing happened, except for a fight he got into at some peeler bar called Pandora's Box."

"That bar wasn't on the list I gave him. Mike is lucky to have gotten out of that dump alive." Josh wanted to say more, but was interrupted by Lila placing drinks on the table.

"Will there be anything else?" she asked.

"Just one thing. Pontiac and I were both marveling at the number of beautiful women on the dance floor last night. You, of course, were the fairest of them all." Josh gave her a quick wink.

"Flattery will get you everywhere."

"Where did all those women come from? I make the rounds, but I can't remember ever seeing such a collection of beauties."

"You obviously travel in the wrong circles." Lila let out a series of high pitched giggles, and then tilted her head as if to say, you can't see the forest for the trees.

"Some of the women at the Rose last night actually work here, but most of them were from the Tiki Club."

"The private club upstairs?" Josh knew the second floor of the Silver Slipper was for Norm Kwan's friends and associates and no one else.

"That's the one."

"Norm decides who climbs the stairs?"

"That's right." Lila rolled her eyes and gave Josh the look, wondering where was he going with this line of questioning, because Kwan's business was not something to be discussed by his waitresses.

"What you think my chances are of becoming a member?" Josh asked.

"Like you said," Lila answered, "it's a private club, and your guess is as good as mine."

"I can take a hint." Josh handed her his platinum Amex card and picked up his Heineken. Pontiac asked if there was a place to smoke, and Lila told him there was a special room, but she would have to come back and take him there.

As she left, Pontiac turned to Josh. "Did I not say only minutes ago that this was where Carrie might be found?" he said, drink in hand.

"You're a human bloodhound, Pontiac." Josh pointed his index finger at his friend. "What's your next move, Sherlock?"

"Convince Lila to join my band." Pontiac had decided he was staying at the Silver Slipper until closing time. Lila would tell him her life story before last call came around, and he would tell her how much he loved her voice; it was just what he needed for his band. Josh tried to picture Pontiac and Lila on the same stage. It was suspect casting; imagine Yoko and Bob Marley performing a duet. It was a scary thought, but then again, if Lila was part of the plan brewing in Pontiac's head, from here on in anything could happen.

Lila soon returned for Pontiac, and he followed her down a hallway that led to the smoker's den. Sure enough, it was a well-furnished room with comfortable tables and bar service along with several HD television sets to entertain sports enthusiasts. Pontiac was far from alone in refusing to give up his nicotine habit; the room was packed with well-dressed patrons, mostly men over thirty. The few women present were waitresses who had finished their shift and were being chatted up by would be suitors.

Pontiac sat by himself, feigning attention to a football game on the screen across the room through a cloud of blue smoke. The Blue Bombers were taking on the Saskatchewan Rough Riders, and the home team was up by a touchdown at half time. Meanwhile, he didn't notice the two women who came over and sat down at his table.

"Do you mind a little company?" Carrie asked a shocked Pontiac, who could only smile in return.

"The company of beautiful women is an offer I never refuse," he replied with tongue in cheek.

"You remember me from last night?" Carrie asked.

"Of course. Carrie, if memory serves me right."

"Yes, and this is Julie," she said, gesturing toward her companion. "We both work upstairs at the Tiki Club."

"Nice meeting you Julie." Pontiac extended his hand to the young Asian woman, resplendent in a red silk dress that complemented her fragile body.

"I overheard you talking about playing at the Tokyo Rose," Carrie said, taking from her purse a package of Player's Filtered.

"That's right. My agent is going to be in touch with Sebastian."

"Sebastian left this morning for Vancouver, then he's headed for Hong Kong."

"Must be nice," Pontiac said. "When is he coming back?"

"I don't know. It could be a week, could be a month. He never talks about business much. I have a feeling it's going to be a while."

"Are you two connected, or is it business?" Pontiac asked bluntly, trying to catch her off guard.

Carrie exhaled a smoky cloud. "Mainly business, but it's complicated."

"Life is complicated. Ain't it the truth?" He noticed that Carrie had that telltale glazed look, which he normally interpreted as a side effect of self-medication. Her friend might have done a few lines of blow, but she was nowhere near as dazed as Carrie.

"Are there any bars open this time of night that would have entertainment? A band, or even a comedian?" Julie asked this question quite innocently after looking over the crew in the smoking room.

"Julie, you are speaking to the midnight prowler," Pontiac said with an aging hipster's satirical arrogance. "And yes, my pretty, there is a blues bar, bluer than the Blue Bombers, that caters to the late night crowd."

"Can we go there?" Julie asked, sounding almost as if she were too young to drive.

"No problem," said Pontiac. "The Batmobile is waiting in the parking lot." Pontiac knocked back the last of his drink, left a twenty on the table, and stood up. "Ladies, the night is calling."

CHAPTER 21

Behind the wheel of his Lexus, Johnny the Greek couldn't believe his passenger was The Blade. He had almost shit himself when he got the driving job; he'd be Sebastian's chauffeur for the duration of his visit to Vancouver. "Whatever it is man, bring it on," Johnny had said when Roberts gave him the job. He picked Sebastian up at the Vancouver Hotel and was now cruising over the Lion's Gate Bridge, headed for the North Shore. This was the dude the biker gangs gave their ultimate respect; he had a rep that came with the name and there was no shortage of stories about how he took care of their enemies. They needed him more than he needed them, an equation that did not happen very often. He didn't like anyone calling him The Blade anymore. His real name was Sebastian.

Today was a reconnaissance trip. A woman in rehab needed to be silenced. The Greek had put in a month at the same rehab, and he told Sebastian it might be dicey getting past the front desk and into the woman's room. There were cops showing up all the time because some meth freak had just gone bananas, plus paramedics all over the place, and the security people were recruited from correctional services. It was high-risk venture, actually better to find an alternative plan if possible. As they drove by the centre, there were no police cars, but a steady stream of people floated through the doors. Suddenly, the scream of an ambulance siren announced its arrival, and when it parked in front of the admissions door, paramedics jumped out of the vehicle and ran into the building.

"Right there, man, is what I'm talking about." Johnny the Greek pointed at the ambulance. "It's always like that. Complete fucking chaos. Makes it difficult for someone to waltz right in and whack someone." He kept his eyes on the front doors waiting for more high drama to unfold. How long it would be until a police cruiser showed up was anybody's guess, but it wouldn't be long. "The only way to get at someone inside is to have one of the patients do the hit. A patient could walk freely through the corridors and enter someone else's room without arousing suspicion. When the job is done, the hitter goes back to their room and nobody knows what happened."

"Slim chance, amigo," Sebastian said, "unless you have someone check in with the express purpose of taking care of this bitch." He liked the Greek's plan, but it meant using someone who wasn't a pro.

"I got it covered dude," the Greek interjected, hoping Delores Delorme was still in town. "Just give me a few hours to put it together."

Kim had stayed up late going over her notes. She had been asked to chair the AA meeting tomorrow, and since she hadn't done much public speaking, she felt better having at least an outline of her life story, which was the topic to be discussed. Rehab was depressing as hell, even though her sponsor tried to make her feel at home. The rooms were sparse, like cells. Nothing stronger than aspirin was given out, and everybody was coming down from some kind of serious substance abuse. Kim shared a room with a young girl, Alice King, who was trying to kick her crack habit. Alice was prone to seizures and throwing fits that gave the impression she was epileptic. Her body bounced around like a rag doll while she mumbled in pain in an unintelligible language, and sometimes from deep in her broken dreams, she screamed out the names of who knows who in the middle of the night. The caretakers never responded quickly. They showed up only when a situation had gotten totally out of control, and then the routine was to manhandle the patient to the showers and make sure no violence erupted between any of the other inmates.

The AA meeting was held at noon in a room filled with addicts. They started with the serenity prayer, "God grant me the serenity to accept the things I cannot change, the courage to change the things I can, and the wisdom to know the difference." Kim's sponsor introduced her to the group, and Kim proceeded to share the story of how she became addicted. She explained that she left her foster home because she was being sexually abused and then was returned to her mother, who was still an addict herself. It was only a matter of time before Kim started experimenting with drugs with her friend Frankie, not realizing an addictive personality is usually hereditary. Within a few years, she was a full-blown junkie working the streets to support her habit.

Finding Carrie George

Kim cleaned up three years later when she found out she was pregnant. She gave birth to a little boy who was given up for adoption, a decision forced on her by social services. She remembered working at a multitude of jobs after rehab: waitress, telemarketer, bartender. The jobs she really wanted were not available because she lacked the education or work experience. She tried going back to school and applied for courses in social work and education, but she was turned down because of her police record. It seemed that every door she wanted to walk through was closed in her face. The post-rehab period was a succession of failures, but she never lost hope that she would someday see her son Clarence again under better circumstances.

When she was forbidden visiting rights to her son, something snapped. For the first time, she realized the game was rigged, and it had been from the moment her father was shot. She would never see Clarence again, and the chance of improving her own life through normal channels was zero. She tried to hold on to those few precious moments when she was still able to believe a miracle could happen. God doesn't listen to a junkie's prayers. The days turned into months, and nothing changed. Finally, she lost all hope and slid back into the world of addiction. Kim thought this would be a good time for a break, but when she checked the faces in the audience she realized everyone seemed to be waiting for her to continue her story.

"What's weird," she went on, "is how screwed up your mind becomes on drugs. There is a moment of freedom when you give up, when you don't give a fuck anymore. You could walk in front of a car and not give a shit if the driver doesn't stop. You lose your will to live. The clock stops. Nothing really matters anymore. The only message that comes in loud and clear: You don't belong on the planet."

Kim let her words echo throughout the room after she stopped talking. She expected a response from someone, but there was dead silence for what seemed an eternity. She was about to start talking again when a woman in her early forties introduced herself as Hillary and asked Kim if she had considered suicide in her darkest hour. Kim smiled softly at her, to let her know she had been in that place, but so far it wasn't an option; she had never considered suicide a solution.

"Taking your own life is tempting," said Kim, "but it seems too easy.

There is an alternative if you're a junkie." She took count of the junkies in the room, most looked down to avoid her stare. "It's a lethal solution, and it only comes from a needle. Every time the needle goes in to your arm, a piece of your soul is sucked into the syringe." She wanted to stop talking because it was bringing on flashbacks, but she continued unfettered.

"Eventually you stop worrying about everything, except where you're next fix is coming from, and you'll do anything not to get dope sick. Rip off your friends, prostitute yourself, boosting, burglary, whatever it takes to get the money to score. And every night when you finally fall asleep, you say a prayer hoping to never wake up. The next morning when you realize you're still here, it starts all over again until you finally realize you need help or you will die, and that kind of slow suicide is the most painful death imaginable."

Kim waited a moment, then picked up her water bottle as applause filled the room. She thanked everyone for listening and felt was relieved it was over; her sponsor told her how impressed people were by her honesty. Kim took the flattery with a grain of salt. Across the room, she noticed a dark haired man in an expensive suit talking to a woman who was new to the group. The man looked to be in his forties and had the aura of money. He hadn't been at the meeting, but now he was engrossed in a conversation with Delores Delorme, a reformed junkie but still a nasty piece of work who had done time for several counts of assault.

Kim left quietly, eager to not be the focus of any more attention. As she walked down the hall, she heard a voice behind her. "Kim, we need to talk." She turned to see Harold Jenkins approaching with another cop. There was a sense of urgency in the Mountie's voice that told her something had happened.

"Is there something wrong?" Kim asked.

"Your life is in danger," Harold said in a low voice. "I'm not sure if this rehab is safe anymore." The man with him was Constable Richard Chang, sent to watch over Kim until Officer Jenkins arrived.

"We can talk in my room." Kim waved at her sponsor, who still stood in the meeting room doorway staring curiously at the policemen. When they arrived on the second floor, the nurse stopped them and asked Officer Jenkins if there was a problem. Harold said he was simply taking precautions and that it was a matter of routine for him to ask Kim a few questions. Constable Chang stood at the door to Kim's room while Harold spoke to her.

"Have you spoken to your boyfriend lately?" Harold asked, not sure if there really was any relationship beyond co-dependency.

"Not since I checked in," Kim said. "I tried this morning. I wanted to know if he picked up my welfare check, but his cell phone's not working." She began to sense there was bad news coming.

Harold took his time. Kim obviously hadn't read the Vancouver Sun or the Province yet, nor had anyone told her what happened to Frankie. "Frankie did pick up your cheque, Kim." For a moment, Harold was unable to continue; he could see from the expression on her face that Kim knew what was coming next. "Unfortunately, someone was waiting for Frankie. Someone who apparently wanted to steal his check and yours."

"My cheque was stolen?" Kim bit her lip, afraid to ask what had happened to her boyfriend.

"Yes," Harold said quietly, "and Frankie was attacked by a vicious dog."

"Is he going to be alright?"

"He's dead, Kim."

"Frankie's... dead?"

"Unfortunately." Harold hesitated. "I think it was Roberts. You mentioned he had a dog." He waited for a response, but none was forthcoming. "You said the dog was vicious, and it chased you down Roberts' driveway."

Kim was caught in a crossfire of guilt and shame that left her numb with fear. She tried to reply, but the tears started flowing. Her boyfriend was dead because Roberts was looking for her. She was the intended victim, not him. She felt gut wrenching guilt; her best friend, dead because of the trouble she had got herself into. Frankie's death made the message clear. Roberts would find her sooner or later. She wasn't waiting around to die here. The rehab centre was history; it was only a matter of time before Roberts showed up. Kim's entire body trembled with fear and grief, her eyes were wet with tears, her lips quivered as she struggled to speak, "I can't stay here."

"I know." Harold had no Plan B. He knew Kim had to leave rehab, but where she was going to go? He couldn't say. Where she could stay, he had no idea. He was always amazed that for so many people who looked as if their situations couldn't get any worse there was always a bottom below the one they were currently sprawled out on, someplace deeper into the gutter. He watched as Kim packed her one and only suitcase, knowing full well she had no home and no one waiting for her.

Frankie had been her best friend since she was twelve years old, and he was the father of her only child. Now, he was dead. Kim closed the suitcase and walked towards the open window in her room. There was a warm summer breeze, and the smell of freshly cut grass filled the air. She had nothing left at this very moment. She was running on empty, and crying didn't stop the pain she felt ripping through her soul.

Harold Jenkins and Constable Chang left for a few moments, and when they returned, Harold explained the plan. Kim would leave by the back entrance where he would be waiting in his cruiser. Everyone in the rehab would think she was still in her room, and Chang would remain in the building as security to authenticate the illusion. Harold was fairly sure Roberts himself would show up tonight. He needed to set the trap and wait for the killer to make his move.

CHAPTER 22

Pontiac's Batmobile was a Honda Civic with a black exterior. Julie took the back seat, and Carrie sat in front with Pontiac, asking him so many questions about himself and his band that he was becoming confused as to exactly what his role was to be for the rest of the evening. He answered politely nevertheless, wheeling the Honda down Market Street as he told Carrie that the Peg was in fact his hometown but that he now resided on the coast. The gigs he played nowadays were usually at festivals or bars that hired bands that were famous in the '70s. For her part, Carrie was trying to be attentive, for although she was genuinely interested, she was also falling in and out of sleep. Julie fired up a joint and gave it to Carrie, warning her to lay off the roofies.

"Did you say roofies, the rape drug?" Pontiac asked.

"Rohypnol, yeah." Julie took the joint back, offered it to Pontiac who declined, then took a haul herself. "Most of the girls who work at the Tiki take them, including my friend Carrie here."

"Why would you do roofies?" Pontiac asked Carrie, as she blew a trail of smoke out of her mouth.

"Because they make me feel good," she said, laughing as she took another toke.

"Management doesn't approve of coke, but pills are no problem." Julie opened her window and threw out the dead joint.

"Leave the window down so we can get some fresh air in here," said Pontiac. The Mad Hatter came into view; its old neon sign still got the job done. Pontiac pulled into the parking lot wondering how often back in the day he showed up at this bar after a gig to trade small talk with fellow musicians until the place closed. He escorted the women to the front door.

Inside, Pontiac was warmly welcomed back to the Peg immediately. The band dedicated a song to him and asked him to join them on stage, so he politely sat in for "The Harder They Come" by Jimmy Cliff. When he returned to his table, Julie gave him a kiss and Carrie told him how much she loved his voice. Pontiac gave Mike a quick call, just to keep him in the loop, and promised to call again when he got back to the hotel. As the evening went on, Carrie remained with him at the table but Julie wandered off with a friend and never returned. When last call was announced, Pontiac and Carrie left the bar assuming that Julie would find her own way home. He drove away in good spirits, but before he had a chance to talk to Carrie alone without all that noise, his passenger was fast asleep. Pontiac had no clue where Carrie lived and didn't have Julie's cell number either, so he decided to bring her up to his room. He carried her into the Carleton Hotel, took the elevator to the third floor, and with a bit of difficulty managed to open the door to Room 348. He laid Carrie gently on the fresh made bed and then, envious of his guest, made his own feeble attempt to sleep on the couch. Sleep would not come easy tonight; there were far too many questions still floating around in his head, and so far none of them had been answered.

Jimmy Secola's phone call came a few minutes after two in the morning, just as Mike had managed to count around half of his sheep. By the time he picked up the phone on the fourth ring, after stumbling blindly around the room in pitch black darkness trying to find the it, Mike was expecting rather a bleaker message than his caller's extremely good news. Jimmy Secola had spoken with the convict Kyle Bennett on behalf of the crown and was surprised when Bennett had told him Candy Webber was responsible for Susan Wabigon's death. Jimmy told Mike how Bennett had taken Susan's overdosed body from Candy's room back to the hotel where Susan had been staying. The plan was to make it look like a suicide. Jimmy had one more meeting with Kyle Bennett to make the deal official, and if everything went as planned, he would arrest Candace Webber and charge her with murder.

Mike wasn't sure if he heard right. This was the same Candy who had pretended Susan's death was such a shocker, and she was actually responsible for her murder? Candy had played him while he was conning her; the only difference was that his play was in the line of duty. She, on the other hand was merely covering her ass, and now the long arm of justice would soon be sending her to jail without a lollipop. What Mike couldn't grasp was her motive. Why would Candy give her friend Susan a lethal injection of cocaine and heroin? It didn't make sense, unless she was dancing on a string, following orders, but who wanted Susan dead? Mike fell asleep pondering the question. His entire knowledge of Candy was a single snapshot taken at the casino. Charlie's profile of her was proving to be the right one. She was a vicious woman with dangerous friends.

Pontiac turned down the volume on the television and watched Carrie nibble on a piece of French toast before putting a cup of coffee in front of her. "How are you feeling?" he asked.

"A little better. I hadn't eaten anything yesterday."

"Good, don't be shy with the coffee."

"Thank you." Carrie gave Pontiac a drowsy smile. "I can't remember if you told me you lived in town."

"Not anymore. I moved to the coast," he said casually. "You're from Victoria, aren't you?"

"How did you know?"

"You'd be surprised how much I know about you." Pontiac was on the verge of letting her know what he was really doing in Winnipeg.

"I can't remember telling you my life story last night." Carrie smiled, but felt a touch embarrassed also, because she often forgot what happened the night before. Memory lapse was happening more and more often, but that hadn't yet convinced her to regulate her use of oxys.

"Don't worry," Pontiac reassured her. "It was nothing you said last night. I knew your life story before I ever laid eyes on you."

"I'm confused. How would you know anything about me?"

"Our meeting wasn't a coincidence, Carrie."

"What do you mean?" Carrie was not sure if she liked what she was hearing. Maybe it was her pill hangover or Pontiac's tendency to mumble his words, but nothing he said made sense.

"My friend is a private investigator. He was hired to find you."

"Was it my parents who hired you? Because if Sebastian finds out, he will kill them." Carrie looked frightened. What kind of mess had she walked into?

"That sounds like a threat." Pontiac was curious as to what kind of hold Sebastian had on her. "Is that how he keeps you and Julie in line?"

"He means it," Carrie said. "I've seen what happens to girls who break his rules. You don't know Sebastian. People are afraid of him for a reason."

"The dude is a gangster," Pontiac said. "The real ones usually carry guns." He could see the pain in her eyes, the kind that only fear can instill in a person. Pontiac wanted to ask her what happened to the rule breakers, but a knock on the door stopped him short. He was expecting the waiter had forgotten something, but it was Mike. Pontiac made the introductions and then gave a short version of the night's events. When he was finished, Mike helped himself to what was left of breakfast: two sausages, scrambled eggs, and cold dry toast.

"I have some news that might interest you, Carrie." Mike put his utensils down. "The RCMP have declared Susan Wabigon's death a murder, and they have a witness who was there that night."

"Dude, did the witness say who put the needle in her arm?" Pontiac interjected.

"He did indeed, and it will come as a great surprise to you, Pontiac."

Carrie spoke up suddenly. "Candy Webber! She was the one."

Mike looked at Carrie. "You already knew she did it?"

"Yes. Sebastian made sure I knew what happened because if I decided to leave, I was next."

"Are you saying he ordered Candy to kill Susan?" Mike asked.

"That's right. She works for him, runs his website, finds women for him, and if he asks, she will kill for him."

"But why?" Pontiac asked, still reeling from the news that Candy was a murderer. "What did Susan do?"

"Susan was not coming back to work for Sebastian, and that broke the cardinal rule." Carrie bowed her head, thinking of her friend.

"When did Susan work for him?" Mike asked.

"We both started working for him in Calgary." Carrie told Mike she had met Sebastian in Cowtown a few months before checking in to rehab.

At the time, she and Susan were going through a gram of heroin every day. They supported their habit by working out of a strip joint called The French Addiction. Sebastian hired the pair for a private party, and he paid them well. The fact they were Native made them exotic and erotic to Asian businessmen, so Carrie and Susan did several of his parties from that day onward.

Out of curiosity, Susan started asking some of the Asian women who worked at The French Addiction questions about the Triads. Carrie then turned to Pontiac and said, "You have to understand. We had no idea what the Triads were. When Susan found out they were hardcore criminals, we both freaked out."

Unfortunately, they were too wired to realize the seriousness of the connection until it was too late. When Sebastian heard the women were in rehab, he came down to tell Carrie that under no circumstance was she or Susan to mention him or his parties, not to the counselors or anyone else. "He was such a hypocrite," Carrie said with a hint of anger, "telling us he approved of us getting off heroin and a job was still open when we left the rehab centre."

Sebastian wasn't aware how Susan had changed since coming off heroin; she wasn't intimidated anymore. After rehab, Susan wanted to lecture to young people in High School about the pitfalls of addiction, and she had already started to write a biography of her life on the streets. Eventually Sebastian found out. Susan had called Candy and told her she wanted to mention her in the book.

That was the exact time Carrie decided she was ready to come home, and her father had paid for the plane fare. The day after she left rehab, Carrie was waiting for her flight when Sebastian found her at the Stampeder Inn in Calgary. He knocked on her door with two of his goons and explained why she should consider his "business offer." Some of his associates had grown to like her, and then there was the money. Carrie went along with him to avoid any violence. A few hours later, she got a call from Susan who was staying in Edmonton in a government-funded house for reformed addicts. She was gathering more stories for her book. Carrie told her about Sebastian's visit, but Susan wasn't worried. She was filled with a born again sense of optimism; she was on a mission to redeem herself by helping others.

"I was on a flight to Victoria," Carrie said slowly, "reading the Calgary Herald when I came across Susan's picture under the heading, 'Woman Found Dead of Drug Overdose.' I couldn't believe Susan had OD'd. When she called me, she was clean and sober."

Carrie took a deep breath and continued, "We had a stop-over in Vancouver, so I booked a room at the Holiday Inn. I needed to pull myself together before seeing my parents. I was in my room for maybe twenty minutes when Sebastian called me. He asked me if I had heard about Susan. I told him I knew she was dead. Sebastian said to me, 'That's what happens to women who give me a hard time.' He said I should take his business proposal seriously. Then he told me if I called my parents they'd be dead before I got to Victoria." Carrie lowered her head, and tears filled her eyes.

Pontiac put his hand on Carrie's shoulder. "It's all history. You can walk away and never look back."

Carrie looked away. "I can't believe that until Sebastian is in jail." She wanted to believe him, just like she wanted to believe Mike, but they didn't know Sebastian.

CHAPTER 23

Harold Jenkins left Kim with Earl at his house, the only safe place available on short notice, plus she needed a friend to help her get over Frankie's death. Earl was the inspiration for Kim's decision to enter rehab in the first place, and now that her life was in danger, hopefully he could provide her with some emotional support and, if need be, a shoulder to cry on. Harold called Constable Chang to see if he had made all the arrangements. It was a done deal; Chang had Kim's rehab roommate moved to another room and stuffed Kim's bed with pillows to give the illusion she was sleeping under the covers. The trap was set. Waiting for the intruder was the hard part, and young Richard Chang felt a sense of relief knowing Officer Jenkins was on the way.

Chang's anxiety was not unusual; he understood someone wanted Kim Lawrence dead, but Harold hadn't given him much background. He knew little about the suspect, his motive, or how dangerous the situation truly was. The question that had been nagging him all night was whether the suspect was a real psycho, because what kind of deranged person would commit murder in a rehab centre?

Constable Chang decided to check out Kim's room one last time before Harold arrived. The night watchman informed him that nothing unusual had gone down; he had just made his last round at ten o'clock curfew, checking all the rooms to make sure everyone was asleep. He would make another round at midnight, but so far so good. It was all quiet in the rehab centre, and since the medical staff hadn't warned him of any potential emergencies, he wasn't expecting anything to change during the night.

Room 207 was dark and silent. Chang took a look around. No one had entered; nothing had changed from his last visit. He walked over to the window that looked out over the parking lot. There were no recent arrivals. He made his way back to the entrance, where Harold and two other RCMP officers were now waiting.

"Richard, I see you have everything under control," Harold said. He had the instincts of a seasoned policeman, a gut feeling for trouble, and right now he could feel it in the pit of his stomach.

"Yes, sir! Nothing so far. How exactly are you expecting your suspect to gain entry? I mean, if he's been watching, he must know we are ready and armed." Chang was still in the grey zone about what was happening,

"The man we're dealing with is a pro," Harold said. "So far, I've underestimated him, and as a result, one man is dead."

"Man's gotta be crazy though, if he thinks he can get away with killing someone in this place."

"His name is William Roberts, and he's a long way from crazy." Harold turned it all over in his head again, the possible alternatives Roberts had to doing the job himself. He sent the two RCMP officers outside to patrol the building in hopes of spotting someone waiting in a car. The night watchman came by to inform the officers he was on his midnight run, a last minute watch to make sure no one getting into trouble.

"Richard, one more thing, your cruiser is still parked in front." Harold pointed through the main entrance door window at what would have been ample warning for anyone who was up to no good. "Could you move it down the street where it won't seem so obvious?"

"I thought that was the plan, to let him know we're here."

"I don't think he's been watching. I'm assuming his plan would be to show up around four in the morning, when things are quiet. If he spots your cruiser, he's gone! But if he thinks no one is awake except the night watchman and everyone else is on the nod, he might feel safe making his move."

"I'll park it a few blocks down the street." Chang was still not convinced the killer hadn't been watching them.

"Good, do it quickly!" These words had barely left his mouth before he regretted what he'd said and that it had come out sounding like a brash order or reprimand when this man had in fact done everything demanded of him. Harold watched the young officer walk out the door; he was a good young cop, but the shit storm hadn't hit him full force yet. No matter what you do with a badge, it doesn't slow down the number of criminals; the ranks just keep swelling. You bust your ass bringing in some dirt bag, and a judge who thinks cops have their own agenda lets him walk. You can turn away, which is what all policemen sooner or later have to accept, or you can drive yourself crazy thinking it should be different.

But when everything you do at your end is undone or overturned, you start wanting to put the judge on trial. Your fuse keeps getting shorter and shorter until some scumbag like William Roberts comes along murdering young women at random, and then the fever starts burning inside of you and you don't give a shit whether there's a search warrant or not because one way or another he's going down.

Maynard Ferguson, the night watchman, moved confidently from room to room. Everyone was fast asleep; the snoring reassured him that everything was normal. The patients seemed all right; no crackheads convulsing as they tried to sleep. Every once in a while it happened that way, and it made everyone's job easier, especially Maynard's. He stopped on the second floor and was about to enter the first room on the left of the elevator when he noticed the door to 207 was ajar. The lights were off, which should have made him suspicious, but the police hadn't given him any information that would have prepared him for any surprises.

Delores Delorme had waited until everyone was out cold before sneaking out of her bed and walking down the stairwell to make her way to room 207. She had spent a good percentage of her life in various penitentiaries and knew how to make a shank with a razor blade and a pencil. It was crude, yet deadly. When Delores saw Kim earlier speaking at the AA meeting, she realized how easy taking her out was going to be. Delores would just cut her open, the pretentious bitch, and let her bleed to death.

The door to 207 wasn't locked. Delores had let herself in and then shut the door without closing it. She'd waited until her eyes adjusted to the darkness before moving slowly towards Kim's bed, the shank in her left hand ready to strike. She was just a few inches away when she looked down at the lump in the bed, then in one swift movement, she slashed at what she thought was Kim's throat. The blade cut through the blanket with no resistance. Delores was furious. She pulled the blankets back to expose a row of pillows, and in a rage she lashed out violently, leaving behind an unmade bed and a mess of synthetic stuffing. She was about to walk out the door when she heard someone coming.

Maynard looked in from the doorway before turning on the light, and at first glance everything seemed in order until he spotted Kim's bed. The mutilated pillows registered danger, and he took a step back just as

Delores jumped out from behind the door with the shank in her hand. He stumbled backwards trying to escape the blade as she swiped viciously at him. She caught him in the left arm, tearing through the flesh from his elbow to his wrist. Maynard screamed in pain as he staggered out of the room, Delores charging toward him. He reached for his baton with his right hand and caught her flush on the nose, which stunned and blinded her temporarily. She fell back against the wall, dizzy and disoriented. Maynard headed towards the exit door, and stumbled down the stairs. He was halfway down to the landing when he looked up and saw Delores at the top of the stairs.

Harold Jenkins was waiting for Chang to come back when he heard a man scream from upstairs. He rushed to the elevator, realizing that the night watchman was in trouble. Harold pulled out his 9mm Smith & Wesson, and unlocked the safety. The elevator arrived at the precise moment an exit door opened down the hallway and Maynard tumbled out, wide-eyed and bleeding, then collapsed on the floor. Before Harold could get to him, Delores came barreling out of the stairwell in a rage, blood dripping from the shank in her hand. She didn't see Officer Jenkins, but she couldn't miss Maynard lying motionless in a pool of blood. She was about to jump the helpless watchman and finish the job she'd started, but Harold had different ideas. There was no time for the conventional warning before he pulled the trigger. Delores was about to slice Maynard's throat. The bullet hit her right shoulder and the impact stunned her. She and the shank fell to the floor in tandem, and as she made a futile attempt to right herself, she gave Jenkins a hate-filled glare.

"Do not make a move!" Harold was standing close now, his arm outstretched with his gun aimed at Delores' head.

"I need a doctor!" she demanded through clenched teeth, as Constable Chang rushed in the front door, gun in hand, followed closely by two RCMP officers.

"Richard, get a nurse down here, pronto! And call 911!" Harold's stare was fixed on Delores. "You have a name?"

"Delores, my name's Delores Delorme," she said, clutching her shoulder in an attempt to stop the bleeding.

"You're under arrest, Delores Delorme, for attempted murder. And if Maynard here doesn't make it to the hospital, we will change the charge to murder. A police officer will accompany you to the hospital to have your wounds looked after. I would advise you not to try anything stupid, although from what I can see here tonight, I'm not sure that's possible."

An ambulance siren wailed in the distance. A nurse bandaged Maynard's arm, while Harold visited Kim's room to confirm what he already knew: Delores had been hired to kill Kim Lawrence. Had Roberts approached her directly or was there a middleman? He would know in a few days. For a reduced sentence, a small time criminal like Delores would drop a dime on whoever paid her, and chances were pretty good that eventually someone would admit to receiving the order from William Roberts.

CHAPTER 24

Johnny the Greek got a call from his lawyer Myron Friedman at eight o'clock in the morning. Delores Delorme was under twenty-four-hour police guard in the hospital with a bullet in her arm, after being arrested for attempted murder. The job had gone bad, and the wrong person got hurt. Delores had sliced up a few foam rubber pillows before trying to hack off a security guard's left arm with a homemade shank. She was charged with attempted murder and, considering the incident happened without provocation, Delores could be spending another ten years in jail. Myron felt it was his duty to let Johnny know since he was paying the bill. Johnny thanked him and asked how Delores was holding up.

"She's tough," Myron said. "Delores is still traumatized by the bullet wound, but she knows she's getting paid, so she going to say she had a meltdown. With her history, it's no big deal that she vented her anger by slashing a few pillows. When the guard walks in, she sees red. Considering she was actually raped by guards in jail, a compassionate judge might just go easy on her."

Johnny made it abundantly clear to Myron that under no circumstances was his name to be mentioned. Delores should be quietly informed the money is going into her bank account, and that she will be taken care of when the trial is over.

"Keep in touch with her," Johnny said. "Make her think everything is cool. And don't let her talk to the cops."

Myron reassured him, "I'll visit her again tomorrow and let her know she's got nothing to worry about."

Maybe Delores had no worries, but Johnny knew he'd have a major problem on his hands the moment Sebastian got wind of what happened. The man didn't tolerate mistakes, and a simple job like the one gone bad could have violent repercussions for someone. Johnny needed some beans; a double cappuccino would help him think straight. He drove his Lexus down Broadway, took a right on Commercial Avenue, and stopped at Starbucks.

For twenty-five years, Johnny the Greek had been the fixer. He never wore the colours, but he had worked for biker gangs in every city from Toronto to Vancouver. The Greek could reliably make someone disappear without a trace. He kept people in line with his fists, and his reputation alone served as a form of blunt intimidation, an immediate deterrent to potential altercations. Still, Johnny was not in the same league as The Blade, and it had been a surprise and a privilege when Johnny had been asked to help take care of the woman in rehab. His failure was not acceptable. Johnny had to figure a way to undo the damage and make up for last night's botched attempt. The rehab must have a record of Kim's transfer and destination, and the pointed toe of a snakeskin cowboy boot in some low-level paper pusher's balls could access the necessary information. He would take care of the problem himself, then Sebastian would appreciate his commitment and forget what happened last night.

Johnny was about to call the rehab centre when his cell phone rang. It was Sebastian, and he wanted to give Johnny the money for Delores. "You heard about last night?" Johnny asked.

Sebastian answered in the affirmative. The money for Delores was to keep her mouth shut in the short run. Sebastian didn't have to expand on the issue; he knew what had gone down, and there was no need to discuss it over the phone. Johnny ordered another double capp before he left Starbucks, then walked through the parking lot toward his car. Just before he opened his driver's side door, a sleek black Mercedes with Sebastian sitting in the back seat slipped in beside him. Johnny opened the right front door of the Mercedes and got in. He recognized the driver as Lefty Burrows, a former employee. Always the extrovert, Johnny politely asked Lefty about his family as the Mercedes left the lot.

Lefty drove down Clarke, then turned left on Bower and entered an industrial park with gravel roads and tall steel fences topped with razor wire around every big ugly red brick warehouse. There were World War II vintage steel Quonset garages and small manufacturing workshops spread out for three or four blocks in each direction. Sebastian took out a sealed envelope and handed it between the seats to Johnny in the front.

"Here's the money for Delores," Sebastian said.

"My lawyer will take care of it," Johnny said, taking the envelope. "I can find out what rehab the hooker has been moved to. I'm waiting for the call right now.

"You let me know the moment you find out," Sebastian said curtly. His right hand slipped into his coat pocket and caressed the cold handle of a German hunting knife.

"I'll take care of it personally," Johnny promised, trying hard to make his point. "Nothing will fuck up this time. This bitch is a junkie, and she's not fully recovered. This time, we don't whack her at a rehab. Instead, we have someone give her a point of heroin. I guarantee she will take it, and a day later when she starts coming down, she will run back to the streets where it will be no problem finding her. End of story; end of problem."

Sebastian didn't reply immediately, but showed a hint of a smile. "I like your plan." He tightened the grip on his knife. "How much time do you need?"

"She's probably scared shitless that someone's trying to kill her, so now is the time to get her the junk. Let me work out the details, but it should all go down in the next few days." The Greek, now in full form, could tell he had The Blade's attention. The plan was solid, and it would make up for last night's little fiasco.

"If you are successful," Sebastian said, "you will get double what Delores was paid, but if you fail again . . ."

"Don't worry, man. This is Johnny-on-the-spot you're talkin' to here. I'll handle it myself this time, and nothing will go wrong, you'll see." The Greek knew this much: Sebastian had no respect for whiners, only winners.

"You have my blessing." Sebastian leaned forward, smiling.

The Greek opened his mouth to say "thank you" just as Sebastian's knife slipped silently across throat. It was over in a second. The Greek's head slumped forward, blood seeping down from his neck staining his shirt. Sebastian whispered to him, "You had your chance, amigo," as he wiped the blade of his knife clean.

Lefty wheeled the Mercedes into the driveway of an abandoned garage where he hauled Johnny the Greek out of the front seat and dumped his body behind the building. Then Lefty hustled back to the car and drove towards New Westminster while Sebastian made a call to Roberts, who was at home waiting for his cleaning woman to finish and leave. Sebastian didn't mention Kim was still alive; he'd save that fact and tell Roberts in person. His next phone call was to Winnipeg. Sebastian spoke to Norm Kwan, letting him know he would be in Hong Kong tomorrow night. The Mercedes seemed to float down the highway, having relinquished some dead weight along the way, and Sebastian made one last call. Somebody didn't come home last night. He wanted to make sure that his best women hadn't made the stupid mistake of running away.

Carrie returned to her apartment with Mike, in case one of Sebastian's goons showed up. She simply wanted to pick up her clothes and leave without any complications. She opened the door and walked in slowly. Mike followed her cautiously but wasn't expecting any real trouble. Carrie found a note from Julie on the kitchen table; she was shopping and would call Carrie later.

"Julie won't call me," Carrie said. "She's not working tonight, so I won't be missed until tomorrow."

"Good," Mike said. "Now get your luggage together. We should be at the airport in the next thirty minutes."

"Don't worry. It won't take me long," Carrie said as she walked into the bedroom.

Mike took stock of the girls' apartment. There was a soft leather couch, Chinese furniture, and a high-def television connected to the stereo. It was all perfect, even the view from the twentieth floor, everything to make a young, impressionable Asian woman from a poor family feel she was living in the lap of luxury. Mike walked into the washroom and checked the cabinet. It was stuffed with pill bottles, a nice assortment of Rohypnol, Percocet, Oxycontin, and a few bottles of Percodan. He expected nothing less. Sebastian's operation worked on intimidation and a pill diet that made the women loyal and addicted. Fear kept the women in line while amphetamines enslaved them to their master. Sebastian was not careless. He ran a tight organization, and the women who accepted his conditions lived well; those who did not were left in an unmarked grave.

Carrie returned from her bedroom with one suitcase, having left much of her wardrobe behind. It was maybe eleven-thirty now. Carrie made one last check to be sure she hadn't forgotten anything precious. When the telephone rang, she wanted to ignore it, but when she saw the number of the caller she thought it wiser to answer.

"Hello, Sebastian? Are you in Vancouver? Everything's fine. Julie's not here. She's gone shopping. Vancouver on the 23rd. Yeah, I'll book the flight. Holiday Inn downtown." Carrie put the receiver down gently. She was glad she took the call, but now she was having serious doubts about leaving. Sebastian was going to Hong Kong and wouldn't be back for a week, enough time for her to disappear from Winnipeg. What terrified her was that the moment Sebastian found out she was gone, he would come after her.

Carrie turned to Mike. "I'm staying here. If I leave he will find me."

"No, he won't." Mike walked up to Carrie and tried to reassure her. "He will be charged with Susan's murder the moment he gets off the plane. This is your one chance to walk out that door with me riding shotgun. Sebastian is never going to come near you again."

"How can you be so sure?" She walked away from Mike who followed her to the washroom and watched as she nervously took the bottle of oxys and dumped two in her shaking hand. She was about to wash them down when Mike took her hand and held it.

"The pills aren't going to change anything, except make you more dependent on them." He stared her down for a few seconds and finally she dropped the pills into the sink.

"Alright, let's go to the airport," Carrie said, leaving the washroom and the pill collection behind.

"That's the plan." Mike watched as she slowly picked up her suitcase. Carrie didn't seem convinced she was making the right decision, but she realized it was too late to change her mind.

"What about Pontiac?" Carrie asked. "He's not flying with us?"

"No, he's leaving tomorrow."

"I feel safer when he's around."

"In that case, you can relax because until the police make a few arrests Pontiac and yours truly are going to be spending some quality time with you, Carrie," Mike said as they walked out the door. He felt a sense of relief as they drove off in the rented Grand Am headed towards the airport.

"Should I get rid of my cell phone?" Carrie asked.

"No, not yet. Just don't answer it. I'm sure Sebastian will leave a message, and that will help the police monitor his movements. You think he was in touch with Candy?" Mike was still curious about Sebastian's business in Hong Kong and his connection with Candy Webber.

"I wouldn't know. The only time he speaks to me is when he wants me to take care of what he calls a *special* person."

"And what is a special person?"

"Usually some Chinese mobster, like that night at the Tokyo Rose. It was Norm Kwan's birthday. The guests were businessmen who work with Kwan; they are the men Sebastian calls special persons."

"And it's your job to keep them happy?"

"That's right, and if the man is dissatisfied, Sebastian will threaten the woman who failed him." Carrie looked away, trying to forget the pain of her own rare failures. "If there is another complaint, the woman is never seen again."

Carrie had noticed several women had disappeared in the short time she had worked for Sebastian. Most of the Asian women were here illegally, a vulnerable situation which Sebastian held over their head, always threatening to expose them if they stepped out of line. The real kiss of death was having to bring in heroin for the Triads. The dope mules were seldom caught by customs, but most of the women disappeared anyway only a short time after they had successfully brought in the contraband. Sebastian didn't trust anyone, and if he had any doubts of a woman spilling her guts to the police, she was dealt with immediately.

The women were expendable. Everyone understood how fragile their own existence was, and survival depended on never crossing the fine line that would put them in danger. Carrie admitted she had planned to escape several times after Susan's murder, but it was too risky. She had seen the casualties, and her only chance was to never give up hope. Through intimidation and pills, Sebastian kept the women loyal, and escape was never discussed by anyone.

CHAPTER 25

Bill Roberts poured himself a cup of java while he listened to Olga, the cleaning woman who came to the house once a week, rant on about the outrageous cost of renting the same apartment she had for twelve years; she could barely make ends meet living alone with the high cost of rent. Roberts finished his coffee without any comment on Olga's subtle attempt at asking for a raise. She had bonds she could cash she said, but Olga enjoyed playing the poor lonely woman from the old country whose husband had died shortly after they arrived, leaving her in a frightful mess. Her grown children had chosen to stay in the new Ukraine to build a nation again. Roberts put up with the old girl when she came to clean the house as she had done for years for the previous owners. At least she could make good coffee.

"Will there be anything else, Mr. Roberts?"

"Not today. Thank you, Olga."

"Alright then. I'll just finish the dishes and see you next week." Olga turned back to her work, humming one of her German melodies as she cleaned.

The sound of Manson barking his head off at Sebastian's Mercedes coming down the driveway prompted Bill to go outside and meet his visitor. Lefty parked the car in front of the garage, and Sebastian emerged from the passenger's seat wearing a long leather coat, the kind the SS loved to wear and every Death Squad in South America had modeled itself after. Roberts took his coffee with him and met Sebastian in the driveway. The two men walked into the garage and closed the door.

"You know what happened last night?" Roberts asked, in a tone as dry as camel shit.

"The woman you wanted dead had been moved from rehab before we got to her."

"What else?"

"Isn't that enough?" Sebastian said sharply. "It was a trap set by the police. They were waiting for the woman I sent."

Roberts grimaced. He had watched all the morning news shows hoping to confirm the hooker was dead, but there was nothing. Now he knew why.

"Was she arrested?"

"Yes, she is in the hospital. She took a bullet, a shoulder wound."

"Who does she know?" Roberts queried. He was sure the police had been speaking to Kim, and now they were probably working on setting a trap for him.

"She knows only the Greek, nobody else. I took care of him before coming here."

"What about the woman?"

"Don't worry. I will take care of Delores."

"Something should happen to her while she's in jail."

"It can be arranged, but she's not a concern right now."

"What the fuck are you saying?" Roberts didn't like being brushed off. "She tried to kill that Native hooker and she fucked up and that's not a problem?"

"Delores is a little loco. She's under arrest because she tried to kill a security guard. How can the police connect you with her?" Sebastian waved his hand in the air. "The police, they got nada! They would have been at your front door a long time ago if there was reason to arrest you. What happened last night had nothing to do with you, as far as they are concerned."

Roberts put down his coffee cup on a workbench littered with tools and bike parts. "I didn't think the hooker had spoken to the police until now, but if the police were expecting someone last night, it means they've already connected Frankie's murder with me. They are waiting for a reason to arrest me."

"No, William! You may be a suspect, that's all. The police have many suspects. If she has spoken to the police, they didn't believe her. You forget this woman is a junkie who sells her body on the street. Why would the police believe such a woman?"

"I don't know, Sebastian, but she has been a real fucking problem." Roberts took a deep breath trying to contain his anger. "The first time I ever came to this city was to eliminate her father. He was moving a lot of coke, living well. Most of the guys in the local chapter respected him, but when they found out he turned informant to avoid jail time, they were pissed off. They called me in to take care of the problem. We found him in his house. He didn't try to run or ask for mercy. He died like a man, even though he was a traitor."

"William, my friend," Sebastian said, "perhaps it is time for a holiday."

"No!" Roberts answered with his teeth clenched. "If this woman disappears, so does my problem, and the police will soon forget she ever existed."

"Please, consider another alternative. She is a junkie; eventually she will be back on the street. She will return to being a junkie, and you know how junkies tend to overdose." Sebastian spoke in the calm voice of reason; a knowing smile creased his face.

"What would I do in the meantime?" Roberts' agitation had settled a little.

"I leave for Hong Kong tomorrow morning. You, William, should come with me. The police will stop thinking of you when you're not around."

"I would need a few days… to make sure nothing's left behind in case the police show up while I'm not here." Roberts said, keeping the real reasons to himself.

Sebastian grimaced in frustration, realizing that William had been careless once again. "William, please tell me the bodies of the women are in the bottom of a lake somewhere miles away from your property!"

"I've buried most of them in the field out there. I never expected anyone to come looking for them." To Sebastian's trained ear, Roberts sounded defensive for the first time in a while.

"What about your trophies?" Sebastian was alluding to Roberts' sick habit of keeping body parts from his victims.

"You know me, all my secrets." Roberts scowled. He hated being questioned by anyone. What he did behind closed doors was nobody's business.

"William, where are they?"

Roberts walked towards the door of the garage and signaled Sebastian to follow him. They went into the house and walked through the kitchen down into the basement. The dead air down there now mixed with the musty stink of old clothes and decrepit furniture. Sebastian felt a wave of nausea. Roberts opened the freezer without a word of warning, and the blue face of Mona stared back at Sebastian. Sebastian's nausea turned into disgust. He looked away for a second and then cupped his nose with his hand.

"Can we finish this conversation upstairs?" Sebastian was unable to spend a single second more in this lunatic's dungeon, the skulls of dead women, body parts like slabs of meat in a butcher's freezer.

"Of course," Roberts replied, slowly closing the freezer door. He led Sebastian through the maze of debris to the stairs and climbed them, lost in thought, to the kitchen where Sebastian made a beeline for some fresh air at the open back door. After a few moments, they both sat down at the table.

"I would suggest you move the freezer." Sebastian said, still feeling a contemptuous sense of anger for what he just seen in the basement.

"Tomorrow."

"I am leaving tomorrow, William! I will expect you to be in Hong Kong in a few days, and you should remain there for at least a month."

"What exactly is your plan?"

"I must return here on business next week. I could make sure this woman is just another junkie overdose. Since you'll be two thousand miles away, you would have the perfect alibi, and the police without their witness would have zero."

"You're probably right." Roberts forced a smile. Sebastian was seldom wrong and never careless, and this was probably the safest means of dealing with the problem.

Sebastian looked Roberts dead in the eyes. "I will see you in Hong Kong in three days."

Theresa always liked the drive to Tsawassen. It was a great excuse to leave the city, and she enjoyed the rural landscape that began the moment Vancouver showed up in the rear view mirror. She looked forward to the underground tunnel that seemed to go for miles before the sun appeared again. It was the halfway point to her destination, and the next exit took her off the main highway through the small towns before she arrived at the ferry terminal. There were farms on each side of the road with cows grazing by old barns and horses trotting through fields, as if they were from a different era.

She tried to replay a conversation she'd had with Mary George. It had been filled with mixed feelings. Mary was almost delirious when she found out her daughter was alive and on a plane to Vancouver, but she couldn't understand why Carrie couldn't come home right away. It was complicated, Theresa had told her, but Mike would give a proper explanation when they arrived. Theresa quite frankly couldn't understand it herself.

Mary would be fine when Mike explained why Carrie had to remain in police protection. Mary should just celebrate the fact that Carrie was alive and she would soon be able to hold her daughter in her arms again. Theresa watched the passengers leaving the ferry, and there were Mary and her husband carrying suitcases with them. Mike had requested they leave the family car parked in the laneway of their house in Victoria to give the impression the family was at home. Theresa pulled the car up to the passenger's exit, stopping only a few yards from the George family. When Theresa got out of the car to greet them, they exchanged hugs and Mary kissed Theresa's cheek, though her husband looked a bit skeptical. He simply followed behind in silent sufferance.

"Are we going to the airport?" Mary asked, sitting in the front seat with Theresa.

"The plan has changed," Theresa said as she pulled out of the parking lot. "We are now going to the Park Hotel."

"We can't meet my daughter when she gets off the plane?"

"No. Mike said it would be safer for you and Phil not to be seen at the airport."

"I don't understand what's happening." Phil leaned forward. "The police are watching our house, now we can't meet our daughter at the airport. I'd like to know if Carrie is in some kinda trouble."

"I don't know the whole story Phil, but from what I can understand, Carrie was involved with the Triads, and once they discover she has left, they might come looking for her."

"Triads? Never heard of them." Phil said innocently.

"They are the Chinese mafia, very organized and very dangerous. That's all I know about them."

"My daughter is with the mob?" Mary looked at her husband in dismay. "None of this makes any sense. What was she doing with the mob?"

"I know how confusing this must be, but I don't have any real answers. Mike will explain everything. I think we should all be happy that he found Carrie alive and well." Theresa herself wanted nothing more than to change the subject.

"I'm sorry, Theresa." Tears welled up in Mary's eyes. "Your husband has saved our little girl. He's a good man, Mike Morningstar. He's in my prayers. No words can express the gratitude I feel to him right now."

"His only concern is everyone's safety, Mary, and I know Mike. If he's worried, then there is a reason the police are keeping a watch on your house."

CHAPTER 26

The flight left Winnipeg with Mike and Carrie safely on board. She had taken a Valium before boarding and fell asleep on the plane. Mike sat in silence, going over in his mind the plan that was already in motion. The Winnipeg police had e-mailed their file on Sebastian to the RCMP and suggested they monitor his moves while he was in Vancouver. Carrie would have to be kept in a safe house until Sebastian was arrested. The RCMP had already established that someone had given Susan Wabigon a speedball then returned Susan's body to her hotel to make it look as if she had simply overdosed on her own. Mike found out through his friend Jimmy Secola that one of the people who had moved Susan's body was in jail on a trafficking conviction, and he was willing to trade information about Susan's murder for less time. His testimony could seal the fate of Candy Webber, but the RCMP still had not identified the significant connection between Candy and Sebastian, only that her sweetness Miss Candy had set Susan up. It seemed likely that the speedball was given to Susan on Sebastian's order.

Carrie was a key witness in this case, but her testimony could set up a perfect Catch-22, rendering the case a dismal failure. If Candy Webber was arrested first, Sebastian would be long gone with plenty of time to disappear into the extremely thin air of South America or somewhere in Asia. Everything must be timed to absolute perfection. Candy would have to be left alone until Sebastian was behind bars. She wasn't going anywhere anyway. Once she found out her boss was in jail and she would very likely be the next to be charged, chances are she would spill the beans. Sebastian would spend the rest of his life in jail, which would allow Carrie to live in peace without fear of Sebastian seeking revenge. All the pieces to the puzzle would have to fall into place at precisely the correct time; otherwise, the consequences could be deadly serious.

Mike turned towards Carrie. She had just opened her eyes, and her face was the picture of serenity. The family reunion she thought would never happen was only an hour away; she was anxious and ecstatic all in the same breath. She remained silent and motionless, but gave Mike just the tiniest hint of a smile at the corners of her lips as the stewardess stopped nearby with a cart full of juices and sandwiches. Carrie settled for a bottle of Perrier, and Mike took a roast beef sandwich and a can of apple juice. It wasn't much, and he actually had to pay for it. The airline wasn't giving away anything for free these days, a sign of the times; everything now had its price.

"Are we landing soon?" Carrie asked, not sure how long she'd been sleeping.

"Very soon. As a precautionary measure, I've made arrangements with the RCMP for the two of us to enter the terminal through a different entrance."

"You think Sebastian knows I'm on this flight?"

"There's no way. Julie won't know you've gone until later on tonight, and she's the only one who could rat you out. Like I said, it's strictly precautionary. Better safe than sorry."

"What about Pontiac?" Carrie asked. "Julie will tell Sebastian I was with Pontiac the last time she saw me. Shouldn't we be concerned about his safety?"

"Pontiac's taking a later flight tonight, so by the time he gets to Vancouver everything'll be fine."

"That's good. What about my parents?"

"My wife," Mike said with a touch of pride, "is waiting at the airport with them. The Victoria Police have an undercover team watching their home. If Sebastian's friends show up there, they will be arrested immediately." Carrie breathed a sigh of relief that spread from her shoulders down through all flesh and bone ending at her feet pressed tightly to the airplane floor.

"Thank you," Carrie said. "I'm sorry for losing it back at the apartment. It's hard for me not to be frightened and worry about my parents, until Sebastian has been arrested."

"You know what he's capable of doing," Mike agreed. "Your concern is normal, but when he does find out you're missing and tries to find you, the police will arrest him the moment he shows himself."

"What about Candy?"

"She can't be questioned until Sebastian is behind bars. If he gets wind there's a warrant out for his arrest, he will simply disappear." Mike didn't mention that Carrie's testimony would make Sebastian's arrest possible.

"It frightens me to know I will be in the same city as her. Candy's a dangerous woman, and she's in love with Sebastian; she will never testify against him." Carrie was not totally convinced that Sebastian would be arrested. He was clever, and if Candy had to confess in order for Sebastian to be charged, it was not going to happen.

"We have a witness who will testify against Candy." The look on Carrie's face told Mike her fear of Sebastian was not going to disappear.

The pilot interrupted their conversation, announcing that the aircraft was beginning its descent; they would land in twenty minutes. Mike looked out the window. He could see the glow of the city far below. It looked like a field of Christmas tree lights, and in the distance, buildings and highways were tiny toys that took him back momentarily to his childhood. But Carrie was beginning to show signs of anxiety. Surely she wanted to see her parents, but she felt an awful guilt that the reunion came with the threat of death.

"Where will my parents stay while they are in Vancouver?"

"The police have a hotel in mind. I'm hoping you can stay with your parents for at least a few days," Mike said as the plane touched ground and slowly came to a halt.

"I'm sure my mother would appreciate all of us being together."

"It shouldn't be a problem."

The passengers were standing in line down the aisle now, waiting for the exit doors to open. "We have to wait," Mike said under his breath. "We're leaving through the freight door as soon as everyone else is off the plane." Carrie simply nodded. Her mind was filled with paranoid thoughts and also real fear for her parents' safety, in case Sebastian had somehow discovered she was onboard. He could have already kidnapped them at the airport. She didn't dare tell Mike, afraid he would think she didn't trust him. She did trust him, but she knew Sebastian better than the police did. Mike didn't know the depth of his cruelty. He was all charm and grace when you met him, but if you opposed him, the charm was immediately replaced by the sniff of the kill. Only one thing mattered to The Blade, and that was getting in close enough to slice blue steel against the throat of anyone who crossed him.

Finding Carrie George

The stewardess waved at Mike. The middle door was open and ready. He took the suitcases from the luggage compartment above his seat and left the plane with Carrie following him. They were met by two RCMP officers: Mike's friend Jimmy Secola and Paul Richards, who escorted the travelers to a security office inside the airport. Jimmy explained the change in plans. A police cruiser was waiting for Mike and Carrie on the lower level where only RCMP cars were allowed. They would be taken to the Park Hotel on Broadway where Carrie's parents were already waiting. Jimmy would follow them to the hotel, and when everyone was settled in, he would discuss the particulars with Mike. The good news was that Sebastian was on a flight for Hong Kong and was not scheduled to return for two weeks. Carrie turned to Mike and gave him a hug. She had underestimated him, but now with Sebastian two thousand miles away and her parents so close, she wanted to show Mike some real gratitude.

The Park Hotel stood on the corner of Broadway and Vine, a busy street filled with restaurants and businesses. Across the street was the Holiday Inn, Future Shop, and a few blocks south was Toys"R"Us, and nearly every bank had a branch set between restaurants and furniture shops along the street. The Park Hotel had many Native guests, which meant the George family would fit right in without attracting attention. An RCMP surveillance team had a room right across from the family, to make sure the George family had no unwanted visitors day or night.

Mary George stood by the window looking down on the street, hoping to see her daughter step out of a police car at any minute. Theresa was watching television with Phil, a documentary on the history channel about a bona fide Native hero, Elijah Harper. She tried to relax while both parents were fighting the pent-up tension of meeting the daughter they had feared was dead. Theresa ordered a light lunch for everyone from room service. Phil seemed content. Unlike his wife, he seemed to show no real concern. Carrie was alive and kicking; that was the only proof he needed to relax his muscular frame. He had come prepared to protect his daughter from any scumbag who came anywhere near her, whatever baggage came with her survival could be dealt with on the spot. In fact, for Phil, having the police watch his house disturbed him.

There was a knock on the hotel room door. Theresa assumed it was room service and promptly left her comfort zone to answer it. Mary turned back to the window, and Phil was focused on the documentary. Neither was prepared when the door opened and there stood Carrie with Mike at her side. Phil was first to react. He rushed toward the door and took his daughter in his arms. Neither of them spoke until Carrie whispered two syllables dense with meaning: father. Mary turned from the window as her daughter moved toward her and gave her a strong and healthy hug. Their embrace lasted a long time, then Mary stood back as if to take stock, but the tears in her eyes announced the pain she had been living with. Hope that Carrie would be returned to her had now materialized; she wasn't sure if it was still a dream. She stared at her daughter in the same manner she had when Carrie was just a two-year-old and every movement her daughter made was a joy to behold. Theresa was now captivated by precisely those moments as she welcomed her own husband safely home, a sort of hero in her heart and mind. Mike smiled, not wanting to interrupt the George family reunion. He motioned to Theresa, and they both quietly left the room.

CHAPTER 27

Captain Carl Hawkins ran a tight ship. He wanted results, and now having recently taken over the Missing Women's Task Force, he knew he had his work cut out for him. Every officer connected with the case had become more and more fixed upon a final result: putting this scumbag away for a long, long time. But it would only happen if everyone did their jobs and functioned at the highest level of professionalism. The Task Force itself was now in full motion. Captain Hawkins' own office was a clearing house for every bit of information relevant to the case, almost compulsively organized for optimum efficiency, not a single file out of place. He was in the process of compiling a current list of suspects to circulate to all detachments in the lower mainland when Harold Jenkins came through the door silently. Harold stood watching as Captain Hawkins perused his paper work, made no comment, showed not a hint of emotion, just a stone-faced stare at the man behind the desk. This morning he had one simple question for the complex man who was his captain, and the question had only two possible answers but numerous variables lined up to complicate the outcome. Would the captain apply right now for the search warrant Harold so badly needed to check out Roberts' house for hard evidence?

Carl Hawkins was still skeptical; however, of all the officers on the force Jenkins had the most plausible lead by far. In William Roberts, all of the foggy intersections and mean streets of the East Side lit up like a movie set. Things began to make sense, if only in the twisted logic of perversion and addiction. Unfortunately, none of it could be tied together to present Roberts as a real suspect. Hawkins understood why the team at New West had not sicked the dogs on Roberts and why they sent Kim Lawrence to Jenkins. A junkie hooker would likely have a thousand and one skewed reasons for accusing an unhappy john of assault or murder. Mona Yellowbird was finally reported missing, but her family hadn't been in contact with her for years. How would they know she hadn't simply moved to another city? Kim Lawrence hadn't actually witnessed Mona's murder; she had heard some screams while she was running away scared shitless. And according to Kim's own statement, both women had been drinking and smoking crack half the night.

"Sergeant Jenkins, you interviewed the young lady several days ago?" Hawkins asked as he put the file to one side.

"Yes, Captain. I also spoke to Jeff Walker, the innocent bystander who was shot at the SkyTrain. He identified Kim as the last woman to get on the train."

"No witness saw the shooter?"

"No. Nobody has come forward, sir." Harold was already focused on his profile of Roberts and was anxious to get to it. "But if I was to show a picture of Roberts to the Transit Police, one of them might recognize him."

"Go ahead then. I can't believe it. Are people sleepwalking? Someone pulls a gun out in broad daylight and starts shooting in a public place and no one sees him?"

"It happened just as the passengers were getting on the train," Harold said, feeling a little guilty for having spent no time at the train station trying to get into the head of the shooter. "I suspect Roberts is or has been a professional killer. He uses a silencer. A pro could have taken those shots and disappeared into the crowd before anyone knew what happened."

"William Roberts has no previous criminal record," Hawkins reminded Harold, "no complaints from his neighbors, and he has been living there for ten years without a whisper of trouble. If your theory is correct, he must be retired. His accuser and your only witness, on the other hand, is a self-confessed heroin addict and prostitute."

"That's right," Harold said smugly, a bit stung but also pissed off that Hawkins could not comprehend the overall picture of what his Task Force was up against. In this case, witnesses would almost inevitably be prostitutes and junkies because that was the population of the poorest postal code in Canada from which the women were disappearing.

"Roberts is not simply a psychopath," Harold insisted, "he is a trained professional killer, and surely in this situation we cannot expect our witnesses to be socialites. He picks on prostitutes working the East End. Kim Lawrence fits the profile. She'd been picked up by Roberts once before, and she was there at his home with Mona. Mona fits the profile, too. And Kim saw extreme violence perpetrated. If she's not telling the truth, then why have there been two attempts on her life, and why was her boyfriend murdered?"

"You can't prove the shooting at the SkyTrain was an attempt on her life, but the woman at rehab was definitely hired to kill Miss Lawrence. I have no doubts. I'm sure Kim's boyfriend was killed by the same person who gave Delores the order. I believe you're on to something here, Jenkins, but none of it connects, at least not yet. And, since William Roberts has never broken the law, at least to our knowledge, I know a judge will never okay a search warrant."

"One corpse, one missing woman presumed dead, and one wounded security guard. That's not enough to get us a warrant?"

"I understand your frustration. You have a strong case here, but no judge is going to sign a search warrant until you can prove Roberts was directly involved in either the murder of the boyfriend or the shooting at the SkyTrain. The key word here is witness. You need a witness."

"We have a witness."

"Kim Lawrence was at the house, but she saw nothing, and we don't have the body of the supposed deceased. Find me a witness at the SkyTrain or get a confession out of that Delorme woman, and I'll have a warrant in your hand the same day. I can't do anything more than that, and in the meantime, don't cut any corners."

"Yes, well, in that meantime I somehow have to keep Miss Kim Lawrence alive while William Roberts designs a way to shut her mouth for good!" Harold had to put a lid on the anger and frustration that was eating him up morning to night, the kind of anger that drew him dangerously close to fighting fire with fire. It would be easy enough to create a witness with some hard earned savings he had packed away. Kim must know someone who would play along, but this idea was a career killer, and it wouldn't do Kim any good in the long run either.

"I will make sure every precaution is taken to ensure the safety of your witness," Hawkins promised. "What you should do in the interim, sergeant, is pay a visit to Roberts' home. Let him know you were told Mona was last seen in his truck. He will deny it, of course, but it might prevent any more immediate attempts on Miss Lawrence's life. It will make it clear that we're watching him. You know the old saying... give a killer enough rope and sooner or later he'll hang himself."

Bill Roberts was in his garage tinkering with an old Harley when Manson began to growl and bark. Bill snapped his fingers and shouted at the dog to shut up and lay down. A police cruiser was coming down the driveway, but Roberts kept working until Harold Jenkins was standing right in front of him. Jenkins was a big man who could easily tip the scale at two hundred and forty pounds, approximately the same size as Roberts. Harold gave a glance around the property and noticed a padlock on the door to the barn, the first place he would be looking if he had a warrant.

Roberts put his tools down and wiped his hands. "What can I do for you?"

"We're looking for a woman who's gone missing. Does the name Mona Yellowbird mean anything to you, Mister Roberts?"

"Never heard of her," Roberts replied bluntly.

"We have a witness who says she came here with Mona not too long ago."

"She's lying."

"Really?" Jenkins met Roberts word for word. It had turned into an interrogation by virtue of each man's ability to translate thoughts and feelings into curt utterance. "Does the name Kim Lawrence mean anything to you?"

"No, I don't know anyone by that name."

"She's a working girl, said she was here with Mona."

"I hope you didn't believe her." Roberts shook his head in outrage.

"As you probably read in the newspapers, several women have gone missing from Vancouver's East Side. As you can imagine, we're following every lead that comes our way. Mona hasn't been heard from for more than a week, and according to Miss Lawrence, Mona never left your property the night she supposedly came here."

"She was never here, officer, neither was your Miss Lawrence, and I'm not going to say it again." Roberts was no longer in any mood to play police games. He was becoming very impatient with Jenkins.

"Really, you've never seen these women?"

"Never. What did you expect coming out here? Do you have a search warrant?"

"No. I came to ask you a few questions so we can find out the truth." Harold answered the question with as much conviction as he could muster.

"Really? Well officer, I could tell you to hit the road, but instead I'll invite you to look around, if you'd like. Olga is cleaning up the house right now. You can start in there or check out the barn, whatever you wish."

"I appreciate your help, Mr. Roberts." Harold was surprised by his cooperation, but decided to take Roberts up on the invitation. "Okay then, let's start with the barn. I would like you to accompany me though, since your dog doesn't look very friendly."

Harold stepped aside to let Roberts lead the way. The barn had been converted into warehouse space for his vintage motorcycles and spare parts. There were Harleys and Nortons scattered about in various stages of repair and disrepair. The stench of oil and gas permeated the place, but there was nothing out of the ordinary. No sign of Mona, either, not that Harold had thought there would be. Roberts was intelligent, after all, and this little tour of his bike museum was just killing time.

As far as Roberts was concerned, there was no point in increasing the obvious animosity between himself and Jenkins or the police in general, but neither was there any point in getting his nose very far up Jenkins' ass. It didn't hurt to observe the man in action though, get to know his mode of operation. There might come a time in the near future when he would have to stay a step ahead of Jenkins, or come up behind him.

Back at the house, Olga seemed pleased to give the police officer a grand tour. She rattled off a complete and unnecessary history of the house as they went from room to room; it had been home to a family of six once, and Olga had worked for the former tenants until the old couple moved into a seniors' home. Harold checked out the bedrooms, remembering what Kim had said about finding bloodied clothing, but he found no women's clothing upstairs, no clues that might suggest a crime had been committed. When he came downstairs, Roberts was waiting in the kitchen nursing a cup of coffee, a stack of papers laid out neatly in front of him.

"Care to join me for coffee, officer? I have something I would like to show you." Roberts picked up one of the papers from the stack.

"Thanks for the offer, but I have to be back at the station by noon."

"Officer," Roberts said, "you were given access to my property. I expect the same courtesy in return, because what I have to tell you may help to explain your complaint." Roberts waved the sheet of paper in front of him and looked at Olga, waiting for her to pour Jenkins that cup of coffee. A serious tension had begun to build in the kitchen; the walls seemed about to vibrate.

"What is it exactly that you want to show me?" Harold sat down across from his hostile host and Olga placed a steaming cup of black coffee in front of him.

"I bought this place about twelve years ago. I also run the private club down the road. You might have heard of it, The Last Chance. I rent the club out to everyone, from the people in the mayor's office to bike clubs or 'gangs' if you prefer that description. Some of your own people including the Chief of Police have been there, although not in a professional capacity." Roberts pointed to the pictures on the wall, and sure enough, there was the chief with two other officers standing in front of the bar with Roberts.

"I have heard of your club," said Harold.

"Well, I'd be the first to admit that we often keep the place open until four in the morning. It's a private club and I'm not breaking any laws, but I do have rules. And that means certain people I judge to be undesirable, such as junkie hookers, are not let past the front door. I don't care who they're with, Sergeant Jenkins. She could be with the toughest biker sonavabitch in town or some Hollywood big shot. If I think a woman is trouble, she's not walking into my club." Roberts finished his coffee and handed Jenkins the sheet of paper.

"What do we have here?" Harold realized he was looking at a court order.

"One of several complaints I have received over the years, all of which have been thrown out of court." Roberts shoved the stack across the table to Harold.

Where there's smoke there's fire, Harold wanted to say, but he kept the thought to himself. "What you're saying is the complaints are coming from women who were thrown out of your club."

"Fucking right. Most of the women were left stranded in the parking lot because their asshole 'boyfriends' were allowed to stay, and none of them were so much in love that they were gonna ruin their party by drivin' some hooker back to town. These women we're talking about were wired to the tits, and they get pissed at me when they should be taking it out on their boyfriends." Roberts fired up a cigarette, having gotten himself a bit agitated. He nodded at Olga for a refill, and she put down what she was doing to answer his request. One thing seemed clear, Olga and Roberts had an easy relationship. He treated her with respect and paid her well for her services, the necessary foundation for a good cover. She, in return, never asked questions nor did she venture into the basement.

"So you're saying we're dealing with a similar charge here, some junked up woman venting her anger by accusing you of murder."

"You're staring at the proof. I've been down this road before. Talk to your chief; he can fill you in on the history."

"I will include this in my report, as of right now, and I agree with you, sir. This may well have been a crank call meant to get you into trouble." Harold forced a smile and stood up to leave.

"No hookers have been inside my house, last night or any other night." Roberts spoke with conviction, and then walked Officer Jenkins out of the house back to his cruiser. Harold opened the door, but didn't get in the cruiser right away. Instead he looked over at Manson, sitting by his master's side.

"Your dog, is he a Doberman or a Rottwieler?"

"A hundred percent Doberman, according to his papers anyway." Roberts looked over at Manson proudly.

"He looks to be about five years old, that right?" Harold was making small talk so he could check the stats the forensics team had come up with. The dog that killed Frankie Morin was a Doberman weighing approximately seventy kilos and four, perhaps five years old.

"Next month, he'll be five," Roberts answered, suspicious of the dog questions. There had to be five hundred Dobermans in the area the same age, and if Jenkins was trying to link Manson to Frankie's death, he was pissing in the wind.

"Dog looks healthy, anyway, puts down a few squares a day, I guess.

Probably prefers fresh raw, too. That must put you back a few dollars." Harold smiled, got into his car, and drove away thinking that Roberts had been expecting him long ago.

Roberts watched the cop leave, his face void of expression. Harold had found nothing of any real substance to add to his file and had merely wasted everyone's time plus his own. That Roberts had already disposed of Mona's body was no big surprise. Harold looked in the rearview mirror and thought to himself that he would indeed be returning, only next time it would be with a search warrant and a forensics team. The bodies of missing women were buried somewhere on this property, of that he was certain, and the smug Bill Roberts would eventually be held accountable for his crimes.

CHAPTER 28

Back in his office, Mike felt like taking his shoes off. His best dog Benny had his belly to the floor under the desk, staying close to his master, and there was warmth down there even if the private eye's feet were cold. Today, the traffic outside had the ring of familiarity by the time it filtered into the office. Jimmy Secola, here on official duty, sat across from Mike trying to put together inside his head all the pieces of Susan Wabigon's murder before speaking to the convict turned informer. Jimmy was a few years younger than Mike, hair cut short, wearing a dark suit that made him look more like an accountant than an RCMP officer.

Jimmy gave Mike a quick rundown. "The driver who moved Susan Wabigon's body is Kyle Bennett. He's in Kent Penitentiary serving a ten-year sentence for dealing crystal meth. He's also had three prior convictions, and he's willing to give his account of what happened to Susan."

"Which means he's giving up Candy Webber," Mike said with finality.

"The crown is willing to cut a deal with him, knock a few years off his sentence and put in a good word to the parole board."

"Have you told Bennett the good news?"

"No, not yet. I needed Carrie George's statement." Jimmy opened his briefcase and took out a file with "Carrie George" written on the front. "When we sit down today to cut the deal, we tell him Candice Webber is our prime suspect. He should feel a little less inhibited about giving us all the facts."

"What time is the sit down?"

"Four o'clock at the jail."

"Are you sure you want me to be there?" Mike didn't want Jimmy putting himself at risk to help a friend.

"You know more about what happened that night than anyone else on the case. You'll know if Bennett is bullshitting me." Jimmy stood up and put the file on the desk.

"I appreciate what you're doing Jimmy. I'm with you. We'll see what the man has to say. I have a feeling he's decided ratting on Candy is no big deal at this stage of the game."

"I want you to read Carrie's statement, just to make sure we're both on the same page."

Mike looked over the file quickly. "I can read it on the way over there. I'm fairly sure every thing she told me is in here, but just in case. One more thing, you better keep tabs on Candy. If she gets wind of what's happening, she'll be on a flight to Hong Kong before you can arrest her."

"Sebastian Garcia is there right now, yes?" Jimmy had read Garcia's file sent from the Winnipeg police and had been monitoring his movements while he was in Vancouver.

"He is," Mike said, "and he's not expected back for two weeks. Carrie told me if one of his women ever fails to meet his standards, she's dead meat. This Sebastian is a piece of work, and by the time this is all over we should know a lot more about him and his connection to the Triads." Mike was in fact still very curious about Sebastian's past, how he was able to get so close to Norm Kwan. Membership in the Triads was strictly Asian, which meant Sebastian had to fill some pretty big shoes to gain their trust. Of course, there was the off chance that he had some Asian blood in him. There had been a significant Asian presence on the West Coast of South America for decades, generations even. What else could explain a Japanese President of Peru?

"I have a strong feeling," Jimmy said in a worried voice, "that Sebastian is a bigger fish than we realize and the pond is not that small either. Proving that he had anything to do with Susan's death is going to be difficult."

Mike had shared these same sentiments from the moment Carrie told him that Sebastian's methods of keeping women in line were mean to say the very least. Sebastian wasted no time in dealing out punishment, and the act of judicial vengeance was always swift and precise. Kwan quite likely respected this sort of sub-contracting. The less he had to worry about details, the better. Truth be told, he was probably dangerously dependent upon Sebastian, and this could very well alter the balance of power down the road. But for now, everyone on both sides of the line was focused on Carrie George.

"If Candy is charged with murder one," Mike said, "she'll roll over in a cyber-second."

"I've never met her, but biker women have a history of refusing to testify."

"Candy's nobody's fool. She could never handle jail time; she's been too spoiled. Given a choice between witness protection and hard time, she will spill her guts like a wino on Saturday night."

"I hope you're right." Jimmy's gut feeling was not in complete agreement with his old friend's familiar optimism, even though Mike was making perfect sense, as usual.

"At the end of the day, we are not simply dealing with one murder. If what Carrie told me is true, this perp helped several women disappear into the dirt, and you can throw in pimping underage Native girls and smuggling and dealing heroin." Mike was certain that Sebastian's arrest would not only save Carrie from his revenge but it would also expose Sebastian's role with the Triads. He had several theories, but all were from a subjective premise. Before Mike could elaborate, Benny rose from his sleep and stood before the door.

"I assume someone is approaching the office." Jimmy gave Benny a little pat on his furry head.

"I'm not expecting anyone. In fact, you are one of the few people even aware that I had returned." Mike had barely finished his sentence when Charlie Feathers walked through the door with anxiety written all over his face.

"Mike, am I glad you're here! Candy Webber has been to the office three times looking for Pontiac." Charlie gave Jimmy the nod, insinuating he had to talk to Mike in private.

"What's her problem Charlie?" Mike knew Charlie could turn any isolated event into a piece of high drama.

"She knows you're not a scriptwriter. In fact, she might know who you really are, but it's Pontiac I'm worried about. He's not answering his cell phone." Charlie was more agitated than usual, and Mike could sense real fear in his voice. He knew that it was probably justified. Candy's entourage was a dangerous group when they were pissed at someone.

"Pontiac is on a plane coming home, which is why he's not answering his phone. He should be arriving at the airport in about an hour."

"We better pick him up because Candy's friends could be waiting for him at his apartment."

"She's obviously got you rattled, Charlie. So what exactly did she say that's got you so worried?" Mike still thought there was a good chance this was little more than a storm in a teacup.

"First time Candy showed up she was cool, she just wanted to reach Pontiac since he wasn't responding to her e-mails. The next time, which was a few days ago, Candy tells me there's no website for you and she thinks you were bullshitting her all along, then this morning she came to the office again looking for Pontiac."

"How do you think she found out?"

"I don't know."

"Does she know where Pontiac lives?"

"I'm sure she does, and there's probably a couple of biker goons waiting for him to come home."

"Charlie, relax! She's pissed off because she thought she was going to be in my bogus documentary. I'll pick up Pontiac at the airport and make sure she doesn't find him." Mike was more concerned that Candy would see the connection once she found out Carrie had left Winnipeg.

"I don't want to be in the office when she comes back."

"Don't worry, Charlie. Candy's got problems of her own. She could be in jail any day now. So you can stop worrying because she's not in any position to be threatening anyone."

In blue jail scrubs at six-foot-two and just over two hundred pounds, Kyle Bennett was a mean sonovabitch from head to toe. His hair, what little was left of it, was pulled back on his head with a dirty pink cloth-covered elastic band that belonged on a five-year-old girl. His face had aged prematurely because of his deep affection for crystal meth, and his beady eyes shifted rapidly from Jimmy to Mike. He kept breathing in gasps, like a fish pulled out of water. A prison guard stood nervously behind him cradling a twelve-gauge shotgun. Jimmy and Mike sat across from Bennett, and Jimmy put three different files on the table between them. The tension in the air was palpable. Bennett was sizing up his two inquisitors in the vain hope of figuring out what his chances were of coming out of this mess with a good deal.

Jimmy looked hard at Bennett and started the conversation. "You know why we're here Bennett, so let's cut to the chase. You have information pertaining to the death of Susan Wabigon. Is that correct?"

"Ya, that's right. I was there. I can tell you what went down, but I ain't doin' it for nothin'. You know what I mean, right? What's in it for me? What's gonna be the deal?" Bennett gave Jimmy a stare that worked so well in the yard as a warning that violence was next.

"It will depend on the information you are willing to share with us today." Jimmy never looked up from his files, denying Bennett anything beyond what his imagination could manage to work out. Maybe they were interested, or maybe they weren't.

"You got nothin' right now!" Bennett gave Jimmy a contemptuous grunt that indicated he wasn't happy negotiating with some office boy. He then looked at Mike, who had not missed any of Bennett's act.

"That's hardly true, Kyle," Jimmy responded coolly. "We have only recently made public the fact that Susan Wabigon's death was neither an accident nor a suicide. She was administered a lethal dose of heroin and cocaine, which caused her death." Jimmy paused for a few moments, and looked up from his files. "We have new evidence that places the responsibility of Susan's death squarely on the shoulders of Candice a.k.a Candy Webber."

"You got it right, partner. That fat-assed Candy was callin' the shots that night." Bennett smirked. Candy was nothing more than a skank who pimped out the women she called her friends.

"I'm assuming you knew Candy Webber before you showed up in Edmonton the night Susan was murdered?"

"HMS Christ!" Bennett was insulted by the stupidity of the question. "Anyone who showed up at the Angel's Acres parties knew Candy. If she wasn't introducing some sweet piece of ass to one of the members, she was on her knees in front of some biker from Oakland." Bennett chortled loudly. "Shit man, Candy's a legend with the Frisco chapter."

"Her services were mainly of a sexual nature, is that what you're saying?" Jimmy asked, hoping for a straight answer.

"She's a ho, plain and simple. Anyhow, I'm in Red Deer with a few friends, I get a call from Candy. She wants me to drive to Edmonton on

Saturday night, and she's giving me five large for a small favor."

"What happened when you went to Edmonton?"

"I didn't get to Edmonton until ten o'clock. We stopped at the Commercial Hotel on the South Side for a beer. I call Candy, she tells me to show up at eleven sharp. I tell her it's a done deal. Thirty minutes later we're there, room 1189 at the Edmonton House."

"Why was she so specific about the time you arrived?"

"I didn't get it either, but sure enough, she hands me the five large and tells me what the favor is. She tells me some dumb broad has just hit up in the room, and now she's turning blue. I say call an ambulance and let them take care of it. Candy says no, it's not her problem. She wants me to take this woman to the Klondike Hotel. She gives me a key for room 603 and a syringe and tells me to leave the woman on the bed and put the syringe in her hand."

"Would you recognize the woman you took to the Klondike if you saw her picture?"

"Of course, man. I carried her down the back stairs to make sure no one saw us. I figured she died on the way back to her hotel because when I put her on her bed I could tell she was gone."

Jimmy took a photograph of Susan Wabigon from the file and handed it to Kyle. Within a few seconds an expression of recognition worked its way onto his face, but it didn't bring a smile with it. Kyle Bennett had forgotten just how young the girl was. Her face was bloated and turning blue that night, and the one time he was able to take a good look at her was when he left her on the bed.

"Ya, that's her," Bennett said, "but she looked a lot different the night I saw her." He put the picture back down on the table. Jimmy turned to Mike who nodded to indicate Bennett was telling the truth.

"Was she fully dressed when you picked her up?" Jimmy was curious if Susan had been forced to perform sexually before she was given the speedball.

"She was."

"No signs of sexual activity?"

"Hell no, unless Candy was a closet lesbo, which I would have a hard time believing. There were no men in the room, only Candy and one other woman."

"The woman with Candy, can you describe her?"

"Thirty-something ex-stripper. She had some kind of fancy name, but I can't remember." Bennett didn't try very hard to remember her, just another stripper turned biker ho with some stupid name she had stolen from a movie.

"Was her name Chantal?" Mike asked. She was one of Candy's friends he had met at the casino.

"That's it, partner."

"One more thing," Jimmy said as he closed his briefcase, a hint the meeting was nearly over. "Have you been in touch with Candice Webber since the night she paid you?"

"Hell no! I was arrested six months later, and I've been in big house ever since."

"Well Kyle, if you are willing to repeat what you have just told me in court, we have a deal. Two years off your present sentence and the crown will put in a good word to the parole board."

"Sounds good partner." Bennett smiled. He had already served two years and had a meeting with the parole board coming in a few months. This deal bought him a few more years of freedom, and maybe the parole board would cut him a break.

After the meeting, Jimmy drove Mike back to the office in his cruiser. Every once in a while, there was witness like Bennett who came out of the blue and solved a murder for him. It was a rare occurrence, but when it happened it was hard not to feast on the moment and hope it would happen again in the not too distant future.

"You were good back there, Jimmy." Mike spoke in a voice filled with respect. When he was on the force, he'd never had to deal with a convict whose testimony could make a case and was impressed with the way Jimmy handled the prisoner.

"Coming from you, I should take that as a compliment." Jimmy couldn't help but laugh, then he looked at Mike with an expression of guilt. "The only problem I can see down the road is that the front office might want me to arrest Candace Webber immediately. I will include Carrie's testimony in my report, but you better hope Sebastian decides to come back sooner rather than later."

Mike was about to reply when his cell phone rang. Richard Beaulieu was on the line. Sebastian had returned to Winnipeg, but the police hadn't been able to pin him down. Mike reluctantly put his cell phone in his pocket. He would have to spend the night at the Park Hotel because Carrie's life now truly was in danger.

"Bad news," Mike said to Jimmy. "Sebastian is back from Hong Kong."

"He's in town?"

"He was in Winnipeg. The police know he has arrived, but they have no clue where he is at this present moment." Mike called Pontiac to make sure he was with the George family but didn't get a response. Mike sighed deeply. "It's only a few days," he said, "and I'm sure Candy's not going anywhere."

"I know Mike, but remember, this is murder one we're talking about, and a witness like Bennett could change his mind if his biker friends find out he's going to testify."

"Candy is a small fish. Sebastian is a guilty bastard, and he's with the Triads. He's a murderer, a smuggler, and pimp on a large fucking scale."

"Mike, you don't have to convince me, but I know when I hand in my report, there might be a warrant for her arrest the next day and I will have no choice." Jimmy knew how the office worked, and certain rules couldn't be bent no matter how good the reasons.

CHAPTER 29

Harold Jenkins made his way through St. Paul's Hospital. Visitors and new arrivals mixed in with the lucky ones sporting an expression of medicated joy who had put in their time and were now certified healthy. Harold took the elevator to the sixth floor; outside room 638 were two policemen standing guard. Harold showed his badge and walked in the room. Delores Delorme was sitting on her bed holding a newspaper with her left hand, a cast on the upper part of her right arm. She's what they called a big-boned woman, her hair cut short, no make up, and an ordinary face with grey eyes sunk in her head, probably the result of habitual drug use. When she noticed Harold, she put the newspaper down and gave him a look of pure hatred.

"What you want?" she asked, venom dripping from every word.

"Just a friendly chat, Delores. Since you're not going anywhere, I thought you might tell me why you wanted to kill Kim Lawrence."

"Talk to my lawyer. I got nothing to say."

"When you hear the news, you might change your mind."

"My lawyer told me not to talk to cops unless he's sitting beside me." Delores was not interested playing games.

"You don't have a lawyer! Your friend The Greek was found with a bullet in his head. He won't be paying any more of your legal bills." Harold picked up the newspaper on the bed and turned to page 28 in the crime section, and there was Johnny the Greek staring back at him. He showed Delores the page, and her expression of toughness melted into fear.

"I'm gonna call Myron right now," she said, picking up the phone and dialing his number. No one answered; a recorded message came on asking her to leave her number. "It's Delores. You need to call me right away."

"He's not going to call you." Harold's voice rippled with sarcasm. "Legal aid will provide you with a lawyer. You've worked with legal aid lawyers before, Delores. Not in the same league as Myron Friedman, but since you're going to jail anyway, what's a few years more."

"What do you want?" she asked in a flat voice.

"Does the name Bill Roberts mean anything to you?"

"Never heard of him."

"The Greek never told you why he wanted Kim Lawrence dead?"

"I didn't ask, and he didn't tell me. That's the way it works."

"Did he mention who was paying the bill, who gave the order?"

Delores stared at him silently. Harold was content she admitted that Kim was the target, but that was about all Delores knew. She had no idea who wanted Kim dead.

Kim walked slowly past the tombstones, trying to imagine a funeral at which nobody but Frankie's family showed up. She began to cry again, realizing Frankie would have wanted a large funeral that brought everyone he had ever known together. Unfortunately, Frankie had few friends left. His habit had cost him lifetime relationships, and some of the bridges he had burned were still smoldering when he was murdered. It didn't matter anymore. Roberts' psycho dog had made sure Frankie never got the chance to start over again. Kim stopped before the freshly filled grave, a dark marbled tombstone in front of her with words carved in bold: Franklin Morin 1979-2006.

Frankie was resting forever. No more dope sick, no more welfare checks, no more begging his friends and family for money. It was all history. Kim hated Roberts, hated him with the same I'll-cut-your-throat hatred she had felt when her mother's boyfriend tried to rape her and she stabbed him with scissors. She felt the kind of anger that only vengeance can appease. If she had a gun, she would stand up to that sick bastard and make him pay for his crimes. Since the police couldn't come up with enough excuses to avoid arresting him, Kim would feel no guilt, only a sense of vindication.

She said a silent prayer to Frankie, thanking him for all the good times they once had shared and asking forgiveness for allowing Roberts to destroy their relationship by taking his life. She finished with a promise to her departed lover, "He will pay, Frankie, for what he did to you. On your grave, I promise, he will pay."

Earl was waiting in his green Ford SUV near the graveyard, and he noticed immediately the change in Kim's manner. She had been grieving all the way here, but now he could sense she was more angry than sorry. When she returned, she sat silently in the passenger seat as they drove back to Earl's home in Kerrisdale where she had been staying since she left rehab.

"Can we go to Burnaby?" Kim asked, staring out the window. She wanted to see her son, let him know his father would never show up for his birthday anymore.

"Where in Burnaby?"

"The daycare centre on Kingsway and 13th avenue."

"Who do you know at daycare?"

"My son Clarence." Her voice had softened slightly, but the fire was still burning inside her. She had squashed so many emotions simply to survive that the anger she felt at this moment was something new.

"I hate to be the devil's advocate," Earl said in a calm but stern voice, "but aren't you forbidden to see your son since the adoption?"

"I just want to see him. I won't disturb anyone. Please Earl, I need to see Clarence. I know it's not the right thing to do, but I don't care. I need to see him, that's all. I will never ask again."

The Unicorn Daycare Centre was a house that had been painted by hippies with a baby obsession. A unicorn was painted over the door, and on the walls, happy little babies were playing with their toys. The company name painted in canary yellow occupied the centre of the roof, and on both sides of the name were more babies floating on clouds, like in the Cistine Chapel. The only thing missing was a baby Mona Lisa.

Earl parked on 24th Street, right across from the daycare. He wanted Kim to reconsider her planned attempt to visit her son, but she wasn't listening. From the moment the SUV turned on Kingsway, Kim was counting the houses, the blocks, the traffic lights, and checking her watch until she was close to her son.

"I don't think this is a good idea, Kim. Your life is already in danger from some deranged psychopath. You're in the middle of an investigation. You don't want Roberts to know you have a son. To do this would be risking your boy's life."

"No one's going to know we came." Kim left the vehicle and crossed the street. She could hear the voices of children coming from behind the building. She gravitated slowly to the wire fence where she could watch. A group of boys were chasing each other with toy laser guns, and two little girls were pampering their dolls; other children were playing tag. Kim held her breath. There he was… the little boy with the dark brown hair zapping his friend with his space gun. Kim laughed, and for a second all the pain she had felt in the last few hours vanished.

She was caught up in the innocence of her own son, his capacity for joy. Kim wanted to climb the fence, run over, and give him a hug, but would he remember her? It had been a year and a few months since she last saw him. She raised her head and let the autumn air fill her lungs as she filled her memory with one last look at her son. She was about to walk away when she noticed an elderly woman wearing a navy blue raincoat coming toward her using an umbrella as a cane. Her hair, which had been permed recently, was silver white, and the wrinkles under her eyes along with her soft white hands suggested she was in her mid-seventies. She stood near Kim, eyes on the children, and smiled as she spoke, "Is there anything more beautiful than young children playing?"

"I don't think so," Kim said, watching painfully as her son disappeared into the building. She had hoped for some sign of recognition. It saddened her because she couldn't risk making it happen.

"I can remember my son when he was their age." The old woman didn't smile, as if the memory of her son's age of innocence brought only sadness. "When you have your first child, you will know what I mean."

"I have a son," Kim said quietly.

"I'm sorry. You look so young." The woman seemed embarrassed that she might have insulted the young lady. "Boy or girl?"

"Boy. He was playing in the yard a few minutes ago."

"Are you waiting to take him home."

Kim pursed her lips. "We don't live together. He was adopted by a family who wanted a child."

"My poor girl, I am so sorry. My son Jeremy was taken from me on his twentieth birthday. I walk by the Unicorn Daycare Centre everyday just to watch the children. It makes me happy to return to a time when my son was my reason for living."

Kim nodded. "I'm happy for my son. He has a nice home and parents who can afford to bring him up properly and give him everything he needs." She was regurgitating the exact words Social Services had used on her when they took away her baby. She didn't fool the old woman, who gave her a look of pity.

The two women exchanged sad smiles and parted ways. Kim walked slowly back to the SUV. Her exhilaration at seeing Clarence was waning; she felt nothing but loss, as if part of her body was missing and she was operating on automatic pilot. Earl didn't ask any questions. By this time, he could read her moods, and he could tell she was in deep emotional pain. He drove down Kingsway in silence turned left on 12th Avenue. He turned up the radio as Kim simply stared out the window, consumed by thoughts she didn't want to share with anyone.

Finally, she broke her silence and asked Earl to stop on Cambie and 25th Avenue. Kim had a friend who would lend her some money; since she had been cheated out her welfare cheque, she had no cash. Earl was hesitant, but he knew Kim hated borrowing money from him, and since leaving the rehab she'd had no other alternative. He reluctantly agreed, and Kim was grateful. In fact, her mood changed immediately. She sat back and sang along with the radio.

Larry Crowfoot had been one of Frankie's best friends. He stood by him in the last years, tried to intervene and failed, but remained his friend. Larry had served four years in the army, including a stint in Afghanistan, and was an avid hunter with an extensive gun collection. He welcomed Kim at the front door told her how sorry he was about Frankie. She reminded him that Frankie always considered Larry is most solid friend.

"I was surprised you weren't at the funeral, but someone told me you were in rehab." Larry was tall and wiry, and looked younger than his 34 years. He was wearing army pants and a black T-shirt with a picture of Geronimo and three of his Apache warriors across the front with the heading "Homeland Security."

"I was in rehab," Kim said, "until someone tried to kill me." She gave Larry a short version of what had happened to her since the fatal night she and Mona went to Bill Roberts' home. She described the shooting at the SkyTrain and the attempt to kill her (which was foiled only because the RCMP had anticipated the coup). She concluded by telling Larry that Roberts' dog had killed Frankie.

"Why haven't the police arrested this bastard?"

"I don't know, but I need a favor," Kim said. "I want a handgun. I need one because he will find me, and when he does, I want to be able to defend myself."

"You got it. Let me show you my collection." Larry walked her into a small room with rifles on the wall and glass case filled with revolvers. He took out a pistol and handed it to her. She held the gun. It was heavier than it looked.

"It's a Beretta," Larry said. "Excellent weapon."

"I like it. Are you going to show me how to use it?"

"It's easy. Just aim and shoot."

"What about loading it?'

"It's already loaded. All you have to do is pull the trigger."

"I've never shot a gun in my life."

"It's easy to pull the trigger when someone wants to kill you. Here, goes on your ankle." He handed her a small leather holster, and she put the gun inside, it was a perfect fit.

"Great," Kim said as she slipped it inside her boot. "Larry, I have someone waiting outside." She gave him a hug in appreciation. "Thank you."

"If you need my help," Larry said, "call me. If the police can't protect you, I will."

CHAPTER 30

I shot a man in Reno
Just to watch him die,
And when I hear that whistle blowing,
I hang my head and cry.

Pontiac was in Carrie's room with his Gibson Hummingbird acoustic guitar doing his best imitation of Johnny Cash for her father Phil, who had earlier requested Hank Williams. Pontiac finished the classic "Folsom Prison Blues" with Luther Perkins' seminal guitar lick that defined many of Johnny's first hits. Phil applauded loudly; he liked the Métis singer, though he wasn't quite sure what reggae was all about, but anyone who could play Johnny Cash was A-okay with him.

Mary and Carrie were equally appreciative though quiet, and everyone was enjoying themselves, making the best out of a bad situation, cooped up in a hotel room, unable to leave unless accompanied by a policeman. Pontiac didn't mind spending time with the George family, but being forced to be under police protection was rubbing him the wrong way. He was grateful to be safe from Sebastian and closer to home. He wanted to call Candy and set her straight, because Charlie didn't appreciate her surprise visits at the office, but Mike convinced him the timing was wrong. Candy was pissed now, but wait until she'd been arrested and charged with murder, then she would have more serious concerns than having been conned. Candy didn't know that Mike had used her to find Carrie, and Mike was trying to make sure Candy wouldn't realize what happened until she was behind bars.

"Well folks," Pontiac said putting the guitar down much to the George family's protest, "that's it for Johnny, and I have to check in with Mike."

"Is there a problem?" Carrie asked, sensing Pontiac was under some kind of stress.

"Just a little misunderstanding, no big ting." Pontiac picked up the phone and called Mike at the office to make sure it was cool to come downtown. Mike told him stay at the hotel. There was a change in plans he didn't want to discuss over the phone. He wanted to meet Pontiac downstairs in the hotel lounge in thirty minutes.

Pontiac put down the receiver and announced, "I'm meeting Mike at a restaurant across the street." He took his guitar case and placed it against the wall. "Keep an eye on my axe Phil, I won't be long."

"Sure thing." Phil waved as Pontiac walked out the door.

Mike was sitting at the bar in the Fairview Hotel where a hockey game between the Canucks and the Calgary Flames was on the big screen. A fight had broken out; both teams were watching their pugilists slug each other. The announcer gave a blow-by-blow description of the altercation, which only lasted a few minutes. Pontiac sat down on the stool next to Mike and ordered a Mojito, then asked Mike if there was a problem.

"Sebastian returned to Winnipeg last night," Mike said.

"Has he been arrested?"

"Not yet. The RCMP are waiting to see if Candy's willing to admit Sebastian gave her the order. Then they will issue the arrest."

"You're kidding me! Sebastian is walking around a free man, which means my life is worth less than the price of a taco, and the police are waiting for a confession from Candy?" Pontiac felt betrayed. He had been under the impression that the police were going to arrest Sebastian the moment he landed in Canada. His life was now truly in danger.

"I asked Richard to keep a close eye on Sebastian. The Winnipeg police know he's in town, but unfortunately that is all they know. Since arriving in Winnipeg, he has ditched police surveillance. Richard has no idea where Sebastian is, but since he hasn't booked a flight to Vancouver, you have nothing to worry about, at least for now."

"So what do you suggest? Should I remain at the hotel or book a flight to Jamaica? I could hide out with the Rastafarians."

"Forget the Rastafarians. I want you to return to your apartment tomorrow morning," Mike said calmly, as if he was requesting a small favor and this was not a matter of life and death.

"You're losing it, dude. That is the first place Sebastian will check. If he finds me, I'm a long gone daddy."

"Exactly. If he knows you're at home, he will come looking for you rather than Carrie."

"That is brilliant, dude. You set a trap, and I'm the bait." Pontiac stared into his Mojito and shook his head. "Do you have an alternative plan?"

"No. There are no alternatives. I'm hoping he books the flight to Vancouver before Candy calls him."

"All right. I will do it on the condition that a SWAT team moves into my living room." Pontiac had given up on trying to be the voice of reason. He truly wanted to leave the country.

Mike looked at him intently and said, "I'm your SWAT team, and there will be an RCMP crew in plain clothes parked in front of your apartment. Is that good enough?"

"Cool. I'm safe in the hands of Dudley Do Little."

"Thank you. It's nice to know I'm appreciated." Mike knew the plan was high risk, but it was the only way to keep Carrie out of the line of fire. "If the RCMP can arrest Sebastian at the airport, you can relax. If not, our best chance is letting him believe that you're at home and just maybe Carrie is with you."

"I understand the logic, Mike. Don't get me wrong, but what you're forgetting is I'm not a cop. I don't like guns. I hate fucking violence and can't stand anyone who goes around killing people. I want to help Carrie, but what you're asking me to do is something policemen are trained for. Straight up, I'm just a musician, dude."

"Listen Pontiac, so far you've made a major contribution by finding Carrie, but here's our chance to nail this bastard. Setting a trap is always risky business, but I will be in your apartment with you, and my posse is going to be sitting in a car by the building entrance. Sebastian doesn't know we're waiting for him. It will be like watching a rat bite the cheese." Mike was sure Sebastian would show up.

"I don't know much about the guy, but what I do understand about him scares me. I'll go back to my apartment, only because I hope he does show up. Like Carrie, I want this to be over with, and I don't want to worry every time I walk out my front door that someone is going to kill me."

"You're a stand up guy Pontiac."

"You can't change horses in the middle of the stream," Pontiac replied. He was starting to feel a mild rum buzz and finally saw the humor in his situation. He had just escaped the wrath of Candy, now he was in the sights of a Columbian drug-dealing pimp and murderer with a talent for using a knife. Could it get any worse? Better not to ask.

He remembered his grade seven religion teacher's favorite line, "Acceptance can lead to enlightenment." As a musician, Pontiac preferred a more interactive approach: "When the going gets tough, the tough get drunk." It worked for Tom Waits, and it made Keith Richards the living legend he is today. Stick to the tried and true, he thought to himself as he ordered one more from the bartender.

"Another Mojito, make it a double… and a beer for my friend."

"Good call, Pontiac. Let's toast to Candy Webber spending the night in jail and waking up to a RCMP interrogation team," Mike said, the humor gone from his voice.

"In the words of John Shaft, I can dig it."

"One more thing," Mike said. "Carrie and her parents are not to know Sebastian has returned."

"Carrie will freak when she finds out."

"She's not going to, at least not until Candy drops a dime on Sebastian." Mike was concerned that Candy would get in touch with Sebastian before she was arrested.

"I doubt she'll rat him out," said Pontiac, "but if she sees her position is hopeless and Sebastian can't rescue her, maybe. But that's a big maybe. Candy will have the best lawyer money can buy, if she goes to trial. And your best witness is a meth-dealing biker with a record a mile long. Think about it, dude."

The office of "Candy and Friends" was going about business as usual. The night shift was their peak time, and twelve women were performing in front of web-cams tonight. Betty was in charge because Candy took the night off. Betty was sitting at Candy's desk going over the files of women she had interviewed earlier, when the police knocked on the door.

"What's your name miss?" asked the arresting officer, John Miller, as he flashed his badge. Two other officers stood guard at the office entrance.

"Betty... Betty Leroy."

"Well Betty, since you appear to be in charge, tell me, what is Candace Webber's position in the company?"

"She's the general manager." Betty wasn't sure if they were here to check on the business license or if it was something more serious.

"I would like to speak to Miss Webber."

"She's not here, officer. She works the day shift."

"Would you happen to know where Miss Webber is? We've been to her home, and she wasn't there, so I assumed she was at the office working late."

"No, she left here hours ago." Betty was curious about what Candy had done to make the police so adamant in their pursuit.

"You sure Candace is not in the back room putting on a show?" Miller smiled.

"I assure you officer..."

"Miller. John Miller."

"Is something wrong, Officer Miller?"

"We came here to arrest Candace Webber," Miller said firmly, bending over the desk, his face six inches from Betty's. "You can be charged also, Betty, if you are withholding information that could help us find her."

"I've told you the truth, and if you want to come and check out the women who are working right now, go ahead." Betty spoke boldly as she stood up and gestured toward the doorway that led to the private rooms where women performed in front of the cameras. She was wearing red leather pants and a white collarless blouse, and Miller's eyes gave away his appreciation for her voluptuous body. He followed her through the different web-cam rooms where he saw women wearing school girl costumes, leather fetish gear, or dolled up in lingerie and playing with different parts of their bodies.

Miller finally agreed that maybe Betty had been telling the truth and didn't know where her boss was hiding. He gave her his card, and the tour was over. "You can give the card to Candace the minute she walks in the door and tell her to call me," he said. "Otherwise, we can add evading arrest to the murder charge."

"Candy is charged with murder?"

"That's right, Betty. We're not here for unpaid parking tickets."

"I can't believe it." Betty, a portrait of silent outrage, stood face to face with Miller, who was taking it all in stride.

"I don't want to come back, Betty, so you make sure Miss Webber does the right thing and turns herself in."

After Miller and the other two officers left, Betty returned to her desk, still in shock over the news. She called Candy and let her know the police were looking for her, but Betty didn't tell Candy about the murder charge. A few minutes later, Betty received a call from Sebastian. When the conversation was over, she opened her briefcase, took out a Colt 45 with a silencer and put it in her purse, then went to the filing cabinet. She took a spare set of car keys from a file with Candy's name on it. It was going to be a long night. Sebastian had made one other request of her: call Pontiac and soften him up for a visit.

One of the girls, Chantal, walked into the room dressed in a black bustier, fishnet stockings, and a pair of four-inch heels. She asked point blank, "Betty, was the stiff you were just with a cop?"

"Yeah. Officer Miller. He kept staring at my tits," Betty said as she flipped through her personal phone book. "He had two other cops with him. They were looking for Candy."

"Are you serious?"

"The charge is murder. How serious is that?" Betty said sarcastically, looking up at the statuesque Chantal. "I might have to leave early tonight, so you're in charge. And don't worry, the cops aren't coming back."

Chantal was momentarily immobilized by the word "murder." She collected herself quickly and said, "No problem. I can handle it. What is Candy going to do?"

"She's talking to her lawyer."

"Murder..." Chantal sat down across from Betty. "Anyone we know?"

"Miller didn't tell me. When Candy calls back, she will have all the facts. It probably has something to do with the bikers she used to hang with. I'm sure her lawyer can deal with the problem. Why don't you go back to work. Don't mention this to anyone else."

Chantal nodded and walked out of the room. Betty put her phone book down and dialed a number. "Hi, Pontiac. It's Betty, are you surprised? We need to talk."

CHAPTER 31

Candy Webber was sitting in her favorite bar, the Metro, still fuming at Pontiac for not returning her e-mails or her phone calls. She wanted to know why he set her up, why he introduced her to his friend Mike who made her believe she was going to be in his movie. She had made a few inquiries among film circles, and to her chagrin, no one had ever heard of Mike Morningstar.

She was nursing a double Courvoisier, expecting that Pontiac would turn up sooner or later. It was just another boring weeknight, nobody familiar in the bar. She was ready to leave when she received a phone call from Betty, who was working late and sounded agitated. Betty was not calling with the usual update on the night shift's performance, no. She needed a Valium the size of a hockey puck to calm her down because the police had just showed up at the office with a warrant for Candy's arrest. Candy kept her cool and took down the name of the arresting officer then called her lawyer, Howard Coleman, who was fast asleep inside his Shaughnessey mansion. He promised to call the police and find out what she was being charged with and get back to her. Candy was rattled, but there was no reason to panic. She hadn't been in court for years, and she had not broken any laws, at least not lately.

When Coleman called her back, his voice was not filled with optimism. Candy was being charged with the murder of Susan Wabigon, and the police had a witness who was at the scene of the crime. Candy slammed her drink on the table and demanded to know the name of the witness. Coleman told her it was Kyle Bennett and asked if she knew him. Candy gave her lawyer Bennett's history along with his association with biker gangs. He was an acquaintance at best and someone she would avoid under normal circumstances. Coleman advised her that if Bennett was telling the truth, she should turn herself in; he would get her released on bail within 24 hours.

Candy was silent for a moment, then she told Coleman to expect a call back in twenty minutes. She finished her cognac, asked the bartender for a refill, and pondered her fate. Face the music or run. Could she make it through a trial? It would be her word against Bennett, a burnt out meth freak with a jail record a mile long. She took out her cell phone and called Sebastian. She had forgotten when he said he was returning from Hong Kong, but she hoped somehow he might answer, and sure enough he picked up on the second ring.

"Honey, we got a problem," Candy said. "The police have put out a warrant for my arrest, and it's a heavy charge." Sebastian wanted to know if it had anything to do with the website. "No, it's a little more serious. I'm being charged with Susan Wabigon's murder… That's right, and that pig-dog Kyle Bennett is testifying against me." Sebastian told her not to worry; he would take care of Bennett. In the meantime, she should tell her lawyer to stall the police. "Hon, you're my man. You know how to take care of Candy. I'll tell Howard the good news."

Before he hung up, Sebastian had a request of his own. He wanted Pontiac's phone number and address. "I have his work number and his cell phone," Candy said as she took a little red book out her purse. "He lives on 2342 Cotton Avenue, apartment 203. I've been looking for him myself, but he's not returning my calls, the bastard. I've got a few issues with him. Maybe he's still in Winnipeg?" Sebastian told her he was in Vancouver and so was Pontiac.

"Why the fuck are we talking on the phone? I can meet you, baby. The Montemartre restaurant on Main Street. I know where it is. Twenty minutes? Come alone. I wouldn't have any other way." Candy finished her cognac, liquid heat flowing through her veins, her heart beating and her mind clicking. She called her lawyer and relayed Sebastian's message. The police's witness was about to reconsider his date in court.

Coleman told Candy to avoid driving and make sure she didn't try to book a flight somewhere or cross the border to Seattle. He would keep the police convinced that she was ready to turn herself in, but the ruse would have a short life span if the charges weren't dropped. Candy told her lawyer that Bennett would get the message immediately. The cops would be left holding their dicks. In the meantime, she was going to stay on a friend's boat and would call him tomorrow. She hummed him a few bars of "Feeling Alright" and hung up.

The Montemartre catered to the folk crowd. There was a different theme for each night, and tonight a Cuban quartet with a percussionist, stand-up bass, piano, and acoustic guitar were performing their version of Duke Ellington's "Sunny Side of the Street." The audience was a mixture of jazz fans, Cubans, and the regulars who came to the bar to enjoy good music no matter what it was called.

Sebastian sat in the back of the room enjoying a bottle of Santa Christina red and a side order of Brie. He had taken great precautions to make sure no one knew he was in Vancouver. He drove discreetly from Winnipeg to Minneapolis to elude the Winnipeg police who had been tailing him from the moment he returned from Hong Kong. He then booked a flight from Minneapolis to Seattle and decided to take a train to Vancouver. Everything had gone smoothly until now. He would have to deal with Candy before she was arrested and brought him down with her.

Sebastian's musings were interrupted by a phone call from Roberts who wanted to cancel his flight to Hong Kong that was scheduled for eleven in the morning on Thursday. "No, you must go," Sebastian said. "The moment you leave, the police will go away and so will your problem." Roberts reluctantly agreed, and Sebastian told him not to worry, just as Candy entered the restaurant.

"You should have called, honey." Candy bent over and gave Sebastian a kiss, then sat down beside him. "I am so fucking glad you are here! My lawyer had me rattled for a few minutes. Can you believe that rat bastard Bennett?"

"He made a deal to get out of jail," Sebastian said, insinuating it was nothing unusual. "I suppose he didn't know you worked for me."

"I would love to be there when he finds out." Candy gave Sebastian a sordid smile. "So my man, will I be able to go home tomorrow without some dick with a badge trying to haul my ass to jail?"

"No," Sebastian said firmly. "It will be at least two days before the charges are dropped."

"Honey, my lawyer said if I don't turn myself in tomorrow it's game over, the gloves come off. The bulls agreed to wait and let me turn myself in rather than start looking for me everywhere. Tomorrow, that agreement will go up in smoke, and there will be a cell with my name on it."

"You simply need a safe place to hide," Sebastian said with a smile.

"You got somewhere in mind?"

"My friend William owns a house in the country. It will be vacant because he is leaving for Hong Kong. The only other person there is his cleaning woman. In a few days, when the police drop the charges, you can return home."

"A house in the sticks? Honey, I'll go crazy with boredom. I got friends I can stay with who live in the city." Candy poured herself a glass of wine from Sebastian's bottle and finished it in one drink, then told the waitress to get her ass over here.

"The police will question your friends," Sebastian said with a sense of authority. "It would be safer if no one knew where you are. It's only two days. It's the only way to make sure you are not arrested."

"Maybe if you come and stay with me," Candy said laughing as she ordered a double Pernod and helped herself to some Brie.

"Thanks for the invitation, but I have business matters to deal with."

"If you think I will be safe in a house in the country, it's all good, babe. I'm just not used to someone taking care of me."

"I take care of all my people. Comprende?"

"I comprende. We make a good team." Candy picked up her glass of Pernod and waved it in Sebastian's face.

"Ambition is a beautiful thing, especially in a woman."

"Thank you, honey." She gave him her famous pout. "You ain't seen nothin' yet."

Sebastian laughed. "You left your car and came here in a cab?"

"My car is parked in the Metro parking lot."

"Can you have your secretary meet us? You should give her your apartment keys, also, in case you need anything while you stay at William's house," Sebastian said as two policemen walked in the front door. They cased the restaurant then joined the band sitting at a reserved table near the stage.

Candy made a quick call to Betty and asked her to pick up the car and meet them in Slickety Jim's parking lot nearby. "Done deal," Candy said to Sebastian. "Good thing Betty keeps my spare set of car keys. She will take care of everything."

Sebastian forced a smile; his congeniality had suddenly shifted into reverse. He spoke slowly. "If you look behind us, you will see a back door. It is open, because people are allowed to go out there to smoke. I want you to walk out and keep walking until you are out of the parking lot. Down the street to your left is a black BMW. It is my rental car. Wait for me there. Two cops just walked in. They are talking to the band members. Do not look in their direction, and walk casually as you leave."

Sebastian filled his wine glass and asked the waitress for a bill as Candy made her way out of the restaurant, through the crowd of smokers in the parking lot, and onto the street. Candy checked to see if the cops were parked nearby; they weren't. She walked south and spotted the Beamer at the end of the street. The police had upset her. The reality of spending time in jail made the house in the sticks look like the perfect hideaway. She waited in front of the rental car until Sebastian arrived, then they drove down Main Street.

"There's a parking lot across from Slickety Jim's," Candy said. "It's right on the corner of Broadway and Main. Betty will be waiting for me. I'll let her know where I'm staying and give her my keys."

"Excellent," Sebastian replied. "You should have her take your car back to your apartment for you. Then, if the police come to your home and find your car is there, they will believe you are still in the city."

"My sugar daddy is so clever." Candy gently placed her hand on his leg.

Sebastian pretended it wasn't there. "Your secretary, can she be trusted?"

"Betty, she's a ditz, but she gets the job done."

"She knows nothing of our arrangement?"

"Hell no. She doesn't hang with the rest of the girls. Betty actually wants to be a porn star," Candy said laughing. "She is dead serious, too. Betty is sure she's the next Tracy Lords."

Sebastian stopped for a red light on 12th Avenue then turned towards Candy and said, "As long as she can be trusted."

"Betty's no problem," Candy replied.

Slickety Jim's wasn't far. Sebastian parked around the block from the restaurant, and Candy walked down to the parking lot. As expected, her red '68 Mustang was sitting at the end of the lot. Betty wasn't in the car, and it wasn't locked. Candy sat in the driver's seat expecting Betty to come back any minute. She checked the glove compartment where she found a few hits of ecstasy and a gram of cocaine. She put the drugs in her purse and was about to leave when suddenly Betty was standing outside the car. Candy waved the apartment keys at her, then turned back to check the stash under the steering column. She took a quick final look for roaches in the ashtray. Nothing. She closed her purse and put her left hand on the door handle, looking out the window at her secretary. Candy's smile faded when she saw the Colt 45 in Betty's hand. Betty unloaded three rounds, and Candy slumped forward onto the steering wheel, blood streaking her blond hair where the trio of bullets had entered her head. Betty walked out of the parking lot and disappeared into the alley.

Ten minutes later, she got in Sebastian's car. "What's next?"

"It's time for you to deal with your friend Pontiac." Sebastian said as he started the car and drove down Main Street. "What did you find out?"

"Pontiac is not the one behind Carrie's disappearance. The supposed documentary director Mike Morningstar is actually a private dick hired by Carrie George's family." Betty removed the silencer from the 45 to make more room in her purse.

"So, Candy was conned into believing she was going to be in his movie and she told him Carrie was alive. He's a clever man, this Morningstar," Sebastian said.

"He got lucky, and Candy was stupid." Betty's voice rippled with contempt. "She would have fucked a director's monkey to be in a movie."

Sebastian laughed. "Every woman who stands in front of a web-cam thinks she's a star, and every stripper thinks she's a dancer. "

"Women with big tits and small brains," Betty snapped back at him, insulted that he would use Candy as a yardstick to judge the female gender. "Not every woman is so shallow."

"Perhaps not. I certainly didn't mean to include you. I was referring to women who sell themselves to the highest bidder." Sebastian leaned over and gave Betty a kiss on the cheek. "What else can you tell me about Mr. Morningstar?"

"His wife knows Carrie George's family. She works for some women's organization." Betty took a card out of her purse, checked the name, and gave it to Sebastian. "Sisters in Spirit, that's it. I found them online. It's all there, the address and phone number. She probably visits Carrie on a regular basis. If you follow her, she could lead you to your Carrie."

CHAPTER 32

Pontiac lived in a one-bedroom duplex on the second floor of a beautifully maintained heritage house at Cotton Avenue and Second Street, just two blocks from Commercial Drive and some of his favorite restaurants. His home was comfortable, though sparsely furnished. In the main room, he had a white art deco couch and a small dining table decorated with a vase full of plastic flowers. Two electric guitars and a Fender amplifier waited beside an old no-name piano. Pictures of Bob Marley and John Lennon hung on the walls, along with several posters of the bands that Pontiac had played with over the years. The place was cozy, if not a little cluttered. It had been his home for almost a decade, and he had no intentions of moving. Outside, two RCMP officers kept vigil in an unmarked car. Meanwhile, Mike was on the couch reading an old Rolling Stone magazine when Betty called.

Pontiac reluctantly tried to carry on a conversation and finally hung up, still not sure if Betty was trying to save their friendship or playing him for a dummy.

"Can you believe it? That was Betty on the phone."

"What did she want?" Mike asked.

"The cops showed up at the office looking for Candy. Now Betty is freaking because the charge is murder."

"You trust her?"

"I'm not sure which side Betty's on anymore. Candy's her boss, but Betty doesn't travel in the same circles, and she will have nothing to do with bikers."

"I wonder if she knows about Sebastian?"

"Forget it dude," Pontiac said shaking his head. "Sebastian may be Candy's boss, but none of the women working for her know him. Candy acts like she owns the website, and most of the women believe she does, including Betty."

"I hope you're right."

"Betty's cool. She's coming by to talk things over with me."

Mike thought for a moment. "I don't want her to know I'm here. When she arrives, I'll be in the bedroom." Mike was playing it safe, but Pontiac couldn't quite understand his logic.

"Dude there is no reason for you to hide in the bedroom. Betty's alright. I want you to meet her."

"Not tonight. Just in case she does know Sebastian, I don't want her to know that we are waiting for him," Mike said as he checked the layout of the bedroom.

"You don't trust anybody, do you Mike?"

"Not true. I trust my wife and you and most of my friends. Betty, I don't know, and until Candy is arrested, Betty is on the suspect list." Mike called the policemen parked out front and warned them a young lady was coming over to visit Pontiac. She was not to be detained, but he instructed the officers to call him back if anyone was with her.

Pontiac took a few Heinekens out of the fridge and gave one to Mike, then he put an album on the old turntable he had purchased back when Marley was still alive. The first cut was called "Rumble." Pontiac turned it up, sat down, and knocked back his beer. It was a fifties recording, but it didn't reflect the time period. Crunching power chords filled with distortion that sounded more Hendrix than Elvis came out of the speakers; the instrumental was filled with dark imagery meant to capture the violence of the streets circa 1958.

"You're listening to Link Wray," Pontiac said proudly.

"Never heard of him."

"He had Shawnee blood running in his veins. Played guitar in the fifties and gave it that nasty distorted growl. His trick was to play through an amplifier with a broken speaker. That's how he got the distortion. His sound has been emulated by every guitar player from Hendrix to Slash." Pontiac was in his groove. He enjoyed talking about music almost as much as he liked playing. He was about to tell Mike that Jesse Ed Davis (who played with the great blues singer Taj Mahal) was also native, when the intercom rang and a familiar voice came through the speaker.

"It's Betty. Can I come up?"

Pontiac buzzed her in, and Mike retreated to the bedroom where he turned the light off and left the bedroom door slightly ajar so he could hear their conversation. Moments later, Betty stood in the doorway. She's divine, Pontiac thought, those beautiful grey eyes, a killer smile, and the body of a playmate.

Betty gave him a hug and a light kiss on the lips. "I had to see you, Pontiac," she said. "I'm afraid to go home."

Pontiac ushered her inside. "What's the problem?"

"Something's happened to Candy. She's disappeared." Betty's voice sounded fragile, as though she didn't understand what was happening but her intuition was waving the red flag.

"Candy doesn't want to spend the night in jail. She's probably hiding somewhere and avoiding the police so she doesn't get arrested. Why should I give a shit what happened to her? She has been stalking me since I got back from Winnipeg." Pontiac walked towards the window and looked down at the traffic on the street.

"She wasn't stalking you." Betty shook her head and laughed. "She just wanted to connect with your friend who was making the documentary."

"If she's gone missing, I can start celebrating."

"I should leave." Betty turned away for a second, embarrassed. "Is there a chance you could give me a ride home?"

"Betty, I couldn't drive you home even if I wanted to. I'm under house arrest… or police protection, depending on which side of the fence you're on." Pontiac felt sorry he had unloaded on her.

Betty asked, "Are you in trouble?"

"Someone wants to put me in the hospital for talking to his girlfriend. The police want me to stay here where it's safe."

"I'm sorry, Pontiac." She drew him toward her and kissed him deeply, longer and more passionately than before.

Pontiac was delighted, but unfazed. This was Betty's way of getting what she wanted. It was also the green light for some horizontal mambo. "I could ask the police to drive you home," he offered.

"No, I don't wanna deal with cops."

"You can stay here for as long as you want, Betty."

"Thank you." She slid away from him and picked up the remote control sitting idly on the coffee table. "Do you mind if I check out the news?"

"Go ahead." Pontiac went to the kitchen and brought back a Heineken for Betty while she surfed through the local news stations. Finally, she stopped on the Global News channel where Chief Carl Hawkins was telling a newswoman that the RCMP were close to making an arrest in the missing women's case. Then the report shifted back to the anchorman who had breaking news about a recent homicide.

"The body of a woman was found this evening in a parking lot on Main Street. The woman had apparently been shot several times while in her car." The camera panned the scene, ending on a close up of a '68 Mustang with a blonde woman slumped against the steering wheel. Pontiac felt a chill run up his spine. "Police have identified the woman as Candace Webber. Small quantities of illegal narcotics were found in the vehicle, but police have not connected this shooting to recent drug-related gang activity, and no witnesses have come forward."

"I knew something had happened!" Betty started sobbing. "My God, she's dead!" She wrapped her arms around Pontiac, whose face showed mixed emotions.

"Murdered," he said. "Someone pumped a few bullets into her head."

Betty held Pontiac tightly. "I don't understand why Candy was killed, but if this had anything to do with the website, all the girls could be in trouble, including me."

"Candy's death had nothing to do with her website," Pontiac said flatly.

"How can you be so sure?"

"Trust me."

Betty pressed her face against his chest. "Could I stay here tonight?"

"Betty, you don't have to ask." Pontiac would have to explain why Mike was hiding in the bedroom, but that could come later.

"One itty bitty favor, can we take a cab to my place so I can pick up some clothes?"

"Cool, but we can't stay there very long. It's in and out." Pontiac could not see any harm in going to her apartment. He could use a change of energy, a little time to digest the repercussions of Candy's murder.

Betty thanked him with a kiss. "It will only take a few minutes," she promised as she dialed a cab.

Pontiac strolled into the bedroom and without saying a word wrote down Betty's address and handed it to Mike. He went back into the living room and left with Betty when the cab arrived. Mike watched them from the window, then rushed downstairs and followed them in his Eldorado with the RCMP close behind.

Betty was on her cell phone talking to the women working the night shift. She explained what happened to Candy and told them to stay cool; everything would be business as usual soon. In the meantime, they could expect the police to show up again and ask questions. "Loose lips sink ships," Betty reminded one of the cyber queens. The cab made its way down Homer Street past the library with its Neo-Roman architecture as Betty made a call to Candy's lawyer. Coleman seemed as shocked to hear the news as everyone else.

"See what I mean, Pontiac?" Betty said when she hung up the phone. "Nobody can explain what happened."

"The body's not even cold yet."

"What's that supposed to mean?"

"Give the police a few days, they can figure it out." Pontiac was impressed with the way Betty was taking command. He was surprised, but she seemed in total control of the situation.

"I hope so, because I won't feel safe until they do." Betty took out her wallet as the driver stopped in front of a new high rise. She gave him a twenty and asked, "Would you mind waiting for us? We're going straight back to Cotton Street. I just have to pick up a few things."

"If you're back in five minutes, I will be here. If not . . ."

"Just keep the meter running," Betty said as she opened the door.

The Windsor was a new building in Yaletown, a stylish high rise with an indoor gym and pool connected to a garden and playground. Pontiac didn't even want to imagine what the rent might amount to. They took the elevator to the 12th floor of the main high rise, and cautiously approached Betty's apartment. She gave her escort an anxious look before opening the door, and once inside she turned on all the lights, checking everywhere to make sure no one had entered her home. The apartment was filled with plants. Expensive vases held fresh flower arrangements, while other greenery sprouted in clay pots or dangled out of baskets hung from the ceiling. Her furniture was leather and the coffee table was Spanish, and framed Warhol prints flanked a huge flat-screen television mounted on the wall.

"Nobody's hiding under your bed?" Pontiac queried facetiously.

"No," Betty smiled. "I guess I was overreacting. Candy is dead, after all. And a lot of weird shit has happened in the office lately."

"You can tell me later. Grab your clothes, and let's get out of here."

"You're right. The meter is running." She walked into her bedroom just as her cell phone rang.

"Maybe I should go down now and keep the cabbie company?" Pontiac looked down on Cambie Street, searching for Mike and the Eldorado.

"I'm almost ready," Betty said from the bedroom. She peeked her head out the door. "Could you give me a hand? It will speed things up."

Pontiac reluctantly left the comfort of an overstuffed chair and walked into the bedroom. A suitcase was open on the bed, and Betty had changed from leather to denim, wearing black jeans with knee-high boots hugging her calves and a blue shirt left unbuttoned at the top to reveal the wonderful symmetry of her breasts, warming Pontiac's demeanor considerably. She stood in front of her closet, staring at a box tucked away in the upper corner that she couldn't reach.

"Pontiac, you're taller than I am. Could you be a sweetie and get the silver striped box stashed in that corner?" Betty gave him a helpless look.

"Move over," Pontiac said as he stepped into the closet and stood on his toes to retrieve the box. He tugged at it for a while before it gave way. It felt heavy as he handed it to Betty, who was all smiles. She took the box over to the bed and began rummaging through it while Pontiac took stock of what remained in the large closet: a colorful wardrobe that leaned heavily toward the erotic. He was about to tell her she had excellent taste in lingerie when he felt the cold steel barrel of a Colt 45 pressed against the back of his head.

"You can turn around, Pontiac," Betty said, the warm gravel of love gone from her voice. "Any sudden moves and there goes our friendship."

"Relax, Betty." Pontiac turned slowly. "You can put that down."

"Not until you answer a few questions." Betty waved the gun at him. "You have a choice, Pontiac. Tell me where Carrie George is hiding, and you can walk out the door. If you don't, Sebastian is on his way over here, and he will find a way to make you talk."

"Your offer is the less painful one." Pontiac knew she was lying through her teeth. If he told her where Carrie was, she would pull the trigger.

"That's right."

"I haven't seen Carrie George since I was in Winnipeg."

"Wrong answer, Pontiac. Let's try one more time." Betty took a step forward, raised the gun until it was a few inches from Pontiac's face, then pulled the hammer back. The pistol was cocked, her finger pressed against the trigger.

"Alright!" Pontiac realized Betty was going to kill him no matter what answer he gave her. "Carrie is in town under police protection. She's called me a few times, but where she is, I swear to God I don't know."

"You have her cell number?"

"I do," Pontiac said resignedly. "You want me to call her?"

"That's right! You're going to find out where she's staying. Tell her you'd like to come visit her." Betty took her cell phone and tossed it to Pontiac.

"Her number is in my wallet." He reached slowly for his wallet and took out several business cards until he finally found the number. He was about to start dialing when a knock on the door made him stop.

"It's Sebastian." Betty gave him a contemptuous smile. "But just in case, why don't you walk out on the balcony? Stay out of trouble." She marched Pontiac towards the balcony, and once he was outside, she locked the glass door. The knocking continued, and when she finally opened the door to an inch see who it was, she was disappointed. Instead of Sebastian, it was the building manager who stood before her, looking disheveled and anxious with his shirt hanging out.

"Betty, it's Ken. The police have been calling for you, and people from your office are out of their minds with worry." He spoke in a low voice so the neighbors wouldn't hear him. "Can I come in? We should settle this matter."

Betty stared at him through the crack in the door, then slipped the gun into the back of her jeans. She wanted to rid herself of Ken as quickly as possible, but before she could think, the door slammed against her with such force that she flew backward, shattering her favorite Egyptian vase. The gun dropped out of her jeans and slid across the floor. Mike burst through the doorway as she lunged for the Colt, and he kicked the gun out of Betty's reach, but as he tried to rescue the weapon himself, he tripped and landed face down on the hardwood floor.

Betty had recovered from Mike's surprise entry, and she came at him before he could stand up, catching him with a boot to the shoulder that knocked him against the wall. She did a spin and came back with another boot aimed at his head. Mike ducked and delivered an elbow to her jaw. She stepped back, dazed but unhurt.

The gun was the prize, and it was five feet away from both combatants. Mike had a black belt in karate, but Betty had apparently also studied martial arts. She was from the school of new fighters who combined boxing with karate and judo. Betty was on the offensive again with a flurry of kicks followed by punches, all executed with lightning speed. Mike parried most of them, but one of her boots grazed his left arm, and in the following kick, he caught Betty's leg and flipped her over the coffee table. She landed awkwardly and screamed in pain as Mike walked over and picked up the handgun before he sat down on the leather couch. Betty lay on the floor moaning. Mike suspected she had cracked a few ribs, which explained why she couldn't move and could barely speak. She looked up him with a painful expression. He pointed the pistol at her and smiled.

"Is this the same gun you used on Candy?" Mike asked her. Betty tried to respond, but couldn't. Her expression grew darker when she saw Pontiac enter the room.

"Mike! Glad you made it in time." Pontiac had been freed from the balcony by Ken, who was busy calling the police. "Sebastian is on the way over. In fact, he should be here any minute."

"I can't wait." Mike checked the Colt 45 to make sure it was fully loaded. "That bastard is in for a surprise."

CHAPTER 33

Sebastian parked in the basement of the Windsor Apartments where Betty kept a spot reserved for him and took the elevator upstairs. He doubted that Betty had been able to convince Pontiac to confess where Carrie was staying. It would take his knife to make him speak, and since Pontiac had conned him and conspired to help Carrie escape, he deserved to be punished. Sebastian was certain now that the police were using Candy to get at him. Now that she was dead, there was no way to tie him to Susan Wabigon's murder... except for Carrie. But once he found her, she would come back to him with a little convincing, then he would send her to his associates in Hong Kong where neither her parents nor the police would ever be able to find her.

The elevator stopped unexpectedly at the first floor and a team of paramedics carrying a stretcher stepped inside. Before the doors closed, Sebastian noticed several police cruisers parked in front of the building. He quickly pushed the second floor button, got off the elevator, and took the stairs back to the basement. His gut feeling told him the ambulance and the police were headed for Betty's apartment.

He returned to his car and pulled around to the front of the Windsor for a closer look. Traffic had slowed to a crawl with the ambulance occupying the right lane and a line of cars moving slowly around it. Sebastian was four cars down, but he recognized Betty on the stretcher and watched her leave in the ambulance. For a second, he considered going back to Seattle and booking a flight back to Hong Kong. Then he reconsidered. Betty would never rat him out to the police, and since there were no witnesses to Candy's murder, they couldn't link her to the crime.

Sebastian left thinking about William and his hooker. William was going to cheat the hangman one more time. Now, if only this problem could be resolved as easily. He took a long look at the business card Betty had given him, memorizing the address of Sisters in Spirit and studying the picture of Theresa Morningstar. He would see her in person tomorrow, and she would lead him to Carrie. Once he found her, it would only be a matter of time before she was back with him. He hoped she did not become stubborn or provoke him. He took one last look at the ambulance as he drove by. Pontiac obviously had help from someone, because Betty could have easily taken care of him herself. Pontiac and his friend Morningstar were likely in Betty's apartment with the police.

Sebastian guessed right. Mike had waited in the apartment until the police showed up, realizing Sebastian would know he was walking into a trap if he came knocking on Betty's door. She wouldn't have been much help, anyway. The paramedics confirmed she had two fractured ribs, and Mike was still in pain from the few rounds he had gone toe to toe with her.

Now, Mike was busy talking with Jimmy Secola, who was still trying to understand who had killed Candy and why. "Let me get this straight," Jimmy said. "Betty works for Candy, but tonight she decides to blow Candy's brains out?"

"That's right! Betty also works for Sebastian. He didn't want Candy to be charged with murder in case she ratted on him, so he had her killed. Betty was the shooter, and once she finished with Candy, she went to work on Pontiac. She was trying to find out where we're keeping Carrie, and she planned to hold Pontiac captive until Sebastian arrived."

"And where is this Sebastian?" Jimmy gestured in frustration. "Six inches behind the scene and five seconds behind the action. No lint on him, I bet!"

"I don't know where he is now, but we know he was on his way here about an hour ago. We're still waiting. I figure Sebastian has already come by. Maybe he saw Betty go out in the ambulance or saw the cruisers outside. You can take it from there. By now, he's back in his hotel room planning his next move." Mike started to feel the pain in his leg. He stood up with great difficulty, and limped awkwardly over to the window.

Jimmy was livid that Candy Webber was assassinated before the RCMP could arrest her, but he did have the smoking gun. "Betty's gun is on its way to forensics," he said. "If it's the same weapon that killed Candy, she'll be charged with murder and so will Sebastian."

"Good luck finding him."

"If tonight is any indication, this man will go to any length to find

Carrie George. We will wait for him at the hotel; eventually he will come looking for her. The longer he goes without finding her, the more skins that fucking snake will have to shed."

"Let's hope he doesn't show up." Mike wanted to avoid a confrontation in the hotel because Carrie and her parents might be caught in the crossfire. "Right now, Sebastian believes that Pontiac is the only person who can lead him to Carrie, which means Sebastian will come back looking for him. With Betty behind bars, it will be a matter of revenge." Mike had begun to understand Sebastian. It was personal now. For a trained killer, happiness is a warm gun, and Pontiac was just another asshole who had it coming to him.

Bill Roberts watched the Russian movers empty his basement. None of them spoke English very well, and Roberts thought he might have recognized one of them from a club downtown, maybe his own place. They all looked like former Red Army rough-and-readies, tough as nails. Earlier in the day, he had contacted the daughter of the former owner and given her an ultimatum: "Pick up your furniture or the garbage department will take charge." She was gracious enough to send a moving company immediately. The freezer with the body remnants was now at the bottom of Lake Pimachanga, about fifty miles North of Kelowna. He left Manson with a neighbor who would take care of him in a place where that snoopy cop Jenkins would never find him.

Preparations had gone well so far. The only thing left was taking the flight to Hong Kong. He smiled at the thought of Jenkins showing up out here and finding nothing; nobody home, no evidence left behind to incriminate him, not even his dog Manson. Thinking of the look on Jenkins' face made him smirk. Bill waved at the movers. They'd made short work of what could have stretched into an all day affair. He watched as they drove off in high spirits, singing loudly in Russian, hauling away a precious cargo of junk. Roberts went into the living room and sat down in front of his computer. He checked his e-mail and found his travel agent had sent his itinerary. There were several other messages, including one from Sebastian. He had returned from Hong Kong to take care of personal business and would call when he was in the city. Roberts frowned, confused and annoyed.

Roberts would still leave the country, but Sebastian would not be in Hong Kong to welcome him and show him around. Still, he would deal with the hooker now, and that was good news. Roberts' trust in Sebastian made him feel better about leaving with the police on his heels. He would be two thousand miles away for the next month, and when he returned, he wouldn't have to worry about Jenkins or any other cop snooping around his home. He decided to drive into the city and drop off his truck at the garage. He trusted the shop, and the old guy would babysit the truck for as long as Bill was in Hong Kong.

Roberts checked the glove compartment, just to make sure there was nothing in there of any importance. He found several old parking tickets, a small bottle of chloroform, and a bankbook. He put the bottle in his shirt pocket; it might come in handy sometime. Then he opened the bankbook. There on the inside of the cover was the number Frank Morin had given him for Earl, the hooker's friend. Roberts had completely forgotten about it. He thought about giving the number to Sebastian, but then he decided to call it himself. Earl picked up immediately.

"Am I speaking to Earl? How's the day treating you, Earl?" Roberts was doing a fair job of imitating the telemarketing assholes that always called him at home. "My name is Roy. I'm with *The Environmental Revue*, and I was hoping we could send you a free copy of our magazine? That's right, absolutely free. Earl, what is your address?" Roberts made a note in the bankbook: 2811 40th Avenue, #711. "Thank you, Earl. I hope you enjoy our magazine."

Roberts smiled as he put his cell phone away. It was a Kerrisdale address, not hard to find. He drove downtown, leaving the truck at the garage with a list of repairs that could be done in his absence. A few blocks away, he picked up a white Lincoln Mark IV at the Budget car rental on Granville Street and drove down 40th Avenue until he was in front of the Chelsea Arms where the hooker was hiding. It was an older building with a rustic look, like several other buildings on the block. He pulled in at the Seven Eleven across the street and parked the car. Roberts wanted to call Sebastian, give him the good news, and let him deal with the hooker in his own way. Roberts had found the bitch. Her fate was sealed, and the police were fucked.

He was just about to dial when he spotted Kim coming out of the apartment building and walking across the street towards the Seven Eleven. He slipped down in the seat and waited until she had entered the store, then he drove across the street to park in front of the Chelsea Arms. It was close to nine o'clock at night, and there were no streetlights in front of the building and just enough darkness to give him a chance to make a bold move. He could take care of the hooker for good himself. He took the bottle of chloroform out his pocket and emptied what was left onto his handkerchief.

Kim needed to pick up batteries for her cell phone, but she had also just wanted to leave the apartment, to be alone. She browsed through a copy of People's magazine by the cashier as she waited her turn behind a man placing his daily bets. Jennifer Aniston was on the cover again, whining about her ex-boyfriend Brad Pitt. Kim put the magazine back. The visit to Frankie's grave had left her with an empty sense of hopelessness, but now that she had a gun, the odds were evened out just a bit. She wanted all of this to end, even though it seemed impossible. All she needed was a driver who was handy with a rifle, and she had found the perfect wheel man in Larry Crowfoot.

Her plan was simple. She figured Roberts spent most of his time at home alone, and he would never expect her to show up at out at his house. Since he was not afraid of her, Roberts would meet her at the door with every intention of luring her inside. She would smile and play along until she was close enough, then she'd pull out the Beretta and settle the score for Mona and Frankie. If Manson so much as twitched a whisker, Larry would take care of the dog with the rifle.

"Can I help you, miss?" The cashier had caught Kim in her daydream, but after a second she was smiling back at the Asian man behind the counter. She pulled out her cell phone and pointed to a display case behind the cashier where several rows of batteries were arranged.

"I need batteries," Kim said, "cell phone batteries."

"We have some right here." He looked at her cell phone, then turned around and picked up the batteries and gave them to her. "Seven dollars and fifty cents."

Finding Carrie George

"Thank you." Kim handed him a ten dollar bill, took her change, and left. She didn't notice the white Lincoln parked in front of the apartment building as she crossed the street with confidence. She was putting the batteries in her phone and contemplating what to make for supper. She was only about ten feet from the entrance to the Chelsea Arms when suddenly she was grabbed from behind, and big hands pressed a cloth against her face. Before she could react in any manner, her brain short-circuited. She felt paralyzed, her knees buckled, and everything faded to black as she slipped into unconsciousness.

Roberts slipped the chloroformed cloth in his pocket and put his arm under Kim's to keep her upright and give the impression he was helping her walk. They managed to make it to his car without attracting attention. Roberts acted swiftly, and his car was only a few feet away. He propped Kim up in the front seat and wasted no time leaving Kerrisdale. He drove down Granville and took a right on Broadway. The traffic was unrelenting until he got up to Boundary Road. When a bit of space cleared around him, he threw the chloroform-soaked hanky out the window.

Roberts looked over at Kim, her head resting against the window. "Are you enjoying the ride?" he asked. She was completely unconscious, unaware that he wanted to make her last few hours on this earth the most painful of her entire life. He chuckled at her complete lack of response. "I'll take that as a 'no' then. Don't worry, we'll have plenty of time to chat." Now that he was in charge, his mind began to wander. How many ways could he kill her? Where would he leave the body when he was through with her? He could put a bullet in her head right now and drop her in a ditch along some side road. That was too risky. The cops would suspect he was responsible, and leaving town tomorrow would only make him look guiltier. If he gave the hooker a lethal injection and left her body somewhere in the Downtown East Side, the police would find her soon enough and assume she had died from an overdose, no one responsible but herself. The police would never suspect him, and because he would be in Hong Kong, they would eventually forget Bill Roberts ever existed.

"Well bitch, tonight is party time, and when this party is over, you will burn in hell with your old man Frankie." Roberts slammed on the brakes at a red light, and Kim hit the dashboard face first and crumpled onto the floor. He pulled her back up by the hair and shoved her upright against the seat-back.

"Stop flopping around like some fucking rag doll!" Roberts looked in his rear view mirror to see if there were any cars behind him. He noticed one vehicle, but it was not close enough for the driver to have seen what happened. He was close to New Westminster now. He kept driving, looking over at Kim as he hissed at her, "You escaped punishment last time, but not tonight!"

CHAPTER 34

Harold Jenkins left St. Paul's Hospital and drove down Broadway, satisfied that Delores had admitted she was in rehab to kill Kim Lawrence. There was only one person in the world who wanted Kim dead, and that was William Roberts. It would please his supervisor to discover a direct link, but again, there was no way to establish one between Roberts and Delores. The Greek was the only person who could have fingered Roberts, and he was stone cold dead. Delores' confession that Kim was the intended victim didn't really change much of anything. It was a small victory in a dull day of predictable battles that had produced nothing truly worthwhile for the case. A morning meeting with SkyTrain security had been inconsequential; no one remembered seeing Roberts the night of the shooting.

Harold called Kim to let her know he was going to pay her a visit, but it was her friend Earl who answered. He explained that Kim had gone to the Seven Eleven across the street and still hadn't returned. She'd been acting strange all evening, and Earl was afraid she might have relapsed and gone downtown to score. Harold didn't want believe him. He had only known Kim a short time, and he was no expert in drug addiction, but the way she handled Frankie's death and the attempts on her own life had convinced him she had kicked her habit for good. He took a left on Arbutus and drove towards Kerrisdale until he arrived at the Seven Eleven.

"Excuse me, sir." He pulled out his badge and showed it to the cashier. "I am Constable Jenkins. Was there a young woman, light brown hair, medium height, wearing a blue T-shirt and jeans who came into your store about an hour ago?"

"Yes, I remember her. She bought batteries for her cell phone."

"When she left, did you happen to notice if she walked towards the bus stop up the street?"

"Hmm... she crossed the street. I know she lives in the building over there." The cashier pointed towards the Chelsea Arms.

"That's right," Jenkins said. "She didn't return home, and we have reason to be worried about her safety." Harold made it clear that Kim hadn't broken any laws, that she was the one in danger.

"I'm sorry. I don't know where she went," the cashier said, as he turned to a waiting customer.

Harold didn't ask any more questions. He was beginning to form a picture in his mind of what had happened to Kim. He called Earl one more time, but Kim hadn't returned, nor was she taking any calls on her cell. Earl told Harold that he had a visitor named Larry Crowfoot, whom Kim had invited over for supper. There was no way Kim could have forgotten he was coming. Earl was getting worried something had happened to her, and he asked Harold to come over to his apartment because Larry had something important to tell him. Harold left his cruiser in the Seven Eleven parking lot and walked over to the Chelsea Arms.

The apartment was on the fourth floor. The place was built in the early forties, a character building with a sense of spaciousness not found in apartments today. The living room had hardwood floors and large windows on the west and south sides of the room. An older PC and printer sat atop a maple desk in the far corner next to a bookcase filled with books about addiction and psychology. Earl was sitting at the dining table with Larry Crowfoot. The meal was over, and both men were enjoying their coffee when Harold knocked on the door.

"I've known Kim for a long time," Larry told Harold. "She's basically a good person who's had to deal with a lot of problems, and my friend Frankie—God rest his soul—he was not a very positive influence on her."

"She dropped in to see you today?" Harold asked Larry. Earl, unable to remain seated, anxiously paced the living room floor.

"She did," Larry replied. "She was frightened. I gave her a handgun, so she could protect herself. She called me later and asked me if I would go with her to this man's house. Kim said he was the psycho who had killed Mona and Frankie and was trying to kill her."

"Was she going to kill him?" Harold asked.

"She never said it in so many words, but it was more or less understood. Kim wanted me to hear her plan. We were going to discuss it after supper. If she's not here, then she's in trouble."

"I agree Larry, and I think I know where she is." Harold thanked the two men and said he would find Kim. Larry asked him if he could come along, but Harold declined. It wasn't that he didn't need help, but Kim had already been gone for over an hour and Robert might expect someone to come looking for her, and Harold didn't want to see Larry take a bullet because of good intentions.

The Lincoln rolled through New Westminster and closer to Roberts' house. Kim was still unconscious; she hadn't moved a muscle since they left Kerrisdale. The chloroform had knocked her out cold, and she was frozen in time for the moment, but that didn't stop Roberts from carrying on a conversation with her. He enjoyed taunting her, as if it were some sort of psychotic foreplay. The fact that she couldn't hear him didn't seem to matter.

"What made you think a lowlife like you deserves to live? Your boyfriend begged for mercy, and so will you before the night is over." He was on the gravel road now, a few miles from home, and he could feel his adrenaline pumping at the thought of killing the hooker right then and there.

Roberts opened the gate to his property and drove through, closing and locking it behind him. He drove down the old road that led to his house and hid the Lincoln behind the barn so that no one would suspect he was home. He carried Kim inside the house and dropped her comatose body on the sofa in the living room. He checked the phone for messages, then walked into the kitchen, opened a bottle of tequila, and started laughing at how easy it had been to snatch the hooker right off the street and bring her to his house. This truly was a moment to celebrate. He drank from the bottle, then took a syringe full of heroin out of the fridge. He walked over to the sofa and poured tequila into Kim's mouth.

"A little firewater to make you feel at home." Roberts laughed and kept pouring the tequila until Kim started gagging. She choked and tried to spit out the alcohol that threatened to fill her lungs, but Roberts kept pouring until she awakened her from her chloroform coma.

"What's the matter, you don't like tequila?" Roberts snorted.

Kim's eyes opened wide, but she was only half conscious and gasping for air. The tequila was burning her gut and making her nauseous. She felt like throwing up, but she couldn't move her arms or her legs. Her vision was still impaired, but she could see the hazy form of Roberts, frightening and disgusting, then the reality of her situation became clear. She was in the psycho bastard's house, and unless a miracle happened, she wasn't going to leave alive.

"I have a little gift for you," he said, showing her the heroin. Kim stared into the void as her brain slowly transmitted what was going on around her.

"I killed your old man, and now I'm going to rid the world of his junkie, hooker daughter." Roberts started laughing again, still waving the smack around. This time, Kim heard him clearly, and the words stuck in her mind, yet she closed her eyes and remained still.

"Can you hear me? I walked your father into the washroom of his own home, made him get down on his knees, and then I blew his fucking brains out." He gulped a shot of tequila then started pouring it into Kim again. She gasped and swallowed hard, then turned her head as the alcohol ran down her cheeks. Roberts cackled and finished the bottle himself.

"He got what he deserved." Roberts looked down at Kim. He felt drunk and hateful; he wanted to cut her up. "You disgusting little junkie! Did you think your cop friend was going to save you? Stupid bitch, you aren't worth saving! You're just another dick-eating junkie whore. Tonight you'll reap what you sowed. You told the cops on me? Well, it's payback time."

Kim kept her eyes closed, but she could feel her body recovering from the chloroform. For the first time since she passed out, there was warmth in her legs. She could feel the holster strapped to her ankle and remembered the gun was there, waiting.

Roberts turned toward the window, suddenly very tense. He heard the wail of a police siren in the distance. He quickly turned off the lights and ran upstairs, staring out at the road from his bedroom window. He could see a set of headlights and a red flashing light speeding down the road about a mile away, getting closer by the second. Roberts rushed downstairs, took a twelve-gauge shotgun from its rack, and loaded it. It had to be that nosy cop again, and this time he was going to receive a different kind of welcome.

Harold didn't waste any time on his way to Roberts' house. He drove flat out with lights and siren on all the way. He didn't stop for the gate, either. It flew open as he barreled down the driveway and came to a screeching halt in front of Roberts' home. He sat in the cruiser for a brief moment; something was wrong. There was no truck, no dog tied to the garage, and the house was completely dark. Harold realized that Roberts had anticipated his visit, which meant he could be anywhere. He may have taken Kim to some remote location where no one would disturb him. Harold reluctantly stepped out of his cruiser and walked up to the house, one hand on his gun. He knocked hard, waited, then knocked again. There was no answer. Finally, he shouted, "POLICE! IS ANYBODY HOME?"

Dead silence. Harold was tempted to break down the door at first, but he reconsidered. He walked around the house checking the windows for any movement inside. At the back of the building, there was a veranda. He walked up the steps and opened a screen door, then tried the handle on the main door. It wasn't locked, so he stepped to the side and took out his nine milli, then gently turned the doorknob and pushed the door open in one quick motion. Immediately, he tried to move back from the open doorway, but he wasn't fast enough.

The shotgun blast broke the silence of the night, and Harold felt his left arm rip open. Excruciating pain shot through his body, and he could feel blood gushing from the wound. Another shot, this time part of the railing was blown away. Harold emptied two rounds toward the dark living room. He heard glass explode, but that was all. He knew Roberts wasn't hit. Another shotgun blast, and splinters from the side of the door fell like snowflakes. Harold fired back and heard more glass shatter. He needed help, and fast. He moved quickly toward the edge of the veranda and over the railing, landing safely on the ground. The loss of blood was making him weak, his vision was starting to falter, and he had two bullets left in his gun. His only chance was to make it to the cruiser and radio for backup. He leaned against the house, his eyes fixed on the doorway.

Roberts had found the trail of blood and figured the cop was hit, so he stuck his head out the door, hoping to find a dead man on the veranda. Harold saw him and fired, missing Roberts by a hair. By his count, Roberts figured the cop only had one more bullet, and now he was wounded and in real trouble. Roberts reloaded his shotgun and inched his way back to the doorway. He pointed the shotgun just outside the door and started blasting. The railing exploded in a million pieces as Roberts stepped on to the veranda, shooting non-stop as he walked towards Harold who had started running awkwardly toward his car.

Harold made a beeline for the cruiser, and was only halfway there when two distinctly different shots rang out and the shotgun fire stopped. Harold heard the big gun clatter on the veranda floor, and he turned quickly just as a third shot was fired and Roberts came tumbling off the veranda on to the ground, blood flowing from the side of his head. Seconds later, Kim stood on the edge of the veranda looking down at Roberts, wisps of smoke unfurling from the Beretta in her hand. The blank, dead look on her face brightened when she noticed Harold. She was shocked to see the condition he was in, but happy he was alive.

"Are you alright?" Kim asked from the top of the steps.

"I'm fine," Harold said on the brink of passing out. "You made it just in time."

Kim took a long look at Roberts, who was lying in a pool of blood. "Is he dead?"

Harold walked slowly over to Roberts' body and bent down to check for a pulse. "Bill Roberts is shaking hands with the devil as we speak. He's dead. No more terrorizing you or anyone else."

Kim put the Beretta back in its holster. "You should come inside so I can bandage you up, stop the bleeding." Kim left came down to help Harold make it inside the house. He was barely conscious as Kim cleansed his arm and wrapped his wound tightly. "We should go to emergency right away."

Harold could barely keep his eyes open.

"Don't worry," Kim said. "I'll drive."

CHAPTER 35

Mike spent the night at Pontiac's. He didn't expect Sebastian to show up there, but then again anything could happen. It was that kind of night. Candy was dead, and Betty was charged with her murder. She was in the hospital with broken ribs, and Mike was still sore from his confrontation with her. Using Pontiac as a trap to snare Sebastian had failed; he had sent Betty to do his dirty work, and she came close to ending Pontiac's life. Mike's musings were interrupted by a phone call from his wife. Theresa was at the office and planned to meet Carrie and her mother for lunch. Mike agreed to join them and bring Pontiac along, then he gave Theresa an account of last night and warned her to be extra cautious.

Theresa was shocked to hear how Candy was killed, and Pontiac's brush with death frightened her. For a moment, she realized how fragile Carrie's safety truly was. This man was ruthless. Theresa opened a drawer and took out a photo of Sebastian that Mike had given her. Sebastian was handsome in a roguish way. He certainly didn't look like a hardened criminal. Theresa studied the photo for a while and put it away. There wouldn't be any problem identifying him. She was on her way to a meeting about a protest on Parliament Hill. Several native women's organizations from across the country were attending, and accommodations were still available. There were issues that had to be discussed, and a press conference would be scheduled with a guest speaker from Indian Affairs. The meeting would hopefully come to a close at noon. Theresa was looking forward to spending time with her husband. She'd hardly seen him since he had returned from Winnipeg.

When he finished his call, Mike walked back into the living room and sat at the table across from Pontiac, who looked up from the daily newspaper and asked, "What's the plan Sherlock?" He was on his second cappuccino, trying to bring his brain to life, the newspaper was there to remind him what kind of mess the world was in today.

"We're having lunch with Carrie at the hotel," Mike said casually. His mind was trying to figure out what Sebastian's next move was going to be.

"Good call, dude. I haven't seen her in two days."

"Be careful what you say to Carrie. I don't want her to know that the police don't have a clue where Sebastian is. With Candy dead, they won't arrest him unless Betty decides to confess, and that is not going to happen." Mike wanted to call Jimmy Secola to see if he had beefed up the police presence around Carrie. One thing for sure, Sebastian had given up on Pontiac after last night.

"Right on, dude," Pontiac said, finishing his capp, then in his most philosophical voice, he added, "I'm thinking Sebastian's not stupid. Surely he realizes he could go back to Hong Kong and no one would be the wiser."

"I've considered his options, and you're right. If he left now we might never see him again." Mike stood up and stretched, walked over to the window, and looked down at the undercover cops still parked in front of the building. "Problem is," he mused, "Sebastian can't walk away. That's not his style. He's a control freak and doesn't like loose ends. He's not leaving unless Carrie is with him or she's in the morgue."

"That is cold blooded. You really think he would risk everything now that Candy's dead? I mean, Carrie's testimony is nothing without Candy being in court. The cops have no real proof to link him with Candy's death. At this point, even the village idiot would know enough to disappear, and Sebastian is no dummy." Pontiac picked up his cup and walked over to the cappuccino machine for one more refill. He was convinced Sebastian was leaving town and felt it was time to loosen up and resume life as he once knew it.

"The criminal mind works a little different than yours or mine," Mike said, angered that Pontiac gave more respect to a murdering pimp than he deserved. "The fact is, the police are looking for him. There is no warrant for his arrest, but they want to talk to him. He probably realizes what's happening, and he does not want to be questioned by the police. So, if he wants Carrie, he has to make his move now."

"He has to find her first." Pontiac was still not convinced.

"Right, and that is the only advantage we have. The more time he spends looking for her, the more time we have to find him."

"Sounds like you've gotten inside his head."

"Let's say I didn't get much sleep last night. So far Sebastian has

stayed a step ahead of us. My gut tells me we're headed for a showdown."
Mike needed a gun; the Sig Sauer 40 caliber he kept in his desk was
strictly for emergencies. It was his last resort, and he always hoped he
wouldn't have to use it. Certain promises aren't made to be kept, and
he had to be ready. Mike wasn't dealing with Betty anymore. The next
round was with The Blade.

Sebastian sat in the far corner of the dining room in the Radisson Hotel.
He finished breakfast and stared at the Sisters in Spirit website on his
laptop. It didn't take him long to find a picture of Theresa Morningstar.
A very attractive woman, he thought to himself as he studied her face,
repeating the office address to himself so he would not forget. Sebastian
finished his coffee, took out his cell phone, and called Theresa's office.
The receptionist told him Theresa was in meetings and wouldn't be
available until late afternoon. Sebastian smiled to himself. He was just
a few miles from downtown and the office where Theresa worked; he
figured he could be there in twenty minutes.

On his way out, Sebastian picked up a copy of the Vancouver Sun.
Candy was plastered across page three. They had printed a picture
of her in the Mustang with her head resting on the steering wheel,
her blond hair streaked with blood, and a lifeless expression on her
face. The police had a suspect in custody, but were not releasing any
details. The Candy & Friends website was officially closed down, and
Betty's name was never mentioned. He perused the rest of the newspaper
and was about to throw it in the garbage when he noticed a photo of
William Roberts staring back at him under the heading "Policeman
Wounded in Gunfight." The story detailed an exchange of gunfire
between Roberts and RCMP officer Harold Jenkins. The officer was
wounded, and Roberts was killed.

Sebastian drove downtown, still shocked by the news. William Roberts
had been just one day away from leaving the country, and now he was
dead. There was no mention of female victims found on his property,
but Sebastian knew it was only a matter of time. Could the police find

anything to connect him with William? He did call Roberts yesterday, so his cell phone would have to be destroyed, but that was all. Their one meeting was held in secret, and nothing else had transpired to link him with William Roberts.

Sebastian was now on Georgia Street, right in the heart of Vancouver's financial district. He drove past the Royal Centre, the CIBC, and the Bentall building then took a left on Pender Street and stopped in front of a large office building. It was fifteen minutes before noon. He left the BMW, crossed the street, and went into Starbucks where he ordered an espresso and found a comfortable vantage point by the window. He could see anyone leaving Theresa's building, and when the clock struck twelve, people began pouring out of the main doors.

Within a few minutes, he spotted her. She walked up the street and stopped in front of a blue Volkswagen. Theresa looked around, as if she was expecting to meet someone, then got in her car and drove away. Sebastian returned to his BMW and followed the Volkswagen down Nelson Street and across the Cambie bridge. Theresa took a right on Broadway and pulled in at the visitor's parking area of the Park Inn. Sebastian parked down the street and watched Theresa enter the hotel. Then he took out his cell, called the Park Inn, and asked for Carrie George.

The receptionist told him Carrie was in room 411 and connected him immediately. A man answered the phone just as Sebastian hung up. A few minutes later, a red Cadillac pulled in, and two men stepped out. Sebastian recognized one of them; it was Pontiac. He assumed the driver was Morningstar. Sebastian waited in his car for maybe ten minutes and then walked to the back of the hotel. Beyond the freight entrance, he found the back door and went in. Sebastian took the stairs to the fourth floor. He stopped at the door leading to the hallway and opened it barely an inch, just enough to hear people talking by the elevator. Sebastian was certain he recognized one of the voices. He peeked out of the door, and there was Carrie with Theresa Morningstar and an older woman entering the elevator. He waited for a few minutes, then moved slowly down the hallway until he stood in front of room 411.

Carrie welcomed Theresa with a hug, excited to see her. Carrie was dressed casually in blue jeans, a T-shirt, and a Seattle Mariners baseball cap. She seemed relaxed and happy, exuding sense of *joie de vivre* that Theresa hadn't really seen since Carrie arrived. Mary stood beside her quietly. She didn't seem to share her daughter's optimism. Spending too many days cooped up in the hotel with no end in sight was starting to wear her down.

"I'm so happy to see you," Carrie said. "Since Pontiac left, the only people I can talk to are the police. And mom is getting antsy. She wants to go home, and I feel the same way."

"We all want to go home," Phil said with a hint of impatience. "So tell me Theresa, has Sebastian been arrested yet?"

"No. He's in Vancouver, that much I know. Mike will be here in a few minutes. He'll bring you up to speed. I will let him explain what's happening. He never tells me anything unless I threaten him with torture," Theresa laughed. "Will you be joining us for lunch, Phil?"

"No, thanks. I already ate." He strummed a few chords on the guitar Pontiac had left for him. "You ladies have fun. I'll keep myself occupied." He couldn't quite make music, but it was better than watching television.

Mary promised to bring back some dessert for him, and the three women took the elevator down to the restaurant. Carrie asked the hostess for a table for five, then turned to Theresa. "Is Pontiac coming with Mike?"

"He'll be here for certain. He's not allowed out of Mike's sight until this Sebastian guy is in jail."

"I know how that feels," Carrie said as they sat down together. Two small tables had been pushed together to accommodate everyone, and the waitress brought over an extra place setting and chair.

"I just want to go home," Mary said in a pleading voice.

"You will," Theresa reassured her, "but not until it's safe."

Just then, Mike walked in the restaurant with Pontiac and headed towards the table. Mary smiled when she saw him; he made her feel safe despite the circumstances. After the waitress took their lunch order, Mike gave Carrie and her mother a brief explanation of recent events, including Candy's death.

Carrie was stunned. "I can't believe it... Sebastian sent someone to kill her?"

"That's right. Candy was charged with Susan's murder, and Sebastian was afraid Candy would tell the police he was the one who ordered it. When he found out the police were about to arrest Candy, he had her killed."

"So, he's still in town?" Carrie asked Mike. Her spirits were sinking at the thought of Sebastian not leaving until he found her.

"I'm afraid so." Mike noticed Mary was not taking the news well. Her daughter was still in danger.

"Are we just going to wait until he shows up?" Carrie asked Mike.

"He doesn't know where you are. We aren't giving up now, and while he's looking for you, the police are closing in on him."

"What about you Pontiac, are you coming back to the hotel?" Carrie decided to change the subject for her mother's sake.

"I just can't stay away. Where is my main man Phil?"

"He's in the room trying to play your guitar," Carrie said with a grin.

"Are you serious? Phil is up in the room right now playing my axe?" Pontiac laughed. "This I have to see. I'm going upstairs to check it out."

"Yes, do. He'll be happy to see you," Carrie said. She watched him walk out of the restaurant, glad he had returned. Having him around would make things easier; maybe her mother would relax a little more.

Pontiac was humming a tune when he arrived on the fourth floor. He listened for a moment, but didn't hear a guitar, then he knocked on the door of room 411. Phil opened the door without a greeting and barely looked at Pontiac when he came inside. The door slammed behind him, and there was Sebastian with a big toothy smile, pointing a gun at Pontiac's head.

CHAPTER 36

Mike finished his club sandwich. The mood at the table became a bit lighter with the arrival of lunch, and since Pontiac hadn't returned, Mike assumed that he and Phil were jamming up a storm in room 411. Mike informed Mary that his friend RCMP officer Jimmy Secola was on his way with two other policemen to watch over the family. Mary thanked him and apologized for seeming unappreciative. Her daughter was alive and well thanks to Mike. He told her there was no reason to feel sorry; she had every reason to be upset, but the nightmare would end soon.

Theresa said goodbye to Carrie and her mother, and Mike walked her out to the parking lot. When she saw the hideous Cadillac parked beside her beautiful Volkswagen, she pretended to faint. Turning to her husband, she said, "Look, Michael: beauty and the beast."

"You're right. That Volks is not just ugly, it's circus ugly."

"No Michael, the Frankenstein-on-wheels is your Cadillac, or should I say Pimpmobile."

"Stop it with the flattery. I know deep down you love my car. By the way, I will be home tonight." He gave her a kiss as she opened the car door. Theresa smiled and whispered "I love you" as she got behind the wheel.

Mike watched as she drove out of the parking lot and was about to get into his Caddy when Jimmy called him on his cell. He had tracked down Sebastian at the Radisson Hotel, but he wasn't there when the police showed up. The police had no clue where Sebastian was, but they knew he was driving a black BMW (license plate YEV 576) rented from Exclusive Car Rentals. The description was familiar. Mike remembered seeing a black Beamer when he arrived at the Park Inn, but he couldn't remember where. He left the parking lot and looked up and down the block. Cars were parked on both sides of the street. He methodically checked every one, and on the right hand side of the street at the end of the block was a black BMW. He walked closer to inspect it, and yes, it was this year's model, jet black, clean as a whistle, and the plates were a match.

Mike ran back to his car, took his Sig Sauer out of the glove compartment, and placed a call to Jimmy Secola. Mike told him where he had found

Sebastian's car and that he figured the man was headed for Carrie's hotel room. Jimmy said he'd contact the policemen on watch across the hall from room 411 and ask them to check in on the George family.

Pontiac was staring at the barrel of a Colt 45. He had walked right into a trap. Sebastian was standing in front of him, gun in hand, waiting for an excuse to pull the trigger.

"Amigo, nice of you to drop in." Sebastian pointed to the Gibson leaning against a wall and said, "Take your guitar and sit down on the bed." Pontiac picked it up carefully and sat next to Phil, who looked as if he felt guilty for not giving Pontiac any kind of warning.

"Excellent, now sing something. May I suggest 'I Shot the Sheriff?'" Sebastian grinned at Pontiac as if this were some macabre game. "And please, sing it with some feeling. We want anyone walking by the room to think we are having mucho fun."

Pontiac wasted a few minutes tuning up, then went through the chord changes to make sure he still remembered the song before he played the opening lick of the Marley classic that Eric Clapton had turned into a hit.

Sebastian moved back behind the door, as he was expecting the rest of the family to arrive at any minute, and he wanted to make sure they received a proper welcome. Pontiac was into the second verse now, singing as loud as he could with his eyes shut, hoping the police in the room across the hall would venture into 411 to see what was happening.

> *Sheriff John Brown always hated me.*
> *For what, I don't know.*
> *Every time I plant a seed,*
> *He said kill it before it grow.*
> *He said kill them before they grow.*
> *And so,*
> *I shot the sheriff*
> *But I swear it was in self-defence.*

Finding Carrie George

Carrie and her mom could hear Pontiac singing from all the way down the hall as they left the elevator. Carrie smiled, glad that Pontiac and her father were having a great time. She was about to knock but decided she didn't want to interrupt the singing, so she asked her mother for the keycard. She slid it in the slot and a green light came on, a signal to open the door. Pontiac was wailing away, sitting on the bed next to Phil, who was looking down at the floor and didn't notice his wife and daughter enter. Carrie turned to close the door, and there was Sebastian. For a moment, she froze. Her mother made a little noise when she saw the gun, and Sebastian pushed her toward the bed. Phil caught his wife as she stumbled and glared back at Sebastian, seething with anger.

Sebastian grabbed Carrie by her hair and pulled her close to him, the barrel of his gun pressed against her head. "Keep singing!" he snapped at Pontiac, whose voice had trailed off. He ordered Mary and Phil into the washroom and told them to stay there if they valued their daughter's life. Phil hesitated, but his wife wisely prompted him to follow Sebastian's orders. Carrie tried to remain calm, but she knew Sebastian didn't make idle threats.

Sebastian walked over to Pontiac. It was time for a little payback. He slammed the butt end of his gun against Pontiac's head, knocking him out cold. The guitar fell to the floor, and Pontiac crumpled onto the bed.

"Next time, you will think twice before stealing someone else's woman." Sebastian looked down at Pontiac. If the circumstances were different, he would finish him off right now. Carrie rushed to help Pontiac, but she wasn't able to revive him.

"I will do anything you want," Carrie pleaded, "just don't hurt him anymore."

Sebastian let out a contemptuous laugh. "I will take care of him later. We leave now, and let us hope I don't have a reason to come back," he warned her, "because your friend and your parents will die."

As they were about to leave, a knock on the door brought everything to a halt. Sebastian stood behind the door, his gun ready, and motioned for Carrie to open it. She looked out the peephole to see who was there. To her surprise, it was Officer Henry Sanford, one of the policemen assigned to watch over the George family. She opened the door slightly so they could speak.

"Is everything all right in there?" he asked.

"We're fine, Henry. My parents are taking a nap, and I was reading."

"It's all good, then." Henry put his piece back in its holster.

"Yes, same as always, and how are you and your partner?"

"Bored. Steve spends more time in front of a television than anyone I've ever met," Henry said laughing. "Listen, I just took a call from Sergeant Secola. He's concerned that Sebastian Garcia is somewhere in the building."

"Has anyone seen him?"

"No, ma'am. Steve is checking downstairs, so I thought I better make sure he didn't show up at your door."

"He wouldn't dare show his face with you and your partner here. But thank you, Henry. My family and I appreciate your vigilance."

"Just doing my job," Henry said, satisfied that the George family was safe. "I will be in my room if you need me."

"We're okay Henry, but thanks just the same."

Officer Sanford returned to his room, and Carrie took a deep breath. Sebastian looked out of the peephole. The cop was gone, and there was no one else around, perfect time to leave.

"Go into the washroom and tell your mother we are leaving." He waved the Colt in Carrie's face. "If she does anything stupid, like telling the cop we have left, she will die, and so will you."

Sebastian and Carrie left the room quickly, and headed for the stairwell down the hall. Sebastian walked with his arm around Carrie, nudging her with the Colt in his right coat pocket as they made their way down the stairs to the main floor.

Mike didn't wait for Jimmy Secola to call back. He had to get to Carrie's room. He took the back door and was on the second flight of stairs when he heard footsteps and voices. He stopped for a few moments, listening. He recognized Carrie's voice and backtracked downstairs and outside, thinking fast. He had to find a way to take Sebastian by surprise and keep Carrie out of the line of fire. He ran toward the street and noticed a UPS delivery van parked in front of Sebastian's BMW.

Mike crossed the street and ducked down in front of the van. He laid down flat on his stomach and inched his way underneath the van as Sebastian and Carrie came out of the parking lot headed towards the BMW. Mike pulled out the Sig and started counting the seconds until Carrie stood in front of the passenger's door while Sebastian walked around the vehicle to the driver's side. Mike pulled himself up and crouched behind the front of the van. When he heard the electronic sound that meant the BMW doors were unlocked, he stepped out in the open, gun raised, just as Sebastian was about to open the car door.

"DON'T MOVE!" Mike shouted, but Sebastian wasn't listening. With lightning speed, Sebastian pulled the handgun from his coat and fired. Mike saw the 45 come out of Sebastian's pocket and ducked behind the van. The bullet lodged in the side door with a metallic screech. Sebastian let off three more rounds. Bullets grazed the side of the van while Mike bent down on his knees, waiting for his opportunity. When he heard the door of the car opening, he moved into the open again and fired two shots, shattering the driver's side window. Sebastian let out a scream and fell against the BMW, blood dripping from his upper chest. He was wounded, but not incapacitated. He grabbed onto the door, lifted himself up, and raised his gun just as Mike got off another shot. Sebastian's head snapped back as the bullet entered just above his left eye. He slumped to the ground, blood oozing out of his head and chest as his gun clattered onto the street.

Mike walked toward him slowly, the Sig Sauer held at arms length. He looked down at Sebastian, as Carrie came around in front of the car staring at Sebastian's body lying on the street in a pool of blood. She couldn't articulate anything; she was shell-shocked. Mike bent down and felt Sebastian's neck for a pulse but found none. When he stood up, he saw Jimmy Secola getting out of a cruiser with two other policemen, all three with weapons in their hands.

"Are we too late?" Jimmy asked, rushing over.

"He's gone."

"In that case, you can put that cannon away."

Mike unloaded his gun, put it in his pocket and walked Carrie back into the hotel. Carrie moved beside him, head down as she walked in short measured steps, holding on to Mike's arm. Neither of them spoke. Jimmy and his assistants secured the scene and collected Sebastian's weapon in an evidence bag while they waited for the forensic crew to arrive. A crowd had formed at the hotel entrance in the wake of the gunfire.

Once they were safe inside the hotel, Carrie broke down in tears, more from shock than remorse. She had hidden behind the car during the gunfight, unsure what the outcome was until the firing stopped. She hadn't anticipated such violence and death, and now she wanted to get as far away as possible.

When she regained her composure, she took a deep breath and said, "Mike, I can't stay here. Can my parents and I go home now?"

"Of course. Sebastian won't be stalking you or anyone else anymore."

"Thanks, Mike." She hugged him tightly. "For everything."

"I'm glad it's over." Mike could hear an ambulance siren approaching as he escorted Carrie to the elevator. When they entered room 411, Mary and Phil were busy trying to help Pontiac, who was soothing a nasty head wound with a hand towel full of ice. He looked up with a groggy smile on his face and said, "Well, look who's here!"

Mary turned to see her daughter in the doorway with Mike. Her hands flew up to her face, barely containing the emotion she felt. She took her daughter into her arms and held her tightly, sobbing with relief and gratitude. Phil joined them and looked toward Mike, his expression saying more than words ever could.

Mike put a hand on Phil's shoulder briefly, then went to check on Pontiac.

"You okay?" he asked.

Pontiac shrugged. "I'm a lucky bastard. What happened to Sebastian?"

"He wasn't so lucky."

Harold Jenkins woke up to his worst nightmare. He was lying in a hospital bed, surrounded by the afflicted and at the mercy of doctors and nurses. He was lucky to be alive. Surgeons had removed three shotgun pellets from his arm and two from his shoulder. He vaguely remembered leaving Roberts' house in his cruiser with Kim driving. Everything else was fuzzy, except for the vivid image of William Roberts face down in grass with his shotgun lying beside him. In the last moments of the gunfight, when he was wounded and down to his last bullet, Harold had felt the cold breath of the reaper as Roberts came at him from the veranda.

"You have visitors, Officer Jenkins," the nurse said from the doorway.

"That will be fine," he said quietly, just as Kim walked in the door with Larry Crowfoot.

"Anything broken?" Kim asked as she stood by his bed.

"My left arm, more chipped than broken." Harold replied in a medicated voice.

"You're alive. That's all that counts," Kim said, putting her hand on his good shoulder.

"I have you to thank," Harold said with a hint of a smile. "You did a good job with the bandages, and you drove the cruiser to the hospital. I could have bled to death."

"You should have seen the expression on the ambulance driver's face when I drove up to the emergency doors," Kim laughed. She had been terrified during the entire trip, driving a police cruiser with a wounded RCMP officer passed out in the back seat. Remarkably, nobody noticed until she stepped out of the car in front of the hospital emergency entrance.

"Don't worry," Harold said. "I gave a verbal report on what happened."

"I won't be arrested?"

"No. If anything, you will receive a commendation for bravery on behalf of the police department."

"That would be nice." Kim couldn't restrain herself from laughing. A reward from the police was something she never expected in this lifetime. She shook her head in disbelief.

"You saved my life, Kim. That is a debt I can never repay. If you need any kind of assistance to get settled once you're out of rehab, call me."

Kim was touched. "Thank you, but Larry's going to rent me a room and help me get a job.

"That's good. Maybe you can get your baby back."

"When I'm ready."

"You can make it happen Kim."

"If it does, it's thanks to you." She bent over and gave him a kiss on his forehead. "I'll be back on Friday."

Harold thanked her for coming. Kim and Larry left just as his nurse returned.

"You have another visitor," the nurse said curtly. "I told him he could stay five minutes."

"Who is it Miss Kearns?"

"Some policeman who thinks he's a big shot."

"Sounds like my boss. Send him in." Harold smiled at the nurse.

Carl Hawkins sat down in a chair beside Harold's bed, and took a hard look at his officer wounded in action. Jenkins had survived, but not without a few battle scars.

"We found the remains of nine women behind Roberts house," Carl said. "The forensic crew is up there right now going through his house and garage."

"What about Mona?"

"We found her decapitated body. You were right, Harold. Roberts was the sexual predator the task force was looking for. We might have saved a few lives if we had acted sooner." Captain Hawkins spoke with a touch of remorse. He had failed to realize the importance of Harold's investigation and should have forced a search warrant based solely on Kim's testimony.

"Have you contacted Mona's parents?"

"Not yet. No names are to be released until we have identified all the women. That will take some time."

Harold was relieved. Finally, Mona was no longer one of the missing, and her fate would soon be made public. "Make sure the press knows that it was her death that led us to Bill Roberts."

"Don't worry, we can deal with the press later." Carl took a closer look at Harold. "You will be on sick leave for the next month. When you return, I have a new position that might interest you."

"What happened to my present position?"

"The task force is to be terminated within a few months."

"Where does that leave me?"

"I'm choosing three officers to create a new unit that deals specifically with missing women. The problem is not going to disappear just because Roberts is six feet under. The same thing is happening in Edmonton as we speak, a serial killer preying on women." Carl said, giving Harold the stare.

"So, am I one of the lucky three?"

"You, Jenkins, will be in charge," Carl stood up, ready to leave and before Harold could respond, he added, "You can take your time to decide. We can wait until you're back to your old self."

Harold nodded to show his approval, "I appreciate the offer, sir."

He could have given his answer on the spot, but it seemed that Captain Hawkins wanted to make it official at the right time, so Harold thanked him and promised to get in touch once he was discharged from the hospital. In the meantime, healing was his only concern. Harold was looking forward to a long rest before returning to duty. Now was not the time to dwell on the past or the future. Sometimes success was simply survival, and he had survived the closest call of his career. The moment he was discharged from the hospital, it was time to go fishing.

Carrie told her parents the good news. They were finally going home. Sebastian was dead, and the nightmare was over. The family packed up their belongings, stopped at the room across the hall from 411 and said farewell to the two policemen who had stood vigil for them. After a final tearful goodbye with Mike and Pontiac, the family left the Park Inn. As Mike watched them leave in the RCMP cruiser, he felt happy and sad at the same time. He wasn't sure when he would ever see the George family again. A friendship forged in a time of need doesn't always survive when the emergency is over. Life goes on, and for Carrie George, this was a chapter best forgotten. It was time to put her life in order, and she would need all the energy she could muster to succeed. There was no need for her to be reminded of her friend Susan Wabigon's tragic death or how close she herself had come to a similar fate. Life seldom offers a second chance, but when such an opportunity arises, it is better to take full advantage and thank the Creator for his benevolence.

Mike drove Pontiac back to his apartment. Pontiac sat quietly in the Eldorado, his head still throbbing as they cruised down Pender Street. He couldn't believe he was going to sleep in his own bed and wake up tomorrow without fear of Sebastian using him for target practice.

"I have something to tell you, dude."

"Go ahead," Mike said.

"I'm dissolving the partnership. As of this moment, consider me retired."

"Not surprised Pontiac." Mike tried not to laugh. "You did make a difference in finding Carrie, though."

"Seriously dude, when I walked in the room and Sebastian shoved his gun in my face, I thought it was all over. So he didn't kill me, but he did try to open my skull with the butt of his gun." Pontiac opened the window, and breathed deeply. The warm air felt good; it lessened the pain of the headache.

"You're lucky he didn't shoot you," Mike said, as he pulled up in front of Pontiac's building.

"I know. Scary shit, but I'm still vertical, and thanks to you Sebastian is history."

"Give it some time. When you're back onstage, you will forget what happened today."

"No way dude, this is one trip I will never forget." Pontiac gave Mike a handshake and opened the car door. "Thanks for the memories."

"You take it easy partner," Mike said as Pontiac stepped out of the Caddy and walked slowly towards the front door of his apartment building.

Mike waited until Pontiac was safely inside before driving away. He wanted to stop at the office and drop off his gun before going to his own home sweet home. Finding Carrie George proved to him the importance of family. Blood is thicker than water; that truism could redefine one's existence. Being disconnected from those you love—or perhaps more importantly, those who love you—was bound to leave a void in one's soul that is difficult to heal. Trying to fill that kind of emptiness often leads to a person's self-destruction. Mike was grateful he had Theresa, and right now she and Benny were waiting for him to come home. That was all he needed, to feel he belonged, to have a reason to carry on and accept life's hardships and tragedies without breaking down. Family is the core of life, and right now, it felt good to be alive. He turned on the radio. Hank Williams' "I Saw the Light" filled his Cadillac with music; Mike turned up the volume and smiled.